THE MIDNIGHT PROMISE

Zane Lovitt lives in Melbourne. *The Midnight Promise* is his first book.

ZANE LOVITT

THE MIDNIGHT PROMISE

A DETECTIVE'S STORY IN TEN CASES

TEXT PUBLISHING MELBOURNE AUSTRALIA

'Leaving the Fountainhead' won the SD Harvey Short Story Award at the 2010 Ned Kelly Awards for Australian crime writing. It was first published in *New Australian Stories 2* by Scribe Publications in 2010.

'Death at Le Shack' was first published in *The Ellery Queen Mystery Magazine* in February 2012.

'Kahraman' was first published in *The One That Got Away* by Dark Prints Press in 2012.

textpublishing.com.au

The Text Publishing Company
Swann House
22 William Street
Melbourne Victoria 3000
Australia

First published in 2012 by The Text Publishing Company
This edition 2013

Cover by WH Chong
Page design by Imogen Stubbs
Typeset by J&M Typesetting
Printed and bound in Australia by Griffin Press, an Accredited ISO AS/NZS 14001:2004 Environmental Management System printers

National Library of Australia Cataloguing-in-Publication entry
Author: Lovitt, Zane.
Title: The midnight promise : a detective's story in ten cases /Zane Lovitt.
ISBN: 9781922147608 (pbk.)
ISBN: 9781921961182 (ebook)
Subjects: Detective and mystery stories.
Dewey Number: A823.4

This book is printed on paper certified against the Forest Stewardship Council® Standards. Griffin Press holds FSC chain of custody certification SGS-COC-005088. FSC promotes environmentally responsible, socially beneficial and economically viable management of the world's forests

CONTENTS

PROLOGUE

YOU DON'T MAKE promises to do what I do. Not those fat professional promises that doctors make, to do no harm and to wash their hands. Lawyers get sworn in by the Chief Justice of the Supreme Court, *in* the Supreme Court. All I had to do was climb the stairs of a grey government building in Richmond, get my photo taken by a woman with mottled skin who didn't know how to operate the camera. She swore at it and smiled nervously, shot looks at the windows like if it weren't for the bars across them she'd be jumping out of one.

The technical word for that, the one you sometimes see in police reports, is 'defenestration'.

She got the camera working but then the laminator broke. It didn't occur to me that I should see this as some kind of omen; I was too guileless back then, too busy feeling embarrassed for her, which made her more embarrassed, which made me more embarrassed. There we were, locked in an embarrassment loop, when she suddenly broke out in a shrill falsetto voice like a kindergarten teacher, singing: 'Today will be an *awesome* daaaaaaay...'

Someone came and fixed the laminator.

You don't make any promises, you get your photo taken and they laminate it for you. After that, you're a private investigator. I don't even remember signing anything.

Last of all, you leave that grey building in Richmond with a shiny blue pamphlet that tells you all the things you should and shouldn't do now that you're licensed. That pamphlet says, in bold red italics, *You can work effectively without breaking the law*. Statistically, I have not found this to be true. Another thing it says in bold red italics is: *Be sure to invest a portion of every payment in a superannuation fund*. You read this pamphlet and you think, whoever wrote this, bold red italics is what they use when they're feeling *optimistic*.

The truth is, I've had to scrounge and hustle for every dollar I've made. Maybe that's why doctors and lawyers are forced to take oaths. It's a ceremonious way of saying, you're going to make a fortune. Try to have *some* standards.

But the work can help you keep perspective. Last year I was hired to investigate a man so poor his neighbours conspired to have him evicted. They said he drove down the market value of their homes. My job was to find something on him, some form of illegality that would be grounds for a notice to vacate: his flat was public housing and governments love to evict people for illegal use, it makes them look tough on crime. After a month of looking I gathered all these neighbours together like Hercule Poirot and explained that the guy wasn't dealing drugs or fencing goods or managing an unlicensed brothel. There was nothing criminal about his hairy face or the tattered clothes he dried on his balcony or his obsessive hoarding of Green Guides.

They didn't like to hear it, but some of it must have sunk in. Because even today I can drive past those flats and see the same tired underwear flapping in the breeze.

His name was Arthur Carreidas and I caught head lice from him.

You don't have to make promises to do what I do, but I have made one. This was a long time after I got my licence. After I started the drinking and after I was kicked out of my home and after my head got stuck all the way up my arse. I made my promise in a border town in the middle of nowhere, at what was literally my darkest hour. There was even a clock tower chiming midnight, right at the moment I said the words, if you believe it.

The promise I made was that I'd never let it become about me. Or at least, never again.

My mother used to say that in her day a midnight promise was one you made to get what you wanted, not one you actually ever kept. Like what a man says to a woman to get her undressed, or the stuff you say to God when your plane flies through heavy turbulence. I still wonder if I'll really hold to what I swore that night. But I have so far. And it's been years.

I used to lug my stories around with me like caged birds, screeching and crapping and demanding all my attention. I dwelt on my stories, which means I dwelt on myself. And sure, everybody does that, but I was the Super Heavyweight Champion. I was the CEO.

And that's what this is. This is the tumbling road to a single moment that changed all that.

Now, when I think about the future, it's no longer a smorgasbord of the ugly things people do to each other. It's my friend Demetri shouting me a lemonade, or slinging me a job. It's earning enough to put flowers on my mother's grave. It's helping people like Arthur Carreidas.

I know, I know. I should write all this down in bold red italics.

I see the future that way because of the promise I made to myself. I think about it often, perhaps every day. The worst stories may be yet to come, but that pledge is what allows me to say, without irony, without adopting a shrill, falsetto voice: *Let's see.*

AMNESTY

I'M SITTING ON the floor of my one-room flat reading the newspaper when Demetri arrives. This is my local paper, the *Western Gazette*, the kind any suburb has in its laundromats and fish and chip shops, and I've been flicking through it, killing time, mentally urging Demetri to hurry up. He knows the way to my office, he's been there about a thousand times. He's never been to my home.

'Nice place,' he says as he steps inside. 'Where's the rest of it?'

Standing here with his brand-name shirt and his gold wristwatch, Demetri looks like a wealthy parent visiting a college dorm. Eyes travel over the coffee mugs in the sink, the oven full of recycling, the bathroom that reeks of mildew, that's also a wardrobe. He fights a knowing smile, loses that battle when his eyes come back to me.

'How's the private detective business coming along then?'

'I'm doing all right.'

'Are you sure? This is like a shanty town I saw once in the Philippines.'

'I guess some of us are resigned to not being a rich bastard.'

'You should be working for a firm, doing something behind the scenes. Mendes Duke or somewhere like that. Nice discreet little card, John Dorn, Corporate Paralegal.' Demetri shrugs theatrically. His combed grey locks cling to his scalp, unmoving. 'But okay. So long as you're *resigned* to it...'

On the open page of the *Western Gazette* in front of me there's a full-page ad for novelty greeting cards. One of the cards says: 'Congratulations! You Finally Got a Real Job!' You know a lot of parents buy that one. Parents, and people who talk to you like they're your parents.

'How's single life treating you?'

'I'm fine.'

'Have you even had a girlfriend since what's-her-name?'

Demetri remembers her name. Pretending to forget is how he expresses his support. It's how he quietly says, 'Good riddance.'

'Been too busy with work, I suppose...'

I smile at the meaninglessness of my response and he gives a meaningless hum of conclusion.

'If you've asked me here to help with Anton Goldberg...' Demetri says, strolling to the centre of the room and wheeling around to face me. He's got his tough scowl on to show how serious he is. 'John, he's a waste of time. Take it from someone who knows all about wasting time on criminals. Anton's one of the ones who *enjoys* prison.'

Last month, Anton Goldberg was charged with robbing a drycleaner in a western suburbs shopping centre called Highpoint. Anyone who doesn't live around here calls it Knifepoint and, sure enough, Anton was armed with a long machete, the kind you'd use to clear a path through the jungle. He's got more prior convictions than brain cells which means he won't get bail, so he's wallowing in the Metropolitan Remand Centre at Ravenhall, trying to find a lawyer who'll argue that society is to blame.

'If someone had bloody fucken taught me to read,' Anton declaimed on a crackling phone line from Ravenhall, 'then I would have seen the bloody fucken sign that said *Security Personnel Patrol*

This fucken Area. Then I bloody fucken never would of bloody knocked the fucken place over.'

For some reason, criminals in the western suburbs have a reputation for being slow-witted.

I told Anton his case was weak but he insists on going to trial and he's asking for my help. What's good about someone being in jail is, you can't return their calls.

But Anton Goldberg isn't the reason I've asked Demetri to my flat on a dull and windy Sunday afternoon.

'So why *am* I here?' he asks. He seems to be thinking about sitting in my brown armchair, but it's old and sticky and he doesn't trust it. 'Did you want me to help you burn your furniture?'

'I've got something amazing to show you. But first I need a favour. A big one. There's no money in it.'

'Of course,' he says, and the classic Demetri smile breaks through his tough scowl. He loves to be asked for favours; helping people is his nature. I suspect that as a criminal lawyer he doesn't get to help people as often as his nature demands.

Now he tries to get the scowl back, managing only an amiable pout. 'But John, don't you think *you* should get remunerated every now and then?'

'I make money. Not enough to spend on my wardrobe, if that's what you mean. Did you come straight from your club?'

Demetri glances down at his outfit, his tapered trousers and silk socks. It's the kind of casual wear that says, I'd rather be wearing a suit.

'So what's this amazing thing?' he asks. 'Are you going to put on a clean shirt?'

'I need you to come for a walk with me.'

He recoils, turns to the window. What he can see, past other blocks of flats, is a grey sky that's mustering rain. Demetri makes a face. 'Is that necessary?'

'I finally get to show you around my neighbourhood.'

'Is that the favour? Putting up with that, at my age?'

'No. The favour is for someone Anton met inside. Someone you don't know. His name's Gary Blanche.'

Demetri wilts. 'And I suppose he's developed an equally brilliant line of legal reasoning to support his not-guilty plea.'

'He's only just gone into remand. He hasn't made a plea yet.'

'And whatever the charge is, he assures you it's a massive miscarriage of justice with the rights of freedom for corruption and victims, innocent, travesty, persecution, outrage, more justice and then injustice.'

I grab the newspaper I was reading, fold it and tuck it gently into my jacket pocket.

'You'll see,' I say.

Demetri gets an overcoat from his car and together we hike silently into the wind. Footscray is the delta where trucks pour out of the city and spread across the west of Melbourne, so living here means slowly drowning in exhaust and the yawn of diesel engines and bored drivers who watch you in their rearview mirrors. It's what keeps housing cheap and makes somewhere so close to the CBD a home for half of Melbourne's migrant population. Sundays here are like low tide on a coral reef: every shape and colour of life is on parade, hollering into mobile phones and undertaking their own serious mission, just like me and Demetri. I steer him away from the stir of Paisley Street and south under the rail overpass and he's happy, at least for now, not to know where we're going.

I tell Demetri about Gary Blanche.

'He's up on three counts of possession of a prohibited weapon. The police found the guns in his house a week ago after a tip-off. Gary's lawyer told Gary who told me that the prosecutor's after a custodial sentence of one year per count, not concurrent.'

I can't tell if Demetri's grimace is because of the wind or because of Gary Blanche's sad prospects. We turn left onto Broadfield Avenue.

'That sounds right,' he says, wrapping his coat tighter. 'It's part of the State Government's crackdown on getting re-elected. New penalties for possessing firearms, proposed by none other than Her Highness the DPP. She's talking about running for preselection and she wants to look tougher on crime than any of the blokes. But those laws only commenced a fortnight ago. When did your friend get charged?'

'Last Friday.'

Demetri exhales theatrically. 'Sounds to me like he's the winner of this month's unluckiest bastard competition.'

'Gary got my number from Anton and he called me from Ravenhall. He told me he'd been in there once before, for possessing stolen goods, and he didn't think he could last another stretch. I've never met him face to face, but from the sound of his voice I'd say something terrible happened the first time he was inside and he's frightened out of his mind it'll happen again.'

'I can see where this is going,' Demetri shakes his head. 'Perhaps Ravenhall shouldn't be the kind of place it is. But do you think he wasn't planning something terrible himself, John? I mean, what was he *doing* with the guns?'

'Exactly,' I say. 'That is exactly what Gary asked me to find out.'

We turn right onto Farrel Street, a stretch of run-down weatherboard homes and blocks of flats that smell of urine and all seem to slump against each other like penguins in the Antarctic. The ones that have gardens really only have weeds that seep into the cracks in the concrete paths and across abandoned playthings and up to the windows, threatening to breach the walls and ravage the people inside. The dogs that bark at us from behind torn wire fences rattle their chains and demand to know how they ended up living *here*. The street is deserted because it's the kind of place where you don't spend a lot of time outside. Even when it's not as bitterly cold as today.

'What are you talking about?' Demetri demands. If he was out of place in my flat, he's more than out of place here. He doesn't seem to notice. 'He asked you to…what?'

'Gary wants me to find out where the guns came from. And before you ask, yeah, I'm working for free.'

Demetri squeezes his eyes shut. 'He doesn't know where they came from?'

'That's right.'

'Does he live alone?'

'He lives with his father, Gary Senior, but Gary Senior's in a wheelchair and he never leaves the house. They weren't *his* guns.'

'So, your friend's story is that they materialised, inexplicably, within the home?'

'Sort of. Gary Junior's just begun an apprenticeship as an auto-electrician, and with a record like his it's hard to find work, which means he's hysterically happy to get the job and he doesn't want to mess it up. So he goes to work every day an hour before everyone else, just to show them how committed he is, and he's leaving the house bright and early one morning when he opens the front door and finds a point-three-five calibre Beretta, pre–World War Two, sitting right there on the porch steps. From what I've managed to find out, it's a pretty rare gun. Valuable.'

'A Beretta? All by itself?'

'That's right.'

'No note from one of his classy friends who collects antiques?'

'Nothing else. It wasn't even loaded.'

'Right,' says Demetri, moving from confusion to disbelief. He steps around a puddle on the footpath. Nobody clears the gutters on this street and there's dead foliage clogging up the drains—

Demetri's shoes don't look like the kind you get wet. 'So, of course, he took it straight to the police.'

'Gary's got a record and he doesn't imagine the police will be too happy to hear from him. Also, he thinks it's a practical joke. He's a new apprentice so surely this is some kind of initiation prank. That's understandable, isn't it? He doesn't want to come across as a wuss who calls the cops at the first sign of a gun. What he does instead is he takes it upstairs and hides it in his sock drawer. Whoever pulled the prank will reveal themselves eventually and meanwhile he's got to be Mister Super Cool.'

'This is the story he told you?' Demetri asks.

'Yes.'

'And there's no one to corroborate?'

'No witnesses of any kind. He didn't even tell his father.'

'And you believe him?'

'If you heard him tell it, you'd believe him too. So. He comes home from work that same day and finds a point-three-eight self-loading Glock in the mailbox.'

Slowly, Demetri comes to a stop. He tries to give me a doubtful, even offended, look but the wind picks up and stings his eyes and he flinches, blinking.

'Come on,' he says with a defensive step back.

'What?'

'It's my sixtieth coming up...That's what this is about, right? You're keeping me occupied so my wife can build a gazebo or something...'

I don't answer, meet his eyes with patience, which only frustrates him more.

He says, *Where the fuck are we going?*

I nod in the direction we've been walking. 'It's one more block,' I say. 'The scene of the crime.'

'What for?'

'Because I think you need to see.'

'Well, we've got a problem. Because I don't go in for bullshit stories. Even if you do.'

And standing there, he folds his arms.

It's not like Demetri isn't familiar with the traipse through these run-down, frigid neighbourhoods. A lot of his clients come from places like this, and he's always on the lookout for another Jim Yedda. I think it's fair to say that Jim Yedda changed Demetri's life. I think Demetri would say that he did.

What happened to Yedda was he got drunk and fell asleep in St Vincent Place, a lush green park in South Melbourne which is open to the public but exclusive enough that the locals call the police when someone's asleep in there. Two uniforms attended the scene and reported that Yedda was in an 'agitated' state, though they said this might have been the result of the kicks to the knees they administered to wake him up. Turning out his pockets they found seven or eight small scraps of paper that they assumed to be tabs of LSD, and when they asked him what they were he replied, slurring and blinking, that he didn't know. The two policemen promptly drew the conclusion that Yedda was, at that moment, tripping on acid, and they placed him under arrest.

During the interview at the South Melbourne police station, Jim Yedda was charged with possession. Typically, if you're charged with possessing a small quantity of something, the first thing that happens is you're offered a bail application. But Yedda had no fixed address, so even if he could rustle up the money, he could never meet the bail conditions. They told him to sit and wait in Ravenhall, overnight, for the paper to be tested. There's nothing unusual about that for homeless people on remand.

What *was* unusual was that the cross-eyed, overworked

prosecutor who landed the job forgot to tick a box. On the form that goes to the forensic laboratory, there's a box you're supposed to tick when the suspect is in custody—it fast-tracks the tests. If that box isn't ticked, well, the lab has a million more urgent tests to do.

It was two months before the tests came back, and they came back negative. Not LSD, just ordinary scraps of paper.

In those two months, Jim Yedda was sexually assaulted more than once. He witnessed a murder and he lost a finger in an attempt on his own life.

Finally he was released and immediately hospitalised and Demetri took up the case, banged the drum with the press and successfully sued the Director of Public Prosecutions for negligence. Soon there were activists clamouring for the DPP to resign. Even talkback radio seemed to sympathise with Yedda's story. No one minds how awful our jails are, so long as everyone in there is supposed to be in there. And just when the news media was moving on to other scandals, a local musician wrote a popular song called 'Scraps of a Life' about Jim Yedda, and the story became front page news all over again. Demetri did the morning shows. It was a public relations nightmare for the DPP, and it cemented Demetri's reputation as a legal white knight.

You can bet he didn't get paid for that job.

So Demetri's not really annoyed because I'm dragging him through the western suburbs on the crappiest day of the year, and he's not annoyed because he's old or because his shoes are getting ruined. He's done more for people who appear more guilty.

Why he's annoyed is because, it seems to him, some low-life has taken advantage of his friend.

I say, 'Why would Gary beg me to help him if it wasn't true?'

Eagerly, Demetri counts off the answers on his fingers. 'To give him the appearance of innocence. So that you might find something that throws the jury or something that makes the cops look bad—'

'He's not that smart.'

'You wouldn't believe how often I've said that about a client and been wrong. Criminals in the western suburbs aren't as dumb as people think.'

'I told you I've got something amazing to show you. Do you want to see it or not?'

'He's already got a lawyer, right?'

'Yeah, but we need you.'

'Why?'

'You're Demetri Sfakiakopoulos, champion of the lost cause.'

He smiles. It's too cold for him to blush.

'In future, the causes don't need to be this lost.'

'Bullshit,' I say, edging on along the pavement, tempting him to follow. 'I think they need to be exactly this lost.'

Demetri turns to the sky again, looking partly for rain but also maybe to God for guidance. Up there a passenger airline glides by, unhelpful. On windy days they change the flight path so that planes headed for the airport make their approach over Footscray, low and loud and self-conscious. Demetri deflates, gives me a look, swallows, pushes his hands deeper into his pockets and trudges past me, leading the way. 'So he put the Glock in his sock drawer too?'

'The two guns won't fit in his sock drawer now,' I say, skipping to catch up. 'He sticks them under his bed.'

'Was it loaded?'

'No, but the next one was.'

'Christ. The next one.'

Ahead of us there's a small shingle that protrudes from the second storey of a shaky brick edifice rising over a thin laneway. On the shingle are some faded words: The Prince Leopold.

I point at it as we approach.

'This happened the following weekend. He goes to the pub and comes home at three o'clock in the morning and there's an old-fashioned police service revolver on the porch.'

'A cop's gun?'

'Three bullets in it.'

'He's plastered, I assume.'

'Yeah, I think he probably was.'

As we reach the Prince Leopold we step around a discreet puddle of last night's dried sick. Through the tinted window there's the silhouette of a man reading the newspaper, a coffee mug on the bar beside him. He's the only person inside and the chairs are stacked on the tables and the lights are off and the doors are shut. Demetri and I stop to consider him.

'The owner knows Gary, says he was there that night, watching the rugby World Cup on the TV. Says Gary's a harmless pom who wants to be liked and wouldn't have any use for a handgun.'

The publican turns the page. I keep walking. Demetri follows.

'Great,' he says. 'The *bartender* can vouch for him. Gary's English?'

'He doesn't have an accent. He and his dad emigrated when Gary was little. He's still pretty passionate about the old country, though. Can't you tell?'

I point.

'This is it?'

'Yep.'

Four doors on from the Prince Leopold is a path made of broken bricks that staggers through a garden of white ivy and up two steps to a porch. The floor planks are warped and stained, the tiny house itself is flaking white paint and showing a sickly shade of white underneath. Out of the corrugated roof two red-brick chimneys rise like infections, one at the front, another at the rear, the one at the rear being almost completely caved in and seemingly a nest for something. Gary's bedroom is on the upper storey, though that's more of an attic than a storey, and the view of the house from the street is dominated by a St George Cross flag the size of a beach towel. It completely fills Gary's bedroom window, stretched out and pinned in place. Those red crosshairs are where they'll aim the missile when they finally decide to bring down this ruin and replace it with yet another block of flats.

'Right,' says Demetri. 'Not ashamed of being poms, are they?'

'Number twenty-nine,' I say, and point to the number wrought from a single strip of rusted iron and prominently mounted beside the ground-floor window. Though the house number means nothing to Demetri. Not yet.

'So he's got three guns...' Demetri says.

'He's got three guns, and he's starting to get the idea that this is a kind of threat, like a symbolically futile attempt to arm Gary before someone comes and shoots him in the head. He's known some scumbags in his time, but no one who he thinks would actually want to hurt him. He starts carrying the loaded revolver with him when he goes out. Also, he changes the locks on the front door.'

Through the old-fashioned flywire door, where the screen has been partially shredded, there's the shiny glint of a new lock plug.

Demetri looks at me sideways. 'The old man lives here too, right?'

'Yeah.'

'He's in a wheelchair?'

'Yep. He's kind of a shut-in.'

The path leading up to the house is so crooked and unstable that even if Gary Senior wanted to go out there's no way he could ever roll from the front door and down the porch steps and all the way to the street.

Demetri smirks. 'If we knock and ask the old man, what do

you bet he says it was *his* idea to change the locks because in his condition he's vulnerable to burglars and psychopaths?'

'I've been here twice and rung the bell. The old man never answers the door. You're welcome to try.'

He exhales through his nose, shrugs. 'I assume, then, that what Gary wants us to believe is that the party responsible for leaving the guns is the same party that tipped off the police.'

'No,' I say. 'His father called the police.'

Demetri blinks at me. 'His father dobbed him in?'

'Gary didn't think his father ever went upstairs, given how he can't, given how he's in a wheelchair. But his father *does* go upstairs—'

'Did you see that?' Demetri's voice is an urgent whisper. He's staring at the ground-floor window.

'What?'

'The curtain moved.'

The lace curtains are drawn and we can't see beyond them. They've only ever been drawn the times I've been here. I expect they're never open.

'He must have heard our voices.'

We watch for some other movement or even for the front door to open. Nothing happens.

Demetri says, 'Let's go. Loitering makes me uncomfortable.'

He turns wearily and moves slowly in the direction of my flat, expecting me to follow.

'This way,' I call to him. He stops and turns. Stares at me.

I say, 'We're not finished. We have to go to the Movie Hut. It's just around the corner.'

'What on earth for?'

'I can't really explain. You have to see it. It's not far. It's where the amazing thing is.'

From somewhere far away comes a roll of thunder.

Together, Demetri and I walk the stretch of Farrel Street. It hadn't seemed possible but it's grown darker and spirals of dead leaves dance around our feet in miniature tornados, breathlessly co-ordinated. Demetri turns the collar up on his coat.

I say, 'It turns out that sometimes, when Gary Junior goes out, Gary Senior climbs up the stairs using just his arms. Crawls up, I guess. Then he rolls around Gary's bedroom, going through his things. Gary knew the old man opened his mail and listened in on his phone calls, but he didn't know his dad could get up the friggin' stairs.'

'Right…He's one of *those* fathers.'

'Yep. Blames Gary's mother for Gary being a bit slow. Reckons she babied him. Blames her, though she died when Gary was six.'

'And he called the cops?'

'That was the deal they made. Two years ago, after Gary got out of jail the first time, his dad wanted to throw him out. Gary begged him to let him stay, promised his father he'd never run with crooks again, and there were tears, and his father let him stay. So now, Dad finds the guns, and that night when the two of them should be sitting up watching England win the World Cup, instead the police come and search the place and haul Gary away and his dad's yelling something about it being for his own good. How he needs hardening up.'

I was staring out my office window, wondering how to drum up some work and thinking about Japanese food for lunch, when my phone rang and it was a man with a voice pitched so high he might have been a child. He said Anton Goldberg had given him this number and he was calling from Ravenhall, then he spewed out his story and the squeal of his voice meant I sometimes had to pull the phone from my ear.

'Mate, I swear to you, I got no idea how them guns got there. Someone's having a laugh, you know? Playing a trick. The cops don't believe me and me dad won't pay my bail.'

'Well, you've got to talk to him,' I said, searching my desk for my wallet. I'd need at least fifteen dollars if I wanted gyoza as well as soba noodles. 'Tell him you're sorry. Tell him if he posts bail you'll have a chance to meet with a lawyer and the three of you can hash something—'

'You don't get it,' Gary said. 'If Dad reckons I can't hack it in here, he'll just want me to stay longer. He's got this idea in his head, like, if it's bad, then it's good, you know?'

The phone lines at Ravenhall are scratchy and full of hiss, so maybe that's why I thought his voice was breaking, why it sounded like he was trying to stop himself from crying.

'But, you know...' Gary cleared his throat. 'He doesn't know what it's like...'

Even then, I was still thinking of food. Forty per cent of the people who call me, they cry. Not necessarily because of what they've been through, just because someone is finally listening. But now I was about to speak. I was about to pull the string on the talking doll that says I'd love to help but I'm flat out with another case, when softly he said, 'Don't know how long I can last. Didn't last long last time.'

'What happened last time?'

'Just...' Silence. Gary seemed to fight with the words in his head. 'One of the screws, he knows me from last time I was in here. He said I should stop showering, stop brushing my teeth and that, because...' His voice cracked, his throat clenched shut. 'Because if I'm, like, unhygienic and that, the other blokes won't be interested.'

'You can request protection.'

'I did already. They said I can't get protection if I'm just scared of *everybody*.'

Weeks of anticipation might be worse for Gary than the thing itself. His Mickey Mouse voice would only make him more of a target.

'All right,' I said. 'Let's go over this again. But slow.'

As we reach the corner of Farrel Street and Stanley Avenue, I point up at the street sign.

'Farrel Street. That's the street we've been on. That's where they live.'

Demetri gives the rusted street sign a lingering look because he isn't wearing his glasses, then we head along Stanley Avenue, another strip of battered houses, towards the traffic on Glenmaddox.

I say, 'So that's the end of the story. I've been trying to figure out what happened. Where the guns came from. It's been baffling...'

Demetri looks at me now, his head partly bowed against the wind, hands in his jacket pockets and collar turned up like a gangster taking me somewhere quiet to whack me.

'What's baffling is that you've been sucked in by Gary's bullshit.'

'I haven't been sucked anywhere.'

'Oh, really?' He was hoping I'd say that. 'Coming to the house to see his father, getting a value on that Beretta, interviewing the bartender...For goodness sake—'

'This is what I do for a living.'

'For a living. Exactly. Would I be saying this if Gary were likely to pay even *your* modest fee?'

'The only difference between what I do and what you do is I don't give it a fancy name like pro bono.'

'Wrong. The difference is that I work pro bono when there's a genuine need.'

'There's a need here.'

'Come on...' Demetri growls, letting his Greekness creep into that second, elongated vowel. When he's frustrated and when he's drunk are the only times his ancestry shows in his voice. 'Gary was collecting firearms for himself or for some criminal acquaintance—either way he had a specifically nefarious purpose in mind, one which we would most likely have seen re-enacted on *Australia's Most Wanted*. They secreted the guns in Gary's room because they assumed, incorrectly, that no one else had access to that space. And should the day have come whereupon they retrieved those weapons from their hiding place in order to commit a crime, one of those bullets in that police revolver might have finished up lodged in *your* skull, John, or the skull of some other innocent. A pregnant woman, or a grandmother.'

I've been waiting for this part, where Demetri explains why Gary is more like Anton Goldberg and less like Jim Yedda. He continues, 'And furthermore, to spin you a yarn like he's been doing, claiming that the guns magically appeared at his home and he was inexplicably compelled to stockpile them…'

'It wasn't inexplicable. I told you—'

'…is nothing short of deceitful, if not criminal, in and of itself. What's likely is that, far from being the emotional tyrant his son depicts him to be, his father is a witless, frail old man with no idea that Gary is out in the world blaming him for everything. And from someone as allergic to even the vaguest whiff of insincerity as you, John, to be frank, I expected more.'

Demetri should have been a barrister. In fact, as he composes himself and his fingertips gently patrol his chin for saliva, I bet that's what he's thinking.

'Okay,' I say, holding my hands up. 'Save your scolding for after we've been to the Movie Hut.'

'I'm not trying to tell you off…' he says, balancing his tone. 'But I've met some practised liars, John. Geniuses. Sociopaths who could make you doubt your own…'

As we reach Glenmaddox Road another truck rockets past and I can't hear how Demetri finishes. So I look at him. When I do he stops walking and tugs on my elbow, which makes me stop. Then he drives that pale, frosted hand back into his jacket pocket and says, 'I don't want to see anyone make a fool of you, that's all.'

'I know. I know that's what you're worried about.'

His lips are cracked from the cold and they twitch as though he has more to say. But he stops himself. I draw him back from the cliff edge with a jerk of my elbow.

'Come on. We're almost there.'

Another long rattle of thunder echoes from the south, louder than before. We have to slalom single file through the oncoming locals who are rushing to get their shopping done before the rain reaches us. I lead him past the Asian groceries and the Arab haberdasheries and the post office, and Demetri has to shout over the heads of the rest of these pedestrians.

'I'm not saying I won't help,' he says. 'I'm just saying, he's got to come clean about where the guns came from. Maybe he doesn't want to dob people in. That's fine. But you have to tell him, John. You have to tell him that he's a liar and he has to stop being a liar if he wants to get out of jail.'

We reach the entrance of the Movie Hut and a short man with dreadlocks and a bag of DVDs exits, looks fearfully up at the sky. The fluoros that illuminate the shelves of movie titles are blinding compared with the dimness of the daylight. I stop at the entrance while Demetri catches up.

Calmly, he says, 'You know I'm right, don't you?'

There are notices on display to the left of the Movie Hut sliding door, attached on the inside of the store so that you can read them through the glass. One is for a lost dog that answers to the name Puppy. Another is for a rabbit that doesn't seem to have a name. The third is a community notice from Victoria Police that, through the glass, doesn't look too old but really it's been up here for months.

Demetri says, 'Go on,' urging me into the warmth of the store.

I linger and nod at the police notice. 'Have a look,' I say.

Demetri squints. 'What is it?'

'You have to read it.'

With a sigh of victimhood Demetri takes a pair of spectacles from his suit pocket and leans in to read, just as the first drops of rain fall onto the glass.

VICTORIA POLICE

REDUCTION OF WEAPONS IN YOUR COMMUNITY
GUN AMNESTY

New laws in the State of Victoria will increase penalties for firearms possession.

Between the dates of February 12 and April 30, you may attend the Footscray Police Station at 300 Paisley Street, Footscray (open 24 hours) to surrender unregistered firearms.

You may also surrender weapons at:

The Reach-Out Accommodation Centre,
166 Crescent Road, Newport

St Christopher's Church,
Paisley Street, Footscray

The Red Cross Relief Service,
29 Farryl Street, Footscray

You will not be prosecuted if surrendering firearms or ammunition for destruction. Weapons may be submitted in person or left anonymously.

The new laws will come into force on May 1.

If you have any questions contact:
Officer in Charge
Footscray Police 9689 9999

Demetri's eyes skim the page. He shrugs, takes his glasses off and dries them. 'It's a weapons amnesty. They do these all the time. And the commissioner always hails them as a big success, no matter how successful they are.'

'People submit guns. Anonymously.'

'That's right. Believe it or not, it's hard to get rid of a gun. You don't just toss one in the rubbish. So what are you saying? People *submitted* the guns to Gary?'

Demetri smirks.

I say, 'Take a look at that last address.'

Demetri holds the reading glasses back up to his eyes: 'Twenty-nine Farryl Street.' He scowls. 'But it's spelled differently...'

'I called that telephone number, spoke to a Sergeant Malkin. I asked him where else the notice had been displayed. I tracked down as many as he could give me. And I found this.'

I take out the folded newspaper that's been sitting in my jacket pocket, waiting for me to take it out. On page three the same notice is printed among the advertisements.

I point to the typing error, where 'Farryl' has been misspelled.

Demetri squints at the newspaper, then back at the notice in the window, then back at the newspaper. It's raining steadily now, on our heads and jackets and pooling at our feet. Demetri seems to hold his breath and he looks at me.

'Are criminals in the western suburbs really that stupid?'

'Stupid enough to mistake a St George's Cross for the Red Cross? What do you think?'

Demetri thinks hard, can't seem to reach a conclusion. 'What do *you* think?'

'What do *I* think?'

'Yeah.'

'I think it's a massive miscarriage of justice with the rights of freedom for corruption and victims, innocent, travesty, persecution, outrage, more justice and then injustice.'

Demetri nods softly. 'Who else have you told?'

'I only figured it out this morning.'

'You haven't telephoned Gary's solicitor?'

'What's he going to do? He's a year out of law school with a thousand clients and even if he wasn't it'd take him weeks to get Gary actually released. And there's always the chance some hotshot junior prosecutor would want to take it to trial *anyway*, which means Gary stays on remand for six more months. A really good lawyer might have Gary home in a fortnight. But there's only one criminal law solicitor I can think of with the clout to get Gary released today.'

Demetri rolls his eyes. 'Don't try to sweet-talk me, you'll ruin all your hard work. You should know that there's probably not much I can achieve on a Sunday.'

I shrug. 'I called the DPP's office this morning, spoke to an intern, pretended I was you. I said I had something really important to speak with the director about. They said she'll be in her office all day.'

He bites his lip to hide the smile.

'Righto. You thought this through, didn't you...'

'You have to tell her this is another Jim Yedda waiting to happen, and that a negligence suit is one thing, but wrongful imprisonment based on laws that *she* lobbied for is something else altogether, the very year she wants to win a seat in Parliament. You can say Gary's locked up with psychopaths and sex offenders, so if he isn't released today then any injury he sustains will be on her head, and they'll be lining up to write a song about it. Or else I can tell her that. You can be the good cop.'

Demetri bows his head, shakes it with a little laugh.

'No,' he says, looking back at me, then up at the rain. 'If anyone else is there she might bristle, try to prove she can't be pushed around. Better I go alone.'

I fold up the newspaper, hold it out. He takes it, giggles again. I laugh back. 'What?'

'I'll do it on one condition. That this is the last job you ever do free of charge.'

'Not a chance.'

He nods. 'It was worth a try.'

Demetri looks out at the road, a new shine in his eyes. 'Okay. I need a taxi.'

This little walk with Demetri, one day I'll remember this as a kind of apogee. I'll regret that I didn't stop to soak it up, watching Demetri climb into that cab and drive away. But at the time you think that this is your life, that days like this are normal. You don't know a high-water mark until you've seen a lot of low water.

AN ORDINARY JOB

JESSICA LOOKS AT the pictures the way a husband does.

She sits on the front edge of the living-room couch, her feet tucked under her in a way that, if she were a man, would be uncomfortable. What she's doing is she's going through the photographs, one by one, wearing a face to show how unhappy the task is, while Phil and I just wait and watch and look sideways at each other.

She reaches the last and starts back with the first, that face unchanged by the shuffling of each print, each piece of bad news. And what occurs to me is that Jessica isn't a man, you'd never mistake her for a man, but she looks at the pictures the way a man does.

A wife, usually her eyes drift across a page or two and then she waves them away, scared of something, choosing not to see.

A husband needs to see. He sucks the detail from each photo like a prison inmate with a pornographic magazine. And what there aren't pictures of, he imagines—the drunken flirting, the whiff of pheromones, the slipping sound of her underwear. He imagines which of her friends know about it, which of them feel pity for him.

And he'll be nervous like it's a job interview, only he's asking me the questions: what I saw, what order things happened, how long it lasted.

'When was this?' Jessica says, not looking up.

'This'd be lunchtime today,' Phil says. 'And I'm sorry to say it, sweetie, but you can see…he didn't use a johnny.'

'A what?' She looks up now, enough disgust in her voice to make Phil flinch.

'A…a condom, you know?'

She's not a handsome woman, which Phil says is one of the reasons I'm here. He probably means her pimply skin, her proud nostrils, her size. But what's actually unattractive about Jessica Waltraub has crept up in just these last moments, a coldness that descended when her father gave her the pictures, when she realised why we've come.

'Wow, Dad. You must be happy now.' A ball in her throat making it hard to talk.

'Nah. I'm not, love.'

She pushes through the ball.

'You must be *fucking ecstatic.*'

The pictures frisbee across Jessica's living room and slap against the television, a massive flat screen, blank and unmoved.

That TV, that's another clue. Probably there have been a thousand clues over the length of the day, staring at me and then shrugging like they didn't care if the private investigator noticed them or not.

I trawl my memory, the long day it's been, wondering whether the sordid truth about this job was ever as obvious as it is right now. If the clues were there, they were subtle. Like the way Jessica looks at the photographs. Like that big TV. But this morning, when Phil first came to my office, when I first heard the names Ben and Jessica Waltraub, I couldn't have guessed what would be revealed. It didn't occur to me that there would be *clues* to watch out for.

This began as an ordinary job.

My ad in the Yellow Pages says my office hours start at nine, so when someone knocks on the door at eight twenty-eight I don't take it to be a client. Usually when this happens, someone's got the wrong door and they don't know that a white guy works here who only speaks English. Usually, they've climbed the stairs to the third floor looking for an acupuncturist named Chen Lei, whose rooms are down the hall and open at five in the morning. Usually, I point to Chen Lei's door and tell the person to follow the smell of burnt pine cones. Usually, I'm polite.

But today I'm up a ladder.

And I've almost finished painting the office walls, which I thought would take most of Saturday afternoon but instead took all of the weekend and here I am on Monday morning, still up a ladder. There's Swan Egg Matte in my hair and under my fingernails and my shoulder blades are screaming. Whoever-it-is knocks on my door a second time and I answer with a bilious '*Ni zou ba*,' which means 'Go away' in Mandarin and is exactly half of what I've learned of that language since I first leased this third-floor office in Chinatown.

A man's voice shouts through the door, '*Hello?*'

'*Yes?*'

The door knob rattles. If he could see my face he wouldn't be trying to get in.

I yell, '*What is it?*'

'*Hello?*'

'*What do you want?*'

Then he clears his throat and yells, in an accent so broad he

25

might be rounding up sheep: '*I think me daughter's husband's doing the dirty on her.*'

And I guess you don't see an acupuncturist for that.

Two months ago a potential client in the hallway would have rushed me to the door with beverages, biscuits, charm. But summer has been good, thanks mostly to a retired psychiatrist who came to me in tears because she couldn't remember where she'd parked her car. Two days earlier she'd driven into town for a show at the Regent Theatre and when it was over she'd walked the city for hours, trying to trigger her memory. I found the car not far from here, on Little Bourke Street, stretched across the driveway of a place that used to be a grocery store and now isn't anything; it didn't have so much as a parking ticket though it had been there for four days. The psychiatrist gave me an extra thousand dollars to never tell anyone what had happened. I told her I didn't think she and I moved in the same circles. But stigma runs deep.

And DISCREET AND CONFIDENTIAL is something else it says in my Yellow Pages ad.

So that's how come I can afford to finally paint these office walls. Another big job and I'll buy some nice furniture, a printer, one of those tall lamps, maybe something to stop the street noise from pouring in through the edges of the windows. Though really, I like the noise. The sound of Chinatown is soothing when there's no work and nothing else to do but listen.

I yell, '*Could you come back at nine?*'

I climb off the ladder, drag it aside and regard the wall.

'*It's just…*' the voice offers, '*I'm on me way to work.*'

At head height the colour is thick and lovingly applied. Towards the ceiling it thins out, in one corner shamefully. The fumes are strong, but an eight-year-old could snort raw heroin and paint my walls more competently than this.

I tray the roller with disgust. The furniture is blanketed with old clothes because I didn't have a drop sheet, and the clothes are blanketed by a weekend's worth of takeaway containers. I tip the mess off one of the three wooden school chairs and go to the door.

He's got a drinker's nose, swollen and textured like the moon through a telescope. Under his ragged Kmart jacket is a shiny red shirt and his left hand is missing half its pinkie—I would guess a factory accident. Once he's inside and seated, after I've apologised for the condition of the office and after he's politely edged the chair closer to the window and the merciful fresh air, Phil tells me that his daughter married a spoilt little rich kid from a family of German immigrants.

'There's this superiority about him,' Phil says in his kookaburra twang. 'You know what krauts are like.'

My father was born in Stuttgart. I don't mention that.

'So the two of you don't get along.'

'Well, what I come for is I want to find out if he's seeing other birds. And I want proof. Something I can show to Jessie.'

'She doesn't know you're here?'

'Nah, mate.'

'You think they're having problems?'

'Well, I don't know about that. I just reckon if she's married to a prick she's got a right to know. Is this the sort of thing you do?'

'Sure.'

'What's it going to set me back?'

'I'm two-fifty a day.'

'How many days you reckon?'

'Until he fools around again.'

Phil nods, keeps thinking.

'How do you...I mean...'

'I'll follow him around, see where he goes, try to get photographs.'

'He won't catch on?'

'I hope not. If he does, there's no way for him to link me to you.'

'Right then,' he says decisively, pressing his fists into his knees. 'So what do we do now?'

I pick up a pen, search my desk for a blank briefing sheet. I have to sift through clothes and takeaway containers, used plastic cutlery as well as puddles of dried paint. Phil takes now as an opportunity to stop churning through his dislike for his son-in-law and have a good look at this office, at this person he's retaining.

'How come you call yourself a private inquiry agent?' He says, his voice more relaxed and noticeably higher pitched. Perhaps the deep voice is just how he establishes credibility.

'It's the same as a private detective.' I unearth a briefing sheet from beneath a pair of boxer shorts.

'So why don't you call yourself that?'

'My father was a Private Inquiry Agent.'

'Fair dinkum? I supposed he's retired.'

'No. He's dead.' With my pen poised, I ask, 'How do you spell your son-in-law's name?'

'W-A-L-T-R-A-U-B. Benjamin Waltraub.'

'What does he do?'

'He does, like…art stuff for the Port Phillip Council.' His big cratered nose flares like it smells something foul. 'Buys paintings for the mayor. You know…organises art prizes. He rakes it in. You wouldn't believe what he gets paid.'

'Has he been unfaithful to Jessica before?'

'I don't know.'

'How do you know he is now?'

'It's sort of a…instinct.'

'Jessica never mentioned anything to you?'

Phil shakes his head, smiling softly. 'Mate, Jessica's mad for him. He's got charm, you know? He's handsome, got money. I guess that's part of why I wonder about him. I mean…the thing about Jessie is…'

He waits, adjusts himself in the chair. Continues, but slower. 'I'm telling you this because I don't want you thinking I'm one of them fathers reckons no one's good enough for his little girl. She's...' His head bobs side to side, dodging invisible bullets. 'She's not what you'd call a looker.'

'And she's never complained to you? Never mentioned a problem with Ben before?'

'Nah...' Phil stops, again searching for the words. 'Some people only see what they want to see.'

And I hardly hear him when he says it.

But later today, and in days to come, when I look back on this strange little job, it will occur to me, the truth of what he said there, despite the quotable cuteness of it.

Right now, I'm too busy ticking boxes on the briefing sheet.

'If your instinct is wrong and I spend two weeks finding out nothing, you get an invoice from me anyway.'

I hand the sheet to him to sign.

'Yeah, no. I get that, mate.'

'Have you got a recent photo of him? Something you can email me?'

'Yeah, I brung one.' From his crumbling wallet he draws out a glossy colour picture the size of a playing card. Ben is well dressed, sun-kissed, straight-toothed. It might just be the way the sun is hitting him, or the attractive gardens where the photo was taken, but he looks like an underwear model who just happened to be wearing clothes when this picture was taken. I put it in my pocket.

'You do car rentals?'

'How could you tell?'

I point at the Avis logo on his shirt pocket.

'Yeah. I'm on me way there now.'

'You're the manager?'

'Yes, mate.'

'Put your mobile number on that form. I'll call you each day, let you know how things are going. Does anyone else ever answer your mobile?'

'I suppose. Sometimes.'

'If I get someone who isn't you, or if it goes to voicemail, I'll leave a message saying I'm John from Melbourne Premier Florists and you should call me back.'

'I get it. So no one knows. Did your dad teach you that?'

It's a question only an unappreciated father would ask.

'My dad died when I was very young. He never taught me anything.'

Jessica gets to her feet. She takes some steps to the mantel and steadies herself, head hung, chin against her chest. 'Well done, Dad. Finally you get to kick Ben in the balls.'

Phil puts his hands up in surrender. 'You're blaming the wrong bloke here, sweetie...'

'Oh? You're not to blame?' She glowers at him, winding herself up again. 'Your grudge against Ben played...*no role*?'

'Wait on, love. You can't go saying—'

'Let's ask the private detective, shall we?' She turns to me, arms crossed, much more comfortable when she's on the attack. 'What did my father say when you showed him these lovely pictures?'

'Sweetie, you're being—'

'*Shut up, Dad*. Come on, Mister Whoever-You-Are, what did he say? Did he seem *upset* to you? Would you say he was *devastated* by what you'd found out?'

She cocks her head with mock attentiveness.

I rub at my shoulder. 'He said you'd accuse him of trying to ruin your marriage.'

'Liar.'

Phil stands up from the couch.

'Jessica, love. Listen to yourself. It's your mate Ben who's the problem, not me. Who would you rather crack it with, seriously? I'm doing you a favour here...'

Hands on her hips, she raises her face to the ceiling. There are tears welling up through her body and she's trying to breathe above the flood as it reaches her chin. She holds there for a long moment.

'I know you are...' she whispers to the roof.

Water seeps from her eyes and her face dives, defeated, into her hands.

Inside there she groans deeply. 'I'm a silly old cow.' I think that's what she says.

Phil goes to her, stands inches away, hesitates at the challenge of consoling her as she sobs. His hands go out and she slaps them away. He speaks but she only bawls louder. His hands go out again and though she struggles he manages to pull her to him and gets a handful of hair, restraining more than holding. Now she slumps into him and it's only her father's arms that keep her standing.

I linger, awkward.

The St Kilda Town Hall is the palatial kind of civic building you'd more likely find in the tropics, where the parliaments of very poor nations meet surrounded by exotic plants and green, green grass. Somewhere inside is the Right Honourable Alex Mills, Lord Mayor of the City of Port Phillip, no doubt fashioning new ways to lay off public servants and subsidise property developers. He's about as different from Phil Haynes as a white man can be, but it's people like Phil who vote people like Mills into office.

I'm thinking about this, waiting to maybe catch a glimpse of Jessica's husband on his lunch break, when a young woman appears in my rearview, striding purposefully along Carlisle Street, not recognising my car. Her face is awash with freckles, more even than when she and I were, what do you call it, engaged, and she appears generally more tropical now in this tropical setting: her hair a lighter brunette, her arms a deeper brown. She's just as straight-backed and graceful as I remember, she still pulls off that fluffy seventies hairstyle and her outfit is a last-minute combination of bright colours. So she still loves colourful clothes.

Annie Levitan could find a bright side to anything. She used to say that she loved my life-draining, shoebox apartment because you could vacuum the whole place from just one power point. She was always so positive. Right up to the day she stopped being positive.

I adjust the mirror so I can see where she's going, but she just heads right up Carlisle and then she's gone and the whole thing feels more like a distant memory than something that just happened. It occurs to me that this is what break-ups are: glimpses on busy streets, emotional time travel, the sullen reminder that you are, what do you call it, unlovable. I don't get to wallow in it though, because Ben Waltraub is suddenly here.

He's tall and he's stunning, even from a distance. It's as if there's an invisible spotlight that follows him around. His suit is tailored to show off his body and his hair to show off his face, and he struts across the carpark eating a sandwich and he manages to do even that like a movie star. After two bites he drops the rest in a rubbish bin, slides two breath mints into his mouth, gets into a big car the colour of a rain cloud and turns onto Brighton Road, headed south.

He doesn't get far. Brighton Road at lunchtime is a snake of cars lined up like refugees for food. Ben can't stop checking his reflection in his mirror. Either he's this vain all the time, or where he's going he wants to look good. Around us, the traffic isn't moving.

I'm in my Toyota Starlet, sky blue and tiny. If Phil could see the kind of car I drive, he'd wince.

'The thing is,' I'd tell him, 'no one expects to be tailed by a Starlet.'

We go nowhere for about twenty minutes, long enough to ruminate on how no one vacuums my apartment anymore, then Ben turns off at New Street and, after a moment, we're on the Esplanade. The bay is big and still while everything else is small and rushing past, but Ben doesn't slow to appreciate it. He's moving quick, in a hurry, running late.

When you're tailing someone in a motor vehicle, the last thing you want them to do is turn down a cul-de-sac. Ben turns down a cul-de-sac, so I have to drive past, pull over and run casually to the corner, peek around.

It's a street of enormous white houses and carefully planted palm trees that must suffer in the winter. The road curves away and I can't see Ben's car so I run past all the trees to the bend, hope he hasn't pulled into a garage.

He hasn't. His Range Rover is there in the driveway of the big white mansion where the road ends.

I down-gear to a stroll, making sure not to look around, not to act like I've never been here before. Across from the mansion, in his front yard, a man in a nylon tracksuit is watching me through his front gate. It's not apparent what he's doing and it's possible he only came out to inspect this stranger on Affluent Boulevarde. A neighbourhood like this, they'll just go ahead and taser you if you don't look like you belong. I try to act like I'm expected as I waltz softly through the front gate of the white palace and into a minimalist Japanese garden.

I hide behind the terracotta walls for ten seconds, then chance a look over the top: the tracksuit sifts through his mail, turns and goes back inside. Maybe he's used to strange men waltzing in through this particular front gate. Or maybe he thinks that whoever lives here, Ben Waltraub's mistress or his bookie or his masseuse, maybe they could do with a good robbery.

I'm quiet as I pad past the garden that is really mostly raked gravel and I reach a pair of french doors that look into a living room the size of a cathedral. When I see what's happening in there I take the camera from my pocket. My hands shake. They always shake when I do this.

It's never a surprise to find that the person I'm tailing is actually engaging in the extramarital affair my client suspects. In fact, I have never had a case where the person in question was *not* cheating. Never even once. But this scene I've crept up on, this is a surprise. Phil and his talk of 'other birds' was enough to put it in my head that that's what I'd be coming across. But what does Phil know. Because right now Ben is bent over an off-white chaise longue and there's another man behind him, making that familiar face. Their respective pants are bunched around their respective ankles and the other man's shirt tails are flapping gently against his thighs like seagull wings. This guy, he's in his sixties, white-haired, craggy, tanned, and given what he's doing, the room he's doing it in, I'm going to assume he lives here alone.

They didn't waste a moment. All that traffic has cut their time short.

Doing this kind of job is the only time I think of my father. He specialised in matrimonial work like so many private inquiry agents did back then—crouching in ornate gardens and peering through windows was his bread and butter. In the days before no-fault divorce you had to have grounds to dissolve a marriage, and the most popular ground was adultery, which couldn't merely be alleged, it had to be proven. So if you wanted a divorce before 1976, you needed a private investigator to kick down a door, flashbulbs blazing, ready to swing a punch if he had to. And boy, did he get paid. The conservatives of the era, the ones who saw the rise of no-fault divorce as a satanic conspiracy, they wanted the end of a marriage to be as expensive and traumatic as possible. Which was fine with people like my father. He made even more if he could sell the details to a scandal sheet like the *Truth*.

Then along came 'irreconcilable differences' and a thousand private investigators were suddenly out of a job, my father included— for them it must have seemed like a whole other kind of satanic conspiracy. But for Albert Dorn the worst was yet to come. Because what else the new laws meant was that my mother could finally dump the guy who blew all his money at the racetrack, in pubs and brothels, who earned plenty but still couldn't provide for his wife and his baby son.

Two years after that, with me only four years old, my father drank himself to death in a Carlton flophouse.

All I know about him is what my mother told me before she too went and died, and based on her stories, I think he would have loved this, what I'm doing here. I can picture him in a cheap suit like mine, huddled next to me, eyes twinkling at this new discovery, muffling giggles with his Stetson Stylemaster. He could have told you that back then 'sodomy' was its own grounds for divorce. He could have told you that, technology being what it was, there weren't a lot of opportunities to take photos *secretly* in those days. And he could have told you what I've gleaned from years of this kind of work: black, white, fat, thin, rich, poor, straight, gay...When they're doing what these two are doing, all men make the same face.

For my father, this would have been the most ordinary kind of job.

Phil says, 'One way to look at it, love, is wouldn't you rather know now?'

Her face is wedged between her father's back and the couch cushion, an arm slung mindlessly across his lap, blubbering noises muffled by the soft silk of the seat cover.

Phil gently touches her hand and his mouth twitches. He says, 'I mean, sweetie, isn't it better to know now? Don't you reckon it's better than ten years from now?'

That one isn't the only couch made of silk. None of the furniture is cheap and Swedish, none of it was assembled by Jessica or her husband. The carpet is lush, the cabinets ornate, the shelves go all the way to the ceiling. Looking down into the speckled opaque glass of the coffee table is like looking down into the night sky itself. I think of my own office, the paint I've put on the walls.

Phil lowers his tone. 'If Ben is…you know…then fine. Whatever. I haven't got any problem with those people, you know? But where I draw the line, sweetie, is he doesn't have a right to lie to you about it all these years.'

Jessica squeezes her father tighter, bawling into his clothes.

Catching Phil's eye, I point to myself, then jerk a thumb at the door. He stares at me but fails to see my gesture.

'And don't forget Mister Dorn. He's our secret weapon. He can stand up in court and tell them he saw it all himself.'

I scowl at these words, shake my head at Phil—he knows I can't do that. Phil raises a palm, a request for me to stay, to be patient. He says to Jessica, 'These kinds of pictures make a big difference in divorce proceedings.'

Phil knows that isn't true either.

Jessica pulls her sticky face from the couch and drags clumps of matted hair from her eyes.

'I don't want a divorce,' she moans, her voice like a violin in a horror movie. 'I want a normal fucking husband.'

Phil helps her clear the last strands. 'I know, sweetie. I know.'

She doesn't turn to look at me, but her eyes dart across to the fireplace, just long enough to glimpse me in her peripheral vision. She leans in to her father's ear, sniffles back more mucus and whispers something.

Phil replies, 'Nah, nah, nah. John is here to help us. He's helping us, see?'

Jessica slaps a hand against her thigh the way she must have when she was six. Her voice cracks and rises a full octave.

'I want that pervert out of my house.'

To make prints I go to a copy centre in the city because I pawned my printer last year. There's a girl there, Kavneet, who knows what I do, what these photos are, so I pass the memory card to her with the usual guilty face, which is our signal for how no one else can see these images. The first time I came to her I had a card full of pictures of a man going in and out of his house, photographed from a hiding place across the street. That's all they were, him coming and going, and then four pictures showing him dropping his keys, picking them up again. Kavneet guessed, using some gift I wasn't born with and without even a hint from me, that he was claiming insurance payments for an injury at work. She guessed what it was I did for a living and she guessed that this guy's payments were about to come to a sudden stop.

The second time I came to Kavneet, they were pictures like the ones I have today. Adultery. Candid.

I said, 'I've come to you because you know I'm not a peeping Tom.'

And Kavneet said back, like it was her only line in the movie and she'd been rehearsing for months, 'John, maybe you don't get off on these pictures, but you *are* a peeping Tom.'

The real reason I go to her is that having a twenty-two-year-old do your prints at a copy centre in the city makes it all a little less creepy.

So I get the pictures and they're big and pretty and in colour and I hike back to Chinatown, politely navigate the throngs of lawyers emerging from boozy lunches, purchase some takeaway Singapore noodles at Leung Mai and return to the heavy vapours of my office. From beneath a tangle of paint-spattered Explorer socks I unearth my laptop and get to shovelling food into my mouth as it boots up. I do a search on Ben's friend who owns the big white house and whose name, according to the Registrar of Titles, is Charles Daschle.

More Germans.

What there is to know about Daschle depends on which website you read. He's gay or he's a confirmed bachelor. He made his money or it was bequeathed to him. He owns ten vineyards or three, and he produces Allingirra Drop, the kind of wine I'd need a bank loan to get a glass of. He may have been picked up for public indecency one time but if he was he was never charged. He owns between two and five apartments in the one complex on Beaconsfield Parade, as well as about a dozen other houses scattered around Melbourne. He contributed money to Alex Mills's campaign for mayor, and the two are good friends. He may own a yacht that he has never sailed in.

He drinks, he smokes, he gets laid a lot. The end.

There's less information available on Benjamin Waltraub. He was born to Gustav and Frederica Waltraub, a family of Lutherans in Mildura, then came to Melbourne to attend Monash University and, it seems, to rebel against his religious upbringing, largely by way of experimental theatre. He and his troupe focused on 'performance art that exists to challenge outdated perceptions of love, sex and relationships'. At that time in his life I'm betting Benjamin was experimental with more than just theatre.

Skip forward to his job at the City of Port Phillip, where he supervises Alex Mills's Cultural Program. His staff profile tells me exactly nothing, so I turn to my mobile phone and dial a number.

Leo Spaske picks up on the first ring.

'John. How are you, dear sir?'

'Fine, Leo. Have you got a second to run a check on somebody?'

'For you, John, anything at all.' You can hear his chair creak as he leans back into it. 'When have you ever known me to refuse you a favour?'

'This will take two seconds. Nothing special. Taxable income, reduction claims.'

'Absolutely, John. I can't think of any reason why I wouldn't do that for you.'

There's a silence.

'You should be flattered, Leo. You're the private investigator the other private investigators come to for help.'

'Oh, John, I'm touched. I'm deeply touched. And I will do this for you because I know you would do the same for me. It has nothing to do with the fact that you might otherwise alert certain authorities to the access I have to certain databases. I would never dream that you would dob me in, John, or threaten to in order that I might provide you with access to those very same databases.'

'If you're not going to do it, Leo, just say the words—'

'Of course I will, John. Of course I will do this for you. What name?'

'Benjamin Waltraub. W-A-L-T-R-A-U-B.'

The sound of Leo's treefingers typing. I've seen his office just once: everything in there seems miniature compared to his elongated frame. He hunches over his keyboard like a daddy long legs wrapping up a fly.

'Benjamin Waltraub. Total income for last financial year, fifty-seven thousand. No capital gains tax. No reductions. No shares. No bonds. No directorships. Nothing depreciating. Total assets, less than five thousand dollars.'

'That's it?'

'That is everything, John.'

'Thanks for your help.'

'No trouble, John. No trouble at all. Oh, and John?'

'Yeah?'

'How are you travelling without the lovely Annie? That must have been such a *blow*. Did I hear that she's engaged again?'

Now is when I hang up the phone.

But Leo's just shovelling snow. Annie and I only ended last year and I'm still finding strands of brown hair on my couch: it's too soon for her to be engaged again from scratch. Even if she wanted to be she wouldn't do it because that's Annie. I ought to call Leo back with a choice insult. Instead I choose not to think about it.

I call Phil on his mobile, don't have to pretend I'm a florist. He agrees for me to come and visit him at work. As I scoff the last of the noodles, I'm thinking I would love for Phil Haynes to be impressed because I've got him such a clean result in less than a day. But these are pictures of his son-in-law getting bent over a couch by a local socialite, so that's not what I'm expecting when I arrive at the Avis Car Rentals outlet in Caulfield.

'Crikey jeepers...' Phil says, looking through the photos, nodding his comprehension. 'Mate, I reckon you're worth more than two-fifty a day.' And he holds my eyes, his own gleaming.

So he's impressed.

The office is tiny and windowless, dark and littered with piles of folded paper. It's the office of a manager who never means to spend a lot of time in here, would rather be out renting or upgrading or test driving. But one thing leads to another and here he always is, managing.

Phil keeps looking through the pictures, squinting so as to filter out the explicit parts.

I say, 'Technically what I did was trespass. Which shouldn't be a problem, but you need to know that these kinds of pictures aren't any good in the Family Court. When you show them to Jessica, you need to be clear that they won't be leverage in any kind of settlement...If she wants to go that way.'

Phil shrugs. What matters is he was right and he can prove it. After a few more moments of sifting through the pictures, murmuring 'crikey' and 'geez', he asks me, 'Who is this bloke?'

'Charles Daschle. Heard of him?'

He shakes his head.

'High society. Unmarried. Owns a lot of stuff.'

'Poor Jessie,' Phil says. 'She's bloody going to hate me for this. She's going to say I'm trying to wreck her marriage. And it's funny... but she's kind of right about that.'

'I know I asked you already, but she's never mentioned any trouble with Ben? Never said she had an inkling that something might be going on?'

'Mate, they've got the happiest bloody marriage I've ever seen. Until now, she always thought *I* was the problem.' He slips the photos back into their envelope. 'Well, I suppose you want your money. How's three hundred sound?'

'It sounds fine.'

He starts to search his desk.

'I got a chequebook somewhere about...I just saw it...'

He rifles, growing flustered, his exasperation partly fuelled by what I'd guess is embarrassment about the state of the place. Being near a light switch, I flick it on. Phil looks at his watch.

'I'm heading off to see Jessie.' He peeks under a pile of manila folders. Then he stops, thinks, goes over to a filing cabinet in the corner of the room. He opens a drawer and pulls out a whisky bottle, half empty, holds it up.

'You want one?'

'No thanks.'

'Just a toast. To celebrate a job well done.'

'I don't really drink.'

He finds a glass and pours a shot, downs it. He's not celebrating. He's steeling himself.

'Look, the thing is…' He peers into the glass. 'Can you come?'

'With you?'

'Yeah.'

'If you want.'

'Bit of moral support.' He waves a hand at the envelope. 'I don't know about this otherwise…'

I point to the chequebook. It sits on a pile of invoices skewered on a metal pin.

'Bring that along,' I say. 'You can pay me when we're done.'

Phil picks it up. He picks up the photos too.

'I mean…' he says, pulling on a jacket. 'When she sees them, she'll think it's more legit if you're there, right? Isn't that what people usually think?'

'Sometimes. Sometimes they think this is what I do for kicks and try to make it about me.'

'No…' Phil zips up the jacket. 'Jessica's stubborn and she can be hard to control, but she won't have a go at you. I expect she'll be too upset to even notice you're there.'

'Get the fuck out of my house!' Jessica screeches, rising to her feet. And I would if she weren't standing between me and the door. Phil has one hand in the air, placating, but when he tries to speak, she speaks louder. To me.

'Photographing people fucking! You don't even know Ben. You *don't* even *know* him. Hey! Are you even listening to me?'

It's my inability to answer that brings on critical mass. From the coffee table she picks up a ceramic candle holder and aims for my face. But her eyes are so full of tears it doesn't hit its mark, instead it strikes a photo of her and Ben mounted in the corridor. The photo falls to the carpet, cracked.

At the irony, nobody laughs.

The second candle holder is more carefully aimed. My hands go up but somehow the missile makes it through and a sharp edge hits my face and sends me knees-first to the floor.

Phil shouts, '*Jessie*,' and before she can throw anything else he's on his feet and wrenching back on her arms.

'Sweetheart!'

He keeps on speaking but it's drowned out by her last echoing declaration—'Oh fuck off, Dad!'—as she pulls herself free and bolts into the hallway.

With a slam of the bedroom door, there's quiet.

Phil helps me to my feet and I can feel his heartbeat through his fingers. A lazy drip of blood comes from my nose. I wipe it away.

'Sorry about that, mate…' Phil says, smiling awkwardly. 'It's a shock for her, you know?'

I don't know if that's true. But if I told him what I really thought, he'd only think it was sarcasm.

We pull up outside a red-brick terrace in Balaclava, near the station. The street has an old-fashioned milk bar and around a million flyers taped to telephone poles: live music, political events, movies; trendsetters have colonised this part of town. The Waltraub house itself has no front gate or yard, the front wall simply rises straight up from the footpath. It has a newly painted door and a window with bars across it. The bars are freshly painted too.

I ask Phil, 'How long have they lived here?'

'Reckon about a month. They only rent it. I'm always telling

Jessie they should buy. Christ knows they can afford to. But I guess it's good they didn't…if she decides to leave him.'

He rings the doorbell. The pictures are in a folder under his arm. He says, 'Oh Jesus,' staring at the door. 'This won't be fun.'

The door opens and there's Jessica, wearing old tracksuit pants and a jumper-cum-apron. She's carrying an empty cardboard box that swings up to her hip when she plants her fist there.

'Hey, Dad.' She's already, very subtly, backing away. 'What's going on?'

'Hi sweetie. How are you?'

'I'm okay.' She smiles nervously, sensing the drama in the air. 'What's going on?'

Phil says, 'This is John Dorn. He's a private inquiry agent. I've hired him.'

'What for?'

'Can we come in?'

'You've been drinking, Dad. I can smell it. What's this about?'

'Let's come in and sit down, love.'

He gently pushes inside and she lets him through and I follow into a bare corridor of stained floorboards. The bedroom to the left is vacant but for a small mountain of empty cardboard boxes spilling out to the hall.

I look at them and she says, 'We just moved in.'

I nod, smile as pleasantly as I can. Into the pile Jessica throws the box she carried to the door. It's decorated with an elaborate Allingirra Drop insignia. All the boxes are.

'That's a lot of wine.' I say, pointing goofily.

'Yes,' she laughs drily. 'Don't worry, my husband and I didn't drink it all.'

'What did you do with the rest?' I ask, still smiling. Phil's eyes widen at me. He wants us to get to the living room, get on with it.

'Oh, you know...' says Jessica, wistful. 'Gifts...That sort of thing. We gave you a bottle for your birthday, didn't we, Dad?'

He nods as though he's only pretending to remember. 'Yes,' he says, and keeps moving down the hall.

I say, 'Do you know Charles Daschle then?'

Phil stops, turns and stares at me. He can't understand why I'd be so indelicate.

Jessica says, 'Who?'

And she shakes her head, and she turns and leads her father towards the living room. And the whole thing blooms inside my brain, like it must be blooming inside hers. The actuality of it paralyses me for a moment.

Maybe I should pull Phil out of here, tell him what I think is going on before this big confrontation happens. Perhaps the kindest thing to do would be to prepare him for what he might be about to find out. But then there's a sad curiosity that leads me headfirst down the hallway. I want to see what she does.

Back on the footpath I'm wrapping my coat tighter around me and getting ready to ask for my cheque. Phil leaves the front door ajar and comes to me with his eyebrows raised, a mild smirk on his lips, like we just came out of a movie that had more sex in it than we'd expected.

'Hell hath no fury, don't you reckon?'

Because he says this I put my hand to my nose, but it's stopped bleeding.

I ask, 'How often does she get like that?'

'Like *that?* Hardly ever, mate. I mean, she can be difficult. But I never seen her act out like that.' He shakes his head, reaches into his pocket and pulls out the chequebook. 'Guess you can't blame her for taking it bad.'

'Did anything seem strange? I mean…did she seem strange to you?'

Phil opens the chequebook and stops to look at me and there's a voice in my head that's telling me I should get the money before I start breaking things down. But there's a louder voice that says to do this now.

'Of course she acted strange. She just found out her husband's a poof.'

'I mean strange even for that.'

He shakes his head, impatient. 'What?'

'Think about it. Jessica would *have* to know where all this stuff is coming from. The wine, the furniture, the car. Have you *seen* Ben's car?'

Phil blinks. 'Ben paid for it…'

'He couldn't have. I looked him up, Phil. Ben makes fifty-seven thousand a year. He makes less than *you*. His family doesn't have money. He's just a civil servant.'

'That's bullshit. His family's loaded.'

'How do you know?'

'Jessie told me…'

I pause, lead into this as gently as I can. 'I think she told you that because she doesn't want you to know where the money's really coming from.'

Phil's eyes bug out, but I don't give him time to think.

'Why did she look at the pictures that way? Analysing them one at a time. She was buying time, figuring out what to do.'

This is me trying to think of all those clues I missed.

'Charles Daschle owns Allingirra Drop. You saw the boxes. And if Ben is so wealthy, how come they're still renting? Why don't they have a mortgage?'

Phil points absently to the house. 'Wait…You're saying that was…what happened in there was…'

'She didn't have a choice, the two of us showing up the way we did. We cornered her.'

'You're joking, aren't you? What kind of bloody dragon do you think she is? For one thing, Jessie's not going to stay with a bloke who's a bloody homo...'

'Maybe he's *not* gay. Not the way you think. Maybe he and Jessica have a great marriage. You said yourself they're mad for each other. But they're broke. She doesn't work, he's in the arts. Then one day Ben meets Daschle at a fundraiser for the mayor and a pretty sweet opportunity presents itself.'

'No...'

'If Ben *is* gay then what's he doing married to Jessie? Why keep living a lie? He works at the St Kilda Town Hall, half the staff there must be gay. He doesn't need to pretend he isn't. Unless he actually isn't.'

'What are you trying to do?' He asks softly, eyes watery with confusion, hands trembling. His denial seems to be happening all over his body.

'I'll bet you Daschle owns this house. I bet Jessica and Ben live here rent-free. I bet there isn't even a bond lodged with the Bond Authority. And I know a bloke who can find out for us. He'll probably cost a couple of hundred and God knows he can be hard to work with, but—'

'Fuck *that*,' Phil says, his voice so soft and fierce. 'I don't reckon you realise what you're saying. Do you realise what you're saying about Jessie?'

He takes two steps towards me, stops. He's shaking. Something in his face has changed. His eyes flicker left and right and I know he's weighing up whether to hit me.

He says, 'Who the fuck do you think you are?'

I don't have an answer for him. I make a deal with myself that if he strikes me I'll go down and stay down until he's gone. His eyebrows twitch and I can tell that the gentlest summer breeze will be enough to blow him over the edge. I stay frozen. My eyebrows are twitching too.

He turns to the car and lays the chequebook on the roof, writing hurriedly, barely legibly. 'Maybe you think you're smart, but that kind of thing…I *reject* that.'

'No, look—'

'Jessie was right about you,' he says.

'Listen—'

'Shut up.' Staring hard, daring me to say more. 'You are disgusting.'

Then he tears out the cheque, gives it to me. Exactly two hundred and fifty dollars.

Phil lingers a moment, full of a pained energy, glowering at me like he's trying to think of something else to reject. I've got nothing more to say. Really, he's right. Maybe he should have hired a 'private investigator', not some half-arsed 'private inquiry agent'. Maybe that's what he's thinking as he goes back into the house.

He closes the front door.

I bury my hands in my jacket pockets and hike back towards Dandenong Road, brooding on it. Ben Waltraub seems to have accidentally carried over his desire to 'challenge modern perceptions of love, sex and relationships' into his adult life. The student in him would have loved to see Phil's reaction: the confusion, the internal panic. The world goes and changes on men like Phil Haynes, and telling them so doesn't do any good.

Even after the divorce, after my mother had thrown him out, my father would still let himself in and set down his bags and ask, entirely serious, what was for dinner. It got so that my mum had code words arranged with the neighbours that would prompt them to call the police.

On the corner of Inkerman Street and Dandenong Road there's a tram stopped at the lights and I break into a run. Just as I reach it the driver looks at me, looks through me, closes the tram doors and moves off. I'm left here, hugging my jacket tight because summer is over.

Since forever, people only see what they want to see.

Which makes this an ordinary job after all.

KAHRAMAN

I'M AWAKE BY the time anyone comes to my office. It's a boy and his mother, both diffident, both Mediterranean. She wears a cream and black hijab, floral silk flowing out from beneath the headdress. He walks with his arms straight down his sides. If they rang first I didn't hear the phone because of the ringing in my ears. I suppose I should be embarrassed by the state I'm in, but I've been to the toilet to vomit already, so at least that won't happen while they're here. Probably.

I ask them to sit and they do. Hunched over my desk and grimacing, I wonder if I smell as bad as I feel.

'We read about you in the paper this morning,' the boy says. He's barely old enough to drive, with shiny hardened hair and a smile like my fly's undone. 'It was all about that Turkish bloke who got killed. We read about you, what you did.'

I glance across at his mother. She doesn't seem to be put off by my bloodshot eyes.

The boy says, 'My family's Turkish. I mean, we're Muslims. Not like that other bloke. My parents came over from Ankara.'

My head gets suddenly too heavy and I let it fall into my hand. I wait for him to get to the point.

'Ummm…so the other day, my dad went out to buy a new washing machine…' He shifts in his seat. 'This is Monday. He never came home. And we want someone to look for him.'

Either she doesn't know much English or she doesn't consider it her place to speak: the mother does nothing more than gaze longingly at the boy and me.

I nod, respectfully. 'You think he's run off?'

'He wouldn't do that. I mean…but if he did do it, we have a right to know, right?'

His demeanour is self-assured, but his appearance tells a different story. As well as the hair and the pressed shirt, he's cleaned his shoes and left scuffs of polish on his white socks. One ear is pierced, but he's taken the stud out. He's red beneath his chin because he doesn't shave often, but he shaved today.

He's a punk who's dolled himself up for me.

I ask, 'Did he pack a suitcase?'

'Nuh. Nothing like that.'

'Any money missing?'

'We don't know. None of us…He's the only one who can use the bank account.'

'How many of you are there?'

'Us and my two sisters.'

'What's your name?'

'Nazeem.'

'Nazeem, did you ring around the hospitals? Go to the police?'

'Yeah, but Mum reckons the police don't care about us cos we're Turks.'

She shifts in her chair, unhappy with how her son has dobbed her in for being ethnic and paranoid. So she understands English.

'You think he's left you, right?' I say this to her. 'So what this is really about is getting access to the money. Am I right?'

She shakes her head, still doesn't want to speak to me. The boy makes another face.

'Not really. Mum doesn't reckon there is any money. We just want to know, like, where is he?'

'I'm four hundred dollars a day. Can you afford me?'

Pain flashes on his face, as if he's the one whose head beats a lonely, monumental throb. Pieces of last night come back to me like shards of a mirror: me slumped on a bar stool…me ordering doubles, storing it up for winter…me getting stroppy with a bartender…so stroppy I break a cocktail glass. Me being asked to leave.

I came here to sleep because it was closer.

He says, 'Ummm…well, not straight off. But it would only be for a couple of months. I've got a job, at a halal butcher in Coburg. I'm going to get some extra shifts because it's coming up to summer and everyone goes on holiday.'

I pinch my eyeballs with my fingers. 'What can you pay me up-front?'

Nazeem's mother's eyes aren't pleading anymore. With all this talk of money, they're worried.

He says, 'No…I mean, nothing. But it would just be until my extra shifts start. I thought, if you want, we could have a payment plan.'

'That's what you thought?'

Nazeem scowls slightly, interprets my tone as a failure to understand. He tries to explain:

'It was in the paper…what you did. It was all about that crazy Greek bloke whose trial was yesterday.'

'Yesterday wasn't his trial. It was his sentencing.'

'Yeah, well…You know what the newspaper said? They called you *Kahraman*. That's a Turkish word. It means—'

'I know what it means,' I say. Loud enough to make him stop talking. 'It's a word that…'

My hands press against my head, try to control everything inside there. When I glance up, I can't bear to look at that Turkish face anymore. I flick my fingers at him.

'Get out of my office.'

His brown eyes start. 'But...But we read about you—'

'You read about me and thought, here's a soft touch. You thought you could come in here and point out to me how Turkish you are and then I'd solve all your problems for you. Well, I can guess what the papers said and I do not give a shit.'

The shock is there in his teeth, in the way he stares at me. For a moment, he's dumbfounded. Mum looks desperately from Nazeem to me, then she speaks. Her voice is a whispery buzz.

'Please, sir. We have not money. For me it is very important if my husband left me. It is very important. Also, it is important that he pay money for his children.'

I give her my sour face.

She says, 'And we pay you. Nazeem pay you because he works. December, January, he works. He pay you December, January. But now must look for Khalid—'

I can't listen to this. I shake my head.

'It's a little rude, don't you think? Asking me for a favour? I don't *know* you. I don't *owe* you anything.'

'Please—'

'And what if your old man's gone back to Ankara? You think I'm going to pay for a flight over there so I can bring him back? Get the fuck out.'

I wave at the door again. Nazeem is still confused.

'But...It would only be for a month or—'

'*Get the fuck out of here!*'

The sound of my voice hurts my ears, head. It's enough to blow them out of their chairs. She doesn't hesitate, bustles straight out the door and she's gone. Nazeem walks slower, maybe searching for something to get me to change my mind or just to listen. He must realise his options are nil because suddenly the punk in him is back and he says, 'Hey, fuck you, man...'

He leaves, doesn't shut the door.

And I'm still hunched over the desk. I've barely moved since they walked in. It occurs to me that I might vomit again and I decide that if I do, I'm not going to run to the toilet. If it's going to happen, it's going to happen right here where I'm sitting. That, I think, would be appropriate.

A TV cameraman sets up a tripod near us. Then a skinny reporter in a blue suit and red tie, holding a microphone with a network logo on it, positions himself with his back to the courthouse and says, 'Face check.'

The cameraman twists the lens, his eye flat to the viewfinder. 'You're fine.'

'Tell me when you're ready.'

Behind him, the crowd isn't big, but it's enough to block foot traffic along William Street and piss off everyone who's due in court today. Barristers and their clients push through the gathering of mostly Turkish church-goers who weren't there for any portion of the trial; they've come out today because their priest asked them to. Already, some of them are going home, stiffly climbing onto the bus that stops directly beneath Lady Justice, with her scales and her blindfold and her toga. Dennis and I are loitering, away from the crowd, hands in pockets, quiet. I don't know what we're still doing here except maybe bearing witness.

The cameraman silently points his finger. The skinny reporter drops into his TV voice.

'Spiros Angelis was visibly shaken today as Justice Linehan sentenced him to a non-parole period of eleven years in prison.'

Dennis rotates slowly to look at me. When I look back, he flicks his chin at something in the crowd. It's the Director of Public Prosecutions, wearing his massive Soviet-style greatcoat, shaking hands with a circle of middle-aged admirers, all of them Turkish. The old DPP just won herself a seat in State Parliament and already this new guy's glad-handing like he's running for office too.

The reporter says, 'In May, a jury found Angelis guilty of the murder of nineteen-year-old Osman Yusedich, a student and beloved member of the Turkish community. Osman was stabbed to death in a Carrum Downs carpark in the early hours of November fourth last year.'

Dennis lights another cigarette, offers me one. I tell him I don't smoke. When he pockets them, I see the flash of a revolver inside his jacket.

'What did you bring that for?'

'It's the one they gave me at the academy.'

'You bring it to court? Who are you going to shoot, the tipstaff?'

Dennis looks at me with intense boredom. 'If this gets any worse, I'm going to shoot us both right here in front of the press. Don't take your shitty mood out on me.'

The cameraman looks over here. The smoke from Dennis's cigarette is wafting past the reporter and maybe we're talking too loud. But he takes a good look at us and, no, he's not going to tell us off.

The reporter says, 'During the trial, Spiros Angelis claimed to have encountered Osman Yusedich whilst coming home from a Dandenong nightclub. He gave evidence that Yusedich provoked the confrontation which culminated in the teenager's death.'

None of Spiros's family is here and there isn't another Greek within eight city blocks. It's a black day for them and they want nothing to do with it. Zeus himself could appear and tell them, '*Go to the Supreme Court*,' and still they wouldn't be here. What's funny is, even if they all knew what I know, what Dennis knows, they'd still be ashamed. No matter how you look at it, a Greek killed a Turk for no good reason.

The reporter continues: 'Justice Linehan said that despite Angelis's intellectual disability and pronounced psychological immaturity, the nature of the crime demanded the harshest of penalties. Angelis appeared shocked by the decision, hanging his head and wiping away tears. But outside the court there was jubilation amongst members of the Turkish church groups who'd fought for justice, even after police had given up any hope of solving the case.'

Father Orhan Safak doesn't look jubilant, but his moustache has grown so big now that it's possible he is and I can't tell because of all the hair. As I watch, he moves across the crowd of Catholics to the DPP. He shakes his hand, talking earnestly. They hug.

I say to Dennis, 'How does it get worse than this?'

The reporter: 'The victim's mother, Miresha Yusedich, was also in tears as the sentence was read out. She told reporters that her prayers have been answered, and that justice has finally been done for her cherished son.'

Miresha is hunched just this side of the steps leading up to the court, looking stoic, partly because of what happened today, partly because she's deaf and she can't hear what people are saying. She's dressed all in black again and I'm wondering what colour she used to wear before her son was murdered. Holding her hand is Anna, talking to a court reporter, animated, like she's about to snatch away the notebook and write tomorrow's page-six copy herself.

I look at Dennis. He's watching Miresha too. He shrugs.

'At least there's that.'

Anna looks over at me and points. Miresha nods earnestly at the journalist, gestures towards me.

I duck my head, scratch at my brow.

The reporter next to us lowers the microphone, drops his reporter's face and raises his eyebrows at the cameraman. 'How was that?'

The cameraman nods and shrugs. 'That's a print.'

The two of them drift away and I can see the other court reporter, the one who was talking to Miresha. She's wading through the crowd, headed over here. Her eyes are locked on to me and she's smiling, trying to freeze me in her headlights.

I say to Dennis, 'Let's go. Come on. Let's go right now.'

Dennis drops his cigarette on the footpath, grinds it under his shoe.

'Yeah. Let's get fucking drunk.'

'I don't want to drink.'

'Where you want to go? Church? You and I aren't welcome there today. A bar is the next best thing.'

'I don't really drink.'

'Fuck that. You just need to learn how.'

What Spiros does when he's scared is he smirks. It's the same thinning of the lips he'd do if he was blowing on a hot cup of coffee, only with a twinkle in his eye that seems arrogant but is really him floundering, shielding himself with a face that says this is all so funny.

The prosecutor asks, 'Mister Angelis, were you under the influence of drugs on the night in question?'

'No, sir.'

'Not marijuana, speed, ecstasy?'

'No, I don't do drugs.'

'Had you been drinking?'

'No.'

The jury watches him, focused but detached, the way scientists watch monkeys. They're not sneaking any Sudoku today. When the trial started, the judge flat-out told them that it would turn on what Spiros had to say. That their one job was to judge if Spiros killed Osman because his own life was threatened, or just because.

So here they are, with their listening faces on. And there's Spiros, smirking.

The prosecutor says, 'You'd patronised the Vitamins nightclub for four or five hours, but in that time you took no drugs and drank no alcohol?'

'I don't do drugs.'

'Do you drink?'

'Sometimes.'

'Had you had anything to drink that night?'

'Maybe I had a beer.'

'Maybe you had a beer.'

'Yeah.'

'Maybe you had more than one?'

'Maybe.'

'How many beers would you say you had?'

'I don't know.'

'More than five?'

'Nuh. No. Not that much.'

'Okay. But you probably had a couple of beers.'

'Yeah.'

'Even though you said a moment ago that you hadn't been drinking.'

Something else about Spiros is he had ADHD as a kid and went to a special clinic in Ringwood. Earlier this week, a psychiatrist was sitting where Spiros is sitting now. He said Spiros had a mild intellectual disability and sub-average cognitive functioning, which means there was never going to be much that that clinic could do for him. While the psychiatrist gave evidence, Spiros sat in the dock, squeezing his lips together with both hands, and the jury must have been thinking what I thought the day I met him: you don't need a shrink to know there's something wrong with the boy.

'Um…I don't know.'

His eyes look across the courtroom, pleading for help. At first I think he's looking at me, but it's his brother, George Angelis, seated behind me near the entrance to the gallery, that he's appealing to. George is only five feet tall, but what he lacks in height he makes up for in width. He's a bodybuilder, and even now, with him wearing a suit for maybe the first time in his life, it's obvious.

With Spiros's eyes on him, George makes no gesture or movement.

'What don't you know, Mister Angelis?'

'It was last year,' Spiros blurts, shaking more visibly now, his eyes urging the prosecutor to understand. And the prosecutor raises his hand, palm out, as if to say, 'Relax.' But what he's really saying is, 'Look how psycho this psycho is.' He speaks softly, as if to a newborn.

'That's okay. That's okay. Let's change the subject. How would you describe Osman Yusedich?'

Spiros blinks.

'I don't know. What do you mean?'

'How would you describe his body size?'

'He was fat.'

'He was fat.'

'Yeah.'

'Would you describe yourself as fat?'

'I don't reckon.'

'Do you exercise or partake in regular physical activity?'

'I do kickboxing.'

'You're a kickboxer?'

'Yep.'

'How often?'

'I spar four times a week and do cardio every day.'

'Right. You're physically very fit, aren't you?'

Spiros blushes, shrugs like it's no big deal.

'I'm all right.'

One of the prosecutor's favourite tools has been silence. He uses it now, pausing to let the jury take in Spiros's coy pride.

'Have you looked at your statement recently, Mister Angelis?'

'Ummm…'

'The statement you made to police. They provided you with a copy?'

'Yeah. I think…'

'In your statement, you said you left the nightclub at around two a.m. You got into your car and you started for home. You stopped at a traffic light, but when the lights turned green, your way was blocked by a man crossing the road. So you beeped your horn. That's correct?'

'Yes. Yes, sir.'

'Why did you get out of the car?'

'Um. He said…' Spiros stops himself, looks around the room. 'He swore at me.'

'He swore at you?'

'Yes.'

'What did he say?'

Spiros bites his lip. This is a recollection he *does* find funny. Or at least, funny to recollect out loud in a courtroom.

'He said "get fucked" to me.'

'That's all he said?'

'Yes.'

'So you got out of the car?'

'Yeah. I got out. And then he called me a wog.'

'He called you a wog?'

'Yeah.'

'Even though he himself was Turkish.'

Spiros doesn't get it. 'Yeah, I mean...'

'My point is, *he* would have been called a wog, I'm sure, dozens of times in his life. It seems unlikely that he would use such a disparaging term towards someone else.'

'He called me other things too. He called me a faggot.'

The prosecutor was about to continue, but pauses again. The silence is perfect. Then he goes on: 'When you got out of the car, what was your intention? What did you intend to do?'

'I don't know.'

'Was your intention to fight him?'

'I didn't want...I don't know.'

'You must have had a reason to get out of the car.'

'Just...So he'd piss off, you know? Like, to get rid of him.'

'You wanted to intimidate him?'

'No...Yes.'

'So you got out of the car. Are you in the carpark by this time?'

'What?'

'May it please the court, I would like to show the witness Exhibit Thirty-Seven, the diagram of the carpark.'

The judge grunts. Everyone, the judge, the barristers, they all have the identical book of photographs, the front of which is blue with the Victoria Police insignia. Those of us in the gallery don't have these books, but it's not like we need them. A diagram of the carpark would be just a big square drawn on a white piece of paper. In real life, it's an expanse of bitumen running the full length of the block it shares with the supermarket. Carrum Downs doesn't have personality, but it does have space; this particular carpark is like an airport runway when it's empty.

The tipstaff puts an open photo book in front of Spiros.

The barrister asks, 'Are you in the supermarket carpark by this time?'

'Yeah. I mean, no. We're on…Just on the street, like…next to it.'

'How did you get to the carpark?'

'I walked there.'

'You walked there?'

'Yeah. To get away from him.'

'He chased you away?'

'No. Yeah, but I didn't run. I walked.'

'What about your car?'

'What about it?'

'Surely, to retreat from Osman, the best thing to do would have been to get back into your car and drive away?'

Spiros thinks about this using a thick line along his forehead. The prosecutor keeps going.

'Isn't it more likely, Mister Angelis—'

Another man in a wig, Spiros's defence counsel, stands and leans into the microphone.

'The witness should be given an opportunity…'

Justice Linehan, the one with the biggest wig of all, nods with a face of severe constipation.

'Restate the question please, counsel.'

The prosecutor bows. 'Certainly, Your Honour. Mister Angelis, why didn't you retreat back into your vehicle when you realised Osman might be a threat to your person?'

Spiros says, 'Umm…I don't know. I didn't think of it.'

'You didn't think of it? Mister Angelis, isn't it more likely that you produced the knife yourself and pursued Osman *away* from the car, into the supermarket carpark?'

'Nuh. It was his knife.'

'So you've said.'

'It wasn't mine. I don't even own a knife.'

'Isn't it more likely, Mister Angelis, that Osman's insults, whatever they may have been, enraged you? It enraged you that a man of Turkish origin had the temerity to call you names. It enraged you to such a degree that you produced a weapon with the intention of causing injury.'

'Nuh. I didn't care.'

Silence.

'Earlier, you gave evidence that Mister Yusedich was fat. That was the word you used?'

'Yes.'

'Yet despite your obvious physical superiority, you're asking this jury to believe that, in a footrace between the pair of you, you would not have easily outrun him?'

This is just another salad of words for Spiros. He's yanking on his tie, unconsciously, like it's a machine that dispenses correct answers, only it's not working properly and he really needs to *pull* that lever. What's also unconscious is he's showing everyone how bad he is at lying.

Spiros's brother, George, his head is bowed—he can't watch anymore. The others in this handful of spectators are captivated, knowing that every answer Spiros gives is another year on his sentence. Which I suppose is why George can't watch.

Also, he knows Spiros never killed anyone.

The prosecutor says, 'You say he chased you across the carpark, whereupon the two of you struggled, you disarmed him and, fearing for your life, you stabbed him twice in the stomach. Is that accurate?'

Spiros gives the vaguest of nods.

'You need to speak your answers, Mister Angelis.'

'Yes, sir.'

'That summary sounds accurate to you?'

'Yes.'

'After you realised Osman was dead, did you call the police?'

'No.'

'Why not?'

'I didn't...I didn't want to get in trouble.'

'But you claim to have acted in self-defence. Osman's mother, Miresha, waited months without knowing the circumstances of her son's death. In hindsight, do you regret not going directly to the police?'

Spiros shrugs again. 'I don't know.'

'Could you speak up, please?'

Too loud, Spiros yells, 'I don't know.' Then he shrinks at how the microphone has amplified his words, filling this massive chamber.

All day, the prosecutor has been repeating Spiros's answers. He doesn't do that now. He lets the reverberation of Spiros's voice do that for him.

And again, Spiros is smirking. To everyone except me and George, it looks as though he finds it all so funny.

McIvor's is where you drink on King Street if you're a cop. I'm hiking uphill, trying to remember where it is, hoping I'll spot it among the strip joints and the places with beds that call themselves hotels. When I do, I push my way in and scan the room. There are no photos of police officers on the walls, no tributes or police colours or funny cop jokes scratched over the doorway. You wouldn't guess a single one of these drinkers wasn't just an ordinary guy having a beer after work. Which is actually what they all are.

I beeline to the pale, black-haired one huddled at the counter. He's tall and stringy and his eyes say I could shoot him in the face and he wouldn't care. With him is another man of the same age but remarkably overweight, who appears to be telling a joke. I don't wait for him to finish.

'Is it true you've charged Spiros Angelis?'

Detective Burke looks over his pointy shoulder, winces.

I say, 'You told me you were building a case against the brother.'

He glances at his companion, a silent apology for the interruption, then turns back.

'First of all, who the fuck are you?'

This is him trying to put me in my place. To look tough in front of his colleagues. I might not have the most memorable face in the city, but he remembers it. I wave him away from the bar.

'I need to talk to you.'

His fat friend raises his eyebrows, purses his lips. I'm a ten-year-old who just challenged the sheriff to a gunfight. Burke simpers, pushes himself off the beer mat.

'Well…I was just going out for a fag.'

I follow him to the door, feeling the fat man's eyes watching us go. When we reach the footpath I plant my hands on my hips, confrontational.

'You said the investigation was all about *George* Angelis. Not Spiros. So you were just telling me what I wanted to hear, Detective Burke? It was all bullshit?'

He lights his cigarette.

'You should call me Dennis.'

I take a breath. His face is a wall you couldn't blast through with cannons.

'I'm John Dorn. I'm the guy who found the car—'

'I remember you,' Dennis says, heading me off. 'I remember we talked about George. You should know that who I charge isn't up to me. In this case, the DPP made the decision.'

'Why?'

'Because Spiros confessed and the DPP isn't a fucking idiot.'

'People confess all the time. Doesn't mean they did anything.'

'Fuck that. We've got him at the nightclub on the night, the car was photographed nearby, the knife with Osman's blood still on it was under his kitchen sink *and* when I asked him he said, Yeah, I stabbed the Turkish guy. Let's see *you* go tell the DPP not to charge him.'

'But you didn't even consider George—'

'Didn't consider him? Are you out of your fucking mind? You want to know what I found on George Angelis?' Dennis straightens, squares off like we're about to fight hand-to-hand. As he speaks, he counts the fingers on his left hand, the cigarette clamped in his mouth, forcing most of his voice through his nose. Faces from the peak hour traffic lurch past, watching him.

'George's got a prior conviction for unlawful assault, grievous bodily harm with a knife. And who was the victim? A Turkish goalkeeper George played against. There was also an incident on a freeway where a driver accused George of taking a cricket bat to their windshield, but then that complaint was mysteriously withdrawn. I found out George has got a pretty detailed history with methylamphetamine, so if he killed Osman, he was probably off his dial. And yeah...' He pulls the cigarette from his mouth, his eyes weeping from the smoke. 'He was with Spiros at the nightclub before the murder. I spent two months looking into George Angelis. But the *evidence* isn't there, John. And I don't decide who we charge.'

'Did you *mention* any of this to the DPP?'

'Yeah, I mentioned it.'

'What did he say?'

'He told me he's got every Turk in the southern hemisphere calling this a hate crime, and then he told me to go fuck myself. Listen...'

Dennis puts a bony hand to his forehead and draws it down his cheek. For a moment, his face is melting. He lowers his voice.

'Don't put me on the other side of an argument I've been making for six weeks. If it was up to me, I'd put George on the rack and torture him until he confessed. God knows Spiros wouldn't pull a knife, let alone stab someone, with or without his brother egging him on. But it isn't up to me, and Spiros is going to stand trial. So get out from behind me, you arsefucker.'

I slump against McIvor's brick work, look up at the sky.

'So you know Spiros is innocent?'

'I don't know about innocent. He was probably there, saw it happen, didn't do anything to stop it. But Christ man, of course he didn't do it. George was driving, cranked up on ice. A fat Turkish bloke crosses against the lights, cuts them off, gives them the finger. George insults him in Greek, Osman comes back in Turkish, George does his block, chases him, fights him, kills him, rinses the knife and hides it under their kitchen sink.'

'So why is Spiros so happy to take the blame?'

Smoke spools from Dennis's mouth, 'That's the six-million-dollar question.'

He watches a woman in a black leotard, a pole dancer at the end of her shift, skip across King Street to a waiting taxi. The driver opens his door, shoves his KFC box under the car, closes the door.

'It's like every conspiracy charge I've ever worked, right?' He squares off again, eyes lingering on the stripper a moment more before coming back to me. 'Every real-life conspiracy I've ever worked has been one bloke who doesn't give a rat's crack about anybody but himself, and another bloke who's too weak to say no. George has gone to Spiros and said, I've got priors, I won't get off on self-defence, you will. Tell them the Turk tried to kill you and there's no one to call you a liar because no one else was there.'

'Maybe. But George can't really think that's going to work.'

'Maybe he doesn't.' Dennis stamps out his cigarette, exhaling a long breath. 'Think about it from George's point of view. Looking after Spiros all the time. Waking up every morning wondering, how is this retard going to fuck up my life today? Worrying if Spiros is going to somehow get *George* sent to jail. Maybe big brother doesn't mind the idea of Spiros going down. Let someone else take care of him for a while...'

I take a moment to appreciate that all of this must be true. Dennis makes a fart sound through his teeth.

I say, 'So you're just going to *allow* that?'

'There's a billion people out there too dumb to protect themselves. I can't spend my time on just one of them.'

His skinny eyebrows make a deep V, mocking my disgust. The sun comes out from behind a cloud and the tavern's bricks sting my head like ants trying to burrow in.

'There's got to be something we can do.'

'Hey, maybe it'll work. Maybe Spiros will dazzle them when he takes the stand.'

'And what if he doesn't? We've got to find something on George.'

'If you think you can do better than what I did in two months, go for your life.'

'There's got to be something...' I've run out of words.

Dennis digs two hands into his pockets and pushes his shoulder into the door of McIvor's. He stops there, looking at me.

'You could try not blaming yourself. That might work.'

'Why shouldn't I blame myself? This wouldn't have happened if it weren't for me.'

'Don't think about it that way. Think about the money. All that work you did. They must have paid you a small fortune, right?'

My face tells him the answer to that question. He scoffs.

'No wonder there's a wart on your fanny.'

*

In this part of Frankston all the driveways lead up to bungalows, each with a couch on the porch that was never meant for the outdoors, each couch with a person or persons splashed across it like paint, made limp by the heat. They watch me without emotion as I drive by slowly in my Toyota Starlet.

The white Mitsubishi Lancer is parked right there in the driveway. Its rear bumper is a black strip of hard rubber, dented in the middle, directly above the licence plate, perfectly centred so that it might be dented by design. But it isn't. Over these last six weeks, I've looked at enough Mitsubishi Lancers to know precisely how they're designed.

I park at the kerb and stroll cheerfully towards the house.

It's no less ramshackle than the others along this backroad. There's a stack of newspapers as high as my hip yellowing on the yellow lawn. The tip of a surfboard sticks out over the bungalow's roof and there's a mouldy bar fridge where the letterbox should be. About all that sets this one apart is the youth watching me from the couch: he's holding a mobile phone instead of a beer.

I grin at him, shielding the glare from my face, distracted by the rear bumper of the car, thinking to myself this trip to Frankston might actually have been worth the effort.

'Hi,' I say.

His reply is a grunt. I think he meant to say hello but his throat was too dry. He clears it. On his head is a peaked cap advertising an American sports team. His eyebrows are enormous and below them are great pools of unease. I stop in the middle of the lawn, still grinning.

'That your Lancer?'

'Yeah.'

'I'm in the market. You selling?'

'What?'

'The car.'

He cranes, looks intently at the vehicle.

'Nah. Not for sale.'

'Why not?' I ask, still friendly. 'Has it got sentimental value?'

'Um…' He squints at me from the shade of his porch. 'I know it's got four cylinders and a six-stack CD player.'

I point at the car, smiling. 'How'd it get that dent in it?'

'I backed into a pole. I was trying to park, and I just backed into a pole.'

I've done this kind of patter more than a hundred times, but now I don't know what to say. If I ramp up the friendliness, my bet is he won't think it's suspicious.

'Hey, mate. My name's John. What's your name?'

'Spiros.'

'It's really nice to meet you, Spiros. Hot one, isn't it?'

'Hot day?'

'Yeah. I've just been driving around. My car's the only place I've got with air conditioning.'

I smile as broadly as I can manage and this pleases Spiros. He smiles back.

He asks, 'Do you play Call of Duty?'

'Play what?'

'Call of Duty.'

'What's that?'

'A game.'

'A computer game?'

'Yeah.'

'What do you do in it?'

'You're like this soldier in a war. And you get to choose between an American one or this other one. It's good.'

'I guess I don't play it.'

Spiros uses his whole neck and face to shrug.

'That's cool.'

'Mind if I sit down? This heat is such a bugger.'

His legs have been, until now, stretched across the whole couch, showing off the thick hair that grows on his shins. He shifts them, settles his feet on the ground, looks at me calmly, waiting for me to sit. When I do, an empty soft drink can digs into my arse. I remove it, settle back into the burst cushions.

'*I* wasn't allowed *in* to the army,' Spiros says.

'Yeah? You went to join up?'

'They said I didn't have *criteria*.' He works his mouth around the word like he's sneering. But really he's just trying to say it properly. 'I do kickboxing,' he adds as compensation. 'Do you do kickboxing?'

'I'm afraid not.'

'Do you go to clubs?'

'Nightclubs?'

'Yep.'

'Sure. I love clubs. Do you go?'

'Yeah. All the time. We should go one time. If you want.'

He can't be a killer, someone so open and determined to be friends. I've met two or three killers and I never wanted to ruffle their hair or generally improve their self-esteem.

'That'd be good. You're Greek, right?'

'I was born in Australia. My mum and dad are Greek.'

'What do you think of Turkish people?'

Spiros makes a face like I just stuck him gently with a safety pin. 'Nothing. I don't know. Are you Turkish?'

'What if I was?'

'I don't care. Are you?'

'No.'

'I don't care. I can never tell.'

He hugs his knees to his chest, his sneakered feet dangling in the air like they've been lynched. 'My brother can tell.'

I lean in. 'Your brother can tell if someone's Turkish?'

His eyes seem to withdraw into his skull. For a moment I'm sure that he's figured out why I'm here. Then, when he doesn't look at me, when his gaze seems stuck on the lawn, I'm wondering if he's forgotten I'm here at all. I lower my voice to its least threatening tone.

'Does your brother live here with you?'

Just as softly, not looking at me, he says, 'Yeah.'

'Where is he now?'

'At the gym.'

'What's his name?'

'George.'

'Does George drive your car sometimes, Spiros?'

'Sometimes.'

I stop asking questions. With the car and maybe a little help from Spiros, the police can take it from here. I lean back in silence to enjoy the moment, one destined to become a perfect memory. What was that Turkish word Miresha called me?

When I look back at Spiros I'm trying to hide my smirk. He's staring at his dry, dying lawn, and for some reason he's smirking too.

'Just because Osman was Turkish doesn't mean it was racially motivated.'

'Yes, I know this,' Father Orhan says. Anna isn't translating what I'm saying, so Miresha just watches me, unmoved. 'But he was a good boy, Osman. Not criminal. Never make trouble.'

All three of them have crucifixes hung from their necks, the big silver ones that ward off vampires, including Anna, the victim liaison officer, who didn't know Father Safak or Miresha before Miresha's son was killed. What a victim liaison usually does is drink tea with the family, help them manage the media, the police.

It is, I'm guessing, the element of shared faith that has Anna going beyond her job description, showing up to the office of some unknown hustler in a cheap suit with gum stuck to his shoe.

And it doesn't look as though I'm going to be too helpful.

'I understand. But there are lots of stupid reasons to attack a person. Ethnicity is only one of them.'

'The motivation for the crime isn't why we're here,' Anna says. I've sensed her shifting in her seat, unhappy with the priest's approach. She appears to me like one of those unshockable nurses you get in city hospitals, and I find myself choosing my words carefully because of her most of all. When people come to see me and they bring along a friend, it's usually the friend who questions my experience, who haggles and doubts me. They consider that to be their role: the pitbull.

'The reason we're here is that the police have failed. They've simply given up.'

And she plays the role to perfection. If I were Miresha, this is exactly who I'd want the government to send me.

When this trio arrived, Miresha was introduced as not only speaking very little English, but also as mostly deaf. There are bushfires burning to the northeast this week and people have died and all of Melbourne reeks like a crematorium. Miresha, dressed in an old black dress and flesh-coloured stockings that bunch around her ankles, she's well suited to the crematorium theme. Father Safak leads a parish in Springvale and every Sunday he takes a mass there in Turkish for the old guard of immigrants like Miresha. Osman used to drive her there from Cranbourne. These days Miresha catches a taxi. Going to church, Father Safak says, costs her more than fifty dollars a week.

And now, though she can't understand what Anna says, Miresha nods and points to the photograph in my hand, because the chubby teenage face smiling back at me—with a vulnerability in his eyes that makes him, at least in this photo, handsome—is all the information she came to impart: her son is dead.

I nod gravely at her, give it a theatricality I instantly regret.

'The police don't care as much for Turkish boy,' Father Safak says.

I shake my head in defence of the friends on the police force I don't have. 'Father Safak, I promise you, the police work on a system of statistics. Every unsolved murder affects who gets paid what, who gets promoted, who gets a medal. They don't care if Osman was Turkish or Greek or Chinese. If they *have* given up, it was only after they did everything they could to figure out what happened.'

'Not everything,' says Father Safak.

'Not everything,' says Anna.

Their alignment brings a silence. Father Safak, sporting about as good-natured a moustache as any you'd find, nods meaningfully to Anna. She goes searching in her enormous black leather handbag. I show Father Safak my palms, inviting him to explain, but he waits for Anna to finish rummaging.

Anna says, 'I'm not supposed to have this. And you can't tell anyone how you got it.'

It's a brown A4 envelope she pulls from her bag.

She says, 'It's nothing illegal. But the detective who was working on the case, Detective Burke, technically he wasn't supposed to give it to me. Do you know him?'

'Who?'

'Detective Dennis Burke.'

'Never heard of him.'

'He came clean to me one day and told me he'd had to close the case, that they couldn't direct more resources to it. When he told me that…it made me upset.'

I can imagine someone like Anna upset with me. I can imagine myself giving her things, just to calm her down.

'He said this demonstrated how difficult it would be to find Osman's killer.'

She holds it out now. I take the envelope and dutifully prise it open. Inside is a single photograph. I frown at it.

'It's from a red light camera in Carrum Downs,' says Anna.

Electronically burned into the bottom right of the picture is the date and time: November fourth of last year, two thirty-seven a.m. Printed below it are street names and a speed gauge: one hundred and fifty-one kilometres per hour. The image itself is out of focus; it's black and white and it's been digitally resized, blurring the detail even more. It is, to my eyes, a picture of a car travelling through an intersection. It appears to be a white car, and it appears to be nighttime, but even that much is hard to tell.

'This is the night it happened?' I ask.

'The night and the place,' says Anna.

'Before or after Osman was killed?'

'We don't know. The time of death can't be that precise. We think it's after, because the car is moving so fast.'

I nod, breathe in deep.

'Is there *anything* to connect the car to Osman's death?'

Anna holds my eyes, knows the answer but doesn't want to say it. Father Safak leans in, tries to reach the photo, then stands up and takes it from me.

'This is same time...' He points to the bottom right of the picture. 'It is same time.'

'But anybody could have been driving there at that time.'

'*No*,' he says, impatient. 'Is nighttime. No cars. There is no cars here for nighttime.' He sits down on the front edge of his chair, holding the picture to my face.

I can't see the licence plate, the camera angle is too high.

I ask Anna, 'Isn't there another photo, one with a plate number? Don't they use two cameras?'

She shakes her head. 'This was the only camera working that night.'

'So even if this is our guy, no one can identify the car?'

Her face is as glum as mine. 'That's what Detective Burke says. Except...'

Father Safak heads her off, waving the picture at me. 'There is *one* to identify,' he says. 'There is one. There is dent.'

I squint at the image. What might be a defect in the image or a bad paint job could also be a dent in its bumper bar, like the car's been rear-ended by a motorcycle.

'You think the dent was made when Osman was killed?'

'*No*,' he says, rising partly to his feet again. 'But is...to identify.'

I don't want to look at Father Safak, see how obvious he thinks it all is. I wait for Anna to say something. She must have seen enough stories like this to know this one is a lost cause. But it doesn't show. Her hands rest quietly on her lap, waiting for me to offer something the police couldn't.

'Would you translate for me?' I ask, indicating Miresha.

Anna nods, eager.

'Mrs Yusedich,' I say, leaning in, adopting the most sympathetic posture I've got. 'I'm very sorry for what happened to your boy.' Anna translates in a wholly different voice, speaking directly into Miresha's ear. Miresha makes no reaction.

'You have to understand...This is just a car. It probably doesn't have anything to do with what happened to Osman. There's no licence plate. There's no way of identifying the driver. I'm concerned...' My eyes shoot across to Father Safak and back again. 'I'm concerned that you're concentrating on an aspect of the police investigation that isn't going to be fruitful in the long run.'

Miresha doesn't move, but Father Safak can't contain his umbrage.

'You can tell from this picture vehicle type. Make. Model.'

'There could still be thousands of these cars in Melbourne, Father. And that's just Melbourne.'

He says, 'But you are *detective.*'

'I'm no better than the police.'

'You talk to VicRoads, eh? You can maybe—'

'And tell them what? That I'm looking for a white car with a dent in it?'

Anna's translations go up in pitch as she finishes that Turkish sentence and starts an indignant one in English. 'But you can narrow down the search. Location, ethnicity...' She tries to think of more.

'I don't think you realise...And I say this to the three of you... What you're talking about here is an awful amount of work. It's massive. It could take months. And let me be blunt—you can't afford to pay me for the amount of work that this will entail. And *I* can't afford to do it free of charge.'

From a pile on my desk I hold up an unopened letter stamped with Drew James Real Estate.

'Inside this envelope is a notice to vacate. It's not the first one I've received. It means I'm going to get kicked out of my home unless I come up with a lot of money very soon. So I *have* to be making a living, and what you're talking about...It's a process of elimination the *police* wouldn't enter into—'

'The police think it is nothing. They treat it like is nothing!' Father Safak spits.

Then Miresha raises a hand, and the novelty of it is enough to silence us all.

She speaks in Turkish, and her words come out in a soft, fluent stream, despite how difficult it seems to be for her. It's a sharp croaking noise, feminine but pitched deep. It's how she'd speak if now was the first time she'd stopped crying since her son was killed.

Anna isn't stunned like I am that Miresha can talk. She scowls, translates: 'She says, Sir, I am poor. I can afford to pay you very little.'

Miresha pauses to swallow, her old woman's jowls trembling. We all watch her, awaiting judgment.

'Before we speak of money, tell me, sir, do you want to live in a world where a man is killed in cold blood and left to die like a dog in the street? Do you want to live in a world such as this?'

Anna finishes these words and looks at me, wanting an answer. They all seem to want an answer.

I say, 'Of course not.'

Anna starts to translate my response, but Miresha speaks over her and Anna stops to translate: 'My son was murdered. For no reason they did this. He was my only son. I have no children. No grandchildren. All I can hope for is that I might one day have justice. And justice might keep me warm the way my son used to do. Do you understand?'

I nod.

She reaches out across my desk with both hands, straining for mine. I offer them. She grasps me with a sad strength. One of the tears pooling in her eyes breaks free, swims down the cracks in her face.

From Father Safak and from Anna, I sense not tension but relief. This is what we're talking about, don't you see? This is why we're so *angry*.

Miresha's dry croak comes out a whisper. Anna interprets: 'She says she believes you are Kahraman. That is a Turkish word that doesn't have a ready translation into English. It is like a champion, or hero. But also compassionate.'

Anna smiles softly.

I lean towards Miresha, lock on to her eyes, try to seem heroic and also compassionate. But I can't hold back a small splatter of a laugh. I smile, embarrassed.

'Well…How can I say no?'

COMEDY IS DEAD

THE FRONT ENTRANCE is wallpapered with government warnings and disclaimers and it's hard to find the sheet of paper with Comedy's name that's required to be on display where the customers enter the store.

SHANE AMIEL JOHNSON, PROPRIETOR.

I'm glad I find it, but only for my curiosity. He's been known as Comedy for so long I'd forgotten his real name, lost somewhere in the whirlwind of bullshit that surrounds him. These days he's insisting people call him Comedy, so I've heard. Like he's proud of it. Or maybe he's forgotten his real name too.

Right inside the doorway is a life-size blow-up doll wearing a blonde wig and an apron. Her hands are glued to her cheeks and her big round mouth is frozen in dismay; she looks like a housewife watching her stove catch fire. The handwritten placard above her reads:

SHOPLIFTERS! IF YOU ARE CAUGHT STEALING FROM US, WE PROMISE TO TELL YOUR FAMILY EXACTLY WHAT YOU TOOK AND WHAT IT IS USED FOR.

Beyond the doll is the store itself, a warehouse of toys and literature arranged in confrontational order—softcore postcards this end, mechanical hamster dildos the other. I pass an array of appliances and foreign comic books and those ultraviolet lights they use in strip clubs. I pass mannequins in costumes and chocolates shaped like penises and CDs featuring 'real-life' sexual encounters recorded during police interrogations. The tattooed punk behind the desk is counting bills from the register, handfuls at a time. I pass all of this, headed for the mirrors at the back of the store, the small door set between them.

When I knock I catch my reflection. It's been a while since I looked this bad; you'd have to go back six or seven hangovers to the Spiros Angelis case. Waking up that day was like walking head-first into a shard of glass. I rub at my eyes like that will somehow clear them up.

And these are two-way mirrors, which means someone's looking out and seeing what I'm seeing—me, scrubbing at my sagging face in a land of proud breasts and arses, the name of the store flashing on the wall behind me in pink neon squiggle.

THE RAUNCH RANCH.

Over the sound system is a tired dance beat and a girl singing about sunshine.

Darryl opens the door with his good hand. The other hand was crushed by a car about twelve years ago and after that he had trouble finding work. You need two good hands to intimidate people for a living. He landed a job here because of his enormous size, driving Comedy to places where Comedy wants to be seen to have a gorilla working for him. They travel in Comedy's silver GT Falcon with orange go-faster stripes, and once I saw Darryl get out of the driver's seat and waddle all the way around the car and open the back passenger door for his boss. Like in the movies. I guess he still does that.

'Yeah?'

Nobody here has ever met me. Maybe they've heard of me. I doubt it.

'My name is John Dorn. I'm here to see Mister Johnson.'

'What for?' Only one of Darryl's eyes looks at me. The other looks past me at all the porn. Another legacy of the car accident.

'You should tell him it's urgent. It's about Joel Kelso.'

He raises his eyebrows and holds them there, processing. Then he says, 'Hang on,' and closes the door.

While I wait, the sunshine song is replaced by a group of men who sing about how they each, individually, intend to get laid tonight.

Darryl opens the door again, this time making room with his rounded frame to let me past and into the outer office, which is mostly open cardboard boxes full of the same stuff that lines the store shelves. I glimpse DVD titles like *The Three Assketeers* and *World's Greatest Gangbang*. Also there's a desk, a surprisingly wholesome wall calendar and a swivel chair with one leg taped in place. Darryl closes the door and makes a rolling gesture with his finger.

'I'm supposed to pat you down.'

I nod, cooperative, but I don't know what to do—I've never had a pat-down before. I raise my arms awkwardly and flinch at the first touch, but Darryl's not passionate about it and gets it done quickly, doesn't go within two feet of my crotch. He has to bend over to pat my ankles and just this much exertion breaks him into a sweat that he wipes away on his sleeve as he makes for another door.

What we can hear when he opens it you'd guess is a pornographic movie, if you're the type to hear the moans of a fake orgasm and leap to that conclusion. Darryl and I enter a much larger and more thoroughly furnished office where Comedy is sitting on his desk and there's a woman sitting behind it in the heavy desk chair.

They don't look at me. Their blank faces watch a small television set on a table against the wall.

What's on the TV is not pornography.

It's a woman, fully dressed, young and pretty. She faces the camera, vocalising an orgasm as thrillingly as she can, and that's all she's doing. There's no one else in the frame, and behind her is the neutral backdrop of a photographer's studio.

Comedy and his companion watch the screen for a few more moments, then Comedy picks up a remote control and presses a button that prompts the aged and dusty VCR beneath the television to wind forward through what remains of the girl's performance.

His angular face is betrayed by a round, jovial nose and ruddy cheeks and his pot belly looks like an advanced pregnancy as he slouches there on the desk. Last time I saw him his sandy grey hair was long and straight but failed to conceal his hairline like it was supposed to. So now it's cut short, military-style, giving him an appearance of toughness that would otherwise be entirely absent. He's got on a brown and white striped polo shirt and blue jeans—it's mufti day at the Raunch Ranch. The woman behind the desk is about Comedy's age, though she's made up like she's twenty years younger and she's showing a lot of skin that's been turned orange by a tanning bed.

Comedy glances at me for the shortest moment, then his eyes return to the TV.

'Who are you, fella?' he says to the screen.

'My name's John.'

He presses play. There's another girl onscreen now, older than the last. The same neutral backdrop. She's doing her own version of a sexual climax.

'*Oh yes. Oh please. Oh right there. Right there.*'

I have to raise my voice over hers. 'I was hoping to have a word...'

The woman in the chair must be Comedy's wife. She says, 'Bit frumpy.'

Comedy says, 'Bit fucking ugleeeee...' and he winds forward again.

Darryl lopes towards the TV to get a better view, leaving me alone by the door. Comedy waves me forward.

'These are auditions,' he gestures. 'For our new website. We need a girl to be the new online host, yeah? Tell people about our products and so forth. Bring some personality to it.'

I stay where I am, nod.

Watching the TV, he says, 'And what's beautiful is, she doesn't have to take her gear off. So we can get a real actress. Someone sexy but who's...you know. Actually talented.'

He presses play.

This girl's Asian, nineteen or twenty.

'Errrrh. Uuuuuh. Ooooh. Errrrmph.'

Comedy and his wife and Darryl all watch, impassive.

'So,' says Comedy. 'You're here about Joel Kelso?'

'That's right.'

'You didn't come here to sell me something?'

'Nope.'

He looks at me, disbelieving. 'Joel sent you, did he?'

'Nope.'

'But you work for Joel.'

'Nope.'

'Nope.' He repeats, makes a glum face. 'You're not giving me a lot to work with, fella.'

'Well, I'd like to talk to you in private, if that's okay.'

'Mate...' he says, elongating the word like I just took the last lamb chop. 'This is my wife, Lindy. And that there's Darryl. They're my family. Well, Darryl's not. He's...we're not related. But I trust him, yeah? There's nothing you can't say in front of him. No secrets here, mate.'

'I understand. But this really is just for you.'

83

Comedy sighs.

I say, 'Joel gets discharged from Royal Melbourne today.'

In the silence while Comedy stares at me, the Asian girl continues: '*Uuuuuh. Uuuuh. Uuuh. Ooooooh...*'

'She's good.' Lindy points to the television. Her fingers are decorated with enough costume jewellery to look like a girl's knuckle-duster. 'Oriental might be the way to go.'

Comedy frowns at her.

'My dear, would you be so kind as to step out for just a moment? Darryl can show you the new merch.'

She rolls her eyes. Comedy shrugs, grins, flicks a hand at me so she knows who to blame.

'Off you toddle. You too, Darryl.' He's gone from telling me how he trusts them to showing me how he orders them around.

Darryl's eyes stay on the TV as he walks to the door. Even after he's gone through it and back into the outer office, after Lindy has glided past me in a thin sarong that hangs off her like a magician's handkerchief, Darryl's still watching the girl. When you spend all your time around pornography, an ordinary woman wearing clothes must be fascinating. It's me who closes the door.

Comedy stops the videotape and walks around the big desk to his big chair. The television's blue signal bounces off his face as he reclines. 'Sit down. How is poor old Joel?'

I do sit, on a rickety metal armchair this side of his desk. The office isn't large but it's pleasantly decorated, like an office in a furniture catalogue. Attached to the wall there's a ceramic phallus that appears to be autographed, but that's all there is to indicate what gets sold on the shop floor.

'He's all right. The rib is healing. So is the collarbone. Slowly, but apparently that's normal for collarbones. For a while there was urine leaking out of his bladder and the doctors were worried his other organs would get infected. That's why they kept him in for so long. I suppose they'll keep an eye on that one.'

'How shithouse for him. Joel told you all this, did he?'

'I've never met Joel. Joel didn't send me here and I don't work for him. But I've spoken to his doctors. And to other people.'

Comedy licks his lips. 'So…what the fuck is it you want, fella?'

'I just want to find out what happened to him. No one seems to know much, so I'm asking questions. All we can say for sure is that a person wearing a balaclava bashed him with a cricket bat behind a Vietnamese restaurant on Lygon Street. He'd been eating alone and he'd gone out for a cigarette, and that's about the last thing he remembers.'

Comedy doesn't react. I reel off the rest: 'The attack took less than a minute, he wasn't robbed, the laneway was dark, there were no witnesses, his assailant was alone, didn't identify himself. These are the only details I've got.'

'And how is it that I…' He interrupts himself, scowls at me. 'What was your name again?'

'John.'

'I was not there, John. So how the fuck should I know what happened?'

'I'm just asking around.'

'What for? Who *are* you?'

'My name's John. I'm a private inquiry agent. I've been looking into what happened to Joel. And although you say you weren't there…That's not what I've heard.'

Comedy reclines further, pokes his tongue around in his cheek to disguise his grin.

'What have you heard?'

'I heard something different.'

'How different?'

'Pretty different.'

He waits for me to say it.

'I heard you were the man who did the deed.'

He can't stifle the grin any longer and smiles broadly at me.

I ask, 'Is that true, Mister Johnson?'

'Please,' he says. 'Call me Comedy. Everybody calls me Comedy.'

'Have you heard these rumours?'

'Did you come here for a confession, John?'

'No.'

'But you work privately, yeah? Who's your client?'

'As of right now, I'm not retained. But there is a party that may seek to retain me in the future, and if they do, understanding what happened to Joel Kelso is going to be a big part of that job. I don't want to say any more than that.'

Comedy's face says *la-di-da*. 'Okay, Mister Mysterious. But I won't cop to nothing. We can have a conversation, but…'

I show him my palms. 'Just a couple of questions.'

'Shoot.'

Anyone else would have thrown me out for accusing them of something so awful, but Comedy tips back and rests his hands on his belly, a professor granting audience to an eager student. I lean forward.

'What happened between you and Joel in the business world? I heard there was a falling out…'

He licks his lips. 'Me and Joel made a deal for some merch, then he dumped me and sold the gear to SlapTickle. They made money, I didn't.'

'The competition is serious? Between you and SlapTickle?'

'We are close competitors, yes.'

'Does it ever get…underhanded?'

'Course not. It's a healthy business rivalry. SlapTickle and the Raunch Ranch inspire each other to new and bolder heights for our industry.'

It's a company line, an answer he's given before to someone who asked the same question, which someone was bound to have done given how much the two businesses hate each other.

'So Joel could have made a deal with you, instead he went with them.'

'Which he was free to do.'

'What was the product?'

'Twenty thousand battery-operated condoms,' he says, without having to think.

I point to his office door. 'You sell them. I saw them out there on the shelf...'

'Them out there have a total battery life of seven minutes, because the batteries are so small, yeah? I might as well sell them as napkin rings. Joel's ones lasted forty-five minutes. That makes them *in demand*. Him and me were negotiating an agreement, but he made the deal with SlapTickle instead.'

'Why'd he do that?'

'Fucked if I know. Probably got a better price.'

'Do you think the condoms had anything to do with the...' I flap my hand in the air, searching for the word. '...the *tragic* incident that put Joel in hospital?'

Comedy takes a breath, adjusts himself in his chair and leans in.

'Let me just stop you right there,' he says, though I've already stopped. 'I was a stand-up comedian once, few years back, did the circuits. That's how I got the name. I understand a thing or two about what you call *irony*.'

I nod blankly.

He says, 'My uncle Merrick spent his whole life working as a bookbinder. Worked fourteen-hour days and dreamed of retiring at forty. That was the fucking holy grail as far as he was concerned. Then it turned out the glue they used to hold the pages together back then, it had these chemicals in it and cancer took him at thirty-nine. Thirty-nine years old. *That's* fucking tragic. That is what you call *tragic irony*.'

With one hand Comedy holds the tips of his fingers together, to demonstrate the delicacy of his point.

'Now you, fella, are not the only one who hears things. I know for a fact there's a catheter been gouged up Joel Kelso's cock for these last few weeks, all the way into his bladder. It's a bloody painful state that. If he got a stiffy then his dick would snap right off. All the battery-operated condoms in the world are no good to him right now. That, my little mate, is not tragic. That is the *comic* kind of irony.' He fixes me with a practised gaze. 'Also known as poetic justice.'

After holding my eyes for another potent beat, he sweeps up his remote control.

'Joel knew bloody better than to go against me. That's all I have to say on the subject.'

With finality, Comedy swivels in his chair, presses play. The blue TV comes alive again, that same girl as before, whimpering and imploring. Comedy drops the remote control on his desk for emphasis.

'Mmmm...Mmmm-hmmmm...that's it...You're sooooo good...'

He watches, defiant, but he isn't hearing a word this unemployed actress is saying. He scoffs like a teenager and says, his back to me, 'Is that why you asked them two to leave the room? You didn't want them to hear a rumour of what I done to Joel Kelso?'

A new girl appears onscreen. He's facing her so I have to raise my voice again, compete for his attention.

'Joel's got a broken rib, a broken collarbone and a ruptured bladder. They're painful injuries, but they'll heal. Whoever did that to him has a precise touch. They knew how to make it hurt but also how to make it temporary.'

The back of Comedy's head doesn't move.

'The thing is, when people talk about Comedy Johnson, they don't say, "He's got a precise touch." They say other things. They talk about how you never were a stand-up comic, and you got the name Comedy because as a gangster you're a joke.'

'Oooh…You're naughty…Oh…Oh yeah…That's right…Ooooh…'

'They talk about your failed insurance scam and your failed SIM-card scam. They talk about the defamation suit SlapTickle brought against you, which you settled out of court. No one knows how much you paid, but you wound up closing your other store. And they talk about your wife, her appetite for codeine.'

'Just a little more…Just a little more…'

'What they don't talk about is how you had nothing to do with what happened to Joel. The two of you had a falling out, so after he landed in hospital a rumour got started. Comedy Johnson waiting in the shadows with a cricket bat. Which didn't bother you, you were more than happy to take the credit. Make people wonder. Make them respect you. But you couldn't have done something like this. You don't know how. And even if you knew how, you don't have the guts.'

Comedy scratches the back of his head, then turns to face me, blinking slowly.

I say, 'That's why I asked them to leave the room.'

Carefully, he picks up the remote and mutes the television. Without the sound, the girl looks like she's about to be sick. Comedy stares at the remote, flips it in his hand.

Then he says, 'Get the fuck out of my office.'

'Don't kick me out yet. I can help you.'

He snorts again, his face showing how all of him is pushing against what I've said. 'Why would I want help from a shit-stirrer like you?'

'Because right now it's working great. People can believe what they want, right? Since when is it your job to set them straight?

Comedy Johnson beat somebody up and suddenly everyone's a little scared of him. He's jumping the queue at his favourite nightclub and girls half his age are whispering his name. Everyone thinks twice about crossing you. Everyone wants to do right by you.' I pause, raise a finger. 'Except Joel. He's heard the rumours too.'

'Piss off...You think I'm scared of Joel Kelso?'

'Do you know what he's been doing in hospital all this time?'

'I couldn't *give* a shit—'

'He's been getting high, mostly. Sometimes the hospital's drugs, sometimes his own. When his friends come to visit, he tells them he doesn't want revenge on Comedy Johnson. What he wants is peace. He says he's learned his lesson.'

'Sounds like the only person making a big deal out of this is you, John.'

I talk faster. 'He hasn't spoken to the police, and by that I mean he won't even confirm his own name. His girlfriend's been telling her friends, workmates, perfect strangers how incapacitated Joel is, how he can't even walk, how he sleeps sixteen hours a day and needs help just to sit up on the couch.'

'You trying to make me feel guilty?'

'I'm trying to *help* you, if you'll just listen. Joel's young and he's headstrong and there's no way he'll be put in his place by someone named Comedy, let alone *you*. He's got a conviction for running a taxi off the road on Victoria Parade, did you know that? The driver cut him off, so Joel shouldered him into an apartment building. He *seems* quiet and kind of shy, but that's just on the surface. He once beat up a homeless man, just around the corner from here, almost killed him. No one even knows why.'

'Bullshit—'

'And if he is planning to come back at you, he's going about it the right way. Saying he wants peace, telling people he can hardly stand up. Spending his days drugged and unconscious. It's Revenge

101. Eliminate the motive and circulate an alibi. "I'm a cripple, I'm too fucked up to get back at Comedy, even if I wanted to." My guess is, and it's the reason I'm here, he's healthier than everyone thinks. He's capable of much more than just sitting up on the couch and there's been only one thing on his mind since he came to in that hospital bed.'

Comedy turns the remote control over and over in his hands and his nostrils are wide open. It takes two tries to clear his throat before he speaks.

'I've never seen him hurt anyone. I never seen him even fight.'

'He's a dark horse.'

'I think he's a pussycat.'

'You've misjudged someone. Imagine my surprise.'

Comedy leans back in his chair, clasps his hands over his head. What was a whirlwind of bullshit has become a cyclone, spinning behind his eyes. All that hot air forms itself into a sneer.

'You came out here to warn me, did you? Thought you'd do me a favour? Out of the kindness of your heart?'

'I came here to make a suggestion.'

'What's that?'

'Hire me to find the guy who assaulted Joel.'

'Hire you?'

'That's right.'

'You're kidding, aren't you?'

'Joel gets discharged today. I don't think he's going to waste any time.'

'You said you weren't here to sell me anything.'

'I lied about that.'

He laughs, coarsely. 'If you knew how many hawkers I get coming in the door...'

'You've never been offered anything like this.'

'Like what? What would you do for me, exactly?'

'I'd go from here to Joel's house, tell him Comedy Johnson has retained me to find out who was responsible for the attack. I'd say that Comedy has heard rumours of his own involvement and he hopes that retaining me will help to extinguish them.'

'Brilliant...'

'Then Joel will accuse me of scamming you. Then he'll laugh me out the door.'

'I can't imagine why...'

'But it might keep him in a box until I find out who really *is* responsible.'

'And please,' he says, smiling broadly, 'Who *is* it who might be responsible? If not me.'

'Someone too smart to go around taking the credit. Maybe someone who knew you would. Wanted you to.'

There's a mock scowl and a mock nod that embellish the mock concentration he's having so much fun with. I almost want him to kick me out of his office so I don't have to look at him anymore.

I say, 'If your friends at SlapTickle no longer enjoy the bold new heights you inspire, and if they've paid someone to take care of you, then it starts to make sense. They get a professional. Someone like Ted Boyle.'

'Uh-huh,' he smirks.

'Boyle figures that if you disappear, the cops are onto it and all roads lead back to SlapTickle. But Boyle's an opportunist. If he knew about the trouble between you and Joel, and if he knew what Joel was capable of, *and* if he knew that Joel would rather have his eyes gouged out than talk to the police, everything falls into place. Boyle attacks Joel, lets you take the credit, sits back while Joel does his job for him. Granted, this theory requires Ted Boyle to be a sort of genius. But he's the smartest thug I know.'

'Your suggestion is that *I* pay *you* to catch the guy, whoever it is?'

'As a goodwill gesture to Joel.'

'And then maybe Joel doesn't k-k-k-kill me.'

His pretend stutter is very funny to him. Again he talks as he laughs. 'You must have a big heart, fella. To help out like this.'

'I'm about to get evicted. I need the money. You can afford me.'

'Got it all figured out, yeah?'

'Not quite.'

'Really? What else is there? Cash or cheque?'

'I haven't figured out how to get you to come clean, to admit it wasn't you who put Joel in hospital. Until you do...we're going nowhere.'

'Well...' says Comedy, with a face that says, *here comes the punchline*. 'At least we agree on something.'

He hits a button on his telephone and calls into it, 'Darryl, come in here, will you?'

Then he unmutes the TV. It's another girl, barely eighteen, with a massive red bow in her hair to look, I suppose, more innocent. It appears that we've missed the climax of her performance and now she's cooing, post-coital.

'This is your last chance,' I say. 'You've got to give Joel something to show it wasn't you.'

Comedy doesn't take his eyes off the girl. 'There's two ways for this conversation to end. The easy way and the hard way. The hard way's about to come in that door.'

The girl on TV is burbling now, like she's just waiting for someone to yell, 'Cut!' She's played all the chords she knows. So have I.

The door opens and Darryl lopes through it. Comedy hurries to let him in on the joke.

'This prick reckons Joel Kelso's going to come gunning for me. Reckons he's secretly a nut job. Joel Kelso. Of all people.'

Darryl laughs along. 'Joel? He *is* a bit of a nut job, isn't he?'

'Hey?'

'He broke Ant Goldberg's fingers that time, remember?'

Comedy blinks at Darryl. Softly, he says, 'Bullshit.'

'Yeah. Ant was cheating at pool, Joel broke his fingers.' Darryl holds up two fingers and twiddles them in the air. 'You remember he had them bandages.'

'I remember...' Comedy says slowly. 'That was Joel?'

'Yeah.' Darryl nods with a goofy grin. 'But fuck it. You took care of him once.'

Comedy's eyes flick to me, then away. He licks his lips, but he doesn't speak. For the first time, words don't come. Now he tips back in his chair, lost in thought, and it seems we're in the eye of the cyclone, where the bullshit settles, the tough guy face evaporates and the real Shane Amiel Johnson is there to see, sick and frightened.

'How come nobody told *me*?'

It's a schoolyard whine. Darryl's shrugging those massive shoulders again when I say, 'Because you're a spook and a phony. What would you do? Pat Anton on the head and say, there there? You're the original fairy godfather, faking it, the way these girls are faking it. If Joel is coming after you you've got to own up.'

And just like that, the eye passes. It's back to the trenches for Comedy Johnson.

'*Get this poofter the fuck out of here.*'

I feel a tap on my shoulder. Darryl's one good arm preparing to do the work of two. I stand.

Comedy tips back in his chair, rotates away from us. There's nothing for me to do but leave.

From the outer office I glance back. Comedy's about as contemplative as I could imagine him, staring past the television. On it there's a new girl wearing a sheer singlet.

'*Oh God Oh God Oh God Oh God Oh God Oh God.*'

Darryl closes the door.

I've never been frisked before today, but I've been walked out of plenty of places: I know how to do this one. Slow lock-step to the entrance past half a dozen men browsing the shelves, past the hamster dildos and the softcore postcards and the blow-up doll and the notice with Comedy's real name on it. In my jacket pocket I'm fumbling for a pen and a scrap of paper. I find a receipt for yesterday's Chinese food.

We reach the street and Darryl waits to make sure I move on.

I scrawl my phone number on the receipt. 'Give this to Comedy.' I hold it out. 'In case he changes his mind.'

Darryl takes the crumpled paper and shoves it in his pocket, appears to be slowly formulating a response. His lazy eye glares at the chemist across the street.

'Don't hold your breath, mate.'

I'm in the bottle shop the next day when it's on the news. This is the store near my home and for some reason they don't put prices on anything so I'm at the counter, asking the Greek man there which is the cheapest six-pack of beer, when the miniature television he's got shows a silver GT Falcon with the pointless orange stripe crushed against one of the blackwoods that line the Nepean Highway. The impact was so devastating that, looking at the TV, it takes a moment to recognise the car. To even know it was once a car.

The Greek man's being helpful. He's telling me about the special on Carlton Colds and I have to ask him to stop talking and to turn up the volume on the television.

Later that night I'm in bed and I'm drinking. Someone's just moved into the flat next door and he plays his TV loud. I won't miss this place when the sheriff's office finally kicks me out. At one point I can hear a replay of the bulletin I saw in the bottle shop. After I saw it, I passed on the beer and bought a bottle of vodka. I'm taking another sip when my phone rings.

It's Darryl. He speaks softly, like he doesn't want anyone to know he's called me.

'You hear what happened?'

'It was on the news.'

'It's weird…'

'Where were they going, Darryl?'

On the news they showed the car from a thousand different angles, mangled and lonely under the floodlights, as well as an impromptu press conference with a senior constable from the Major Collision Investigation Unit. I can hear him now through the walls of my flat.

'The car was doing a speed of approximately one hundred and fifty kilometres per hour. Both the male driver and the female passenger were killed instantly.'

Darryl says, 'He was all weird after you left. He said them two were going on a holiday in Ocean Grove for the weekend. Lindy didn't know what the fuck was going on neither. Comedy just said they're leaving, and I had the run of the store until he got back. Then they just left.'

'They were on the Nepean Highway. That's not how you get to Ocean Grove.'

'Yeah, mate, that's what's weird.'

On next door's TV, Senior Constable Fellows is saying that the driver was speeding and lost control of the vehicle. Darryl asks me if I think it was Joel Kelso.

I say, 'He's done it before.'

Darryl snorts into the receiver, which comes through my end as a blast of static. 'Comedy bashing him like that. That's weird too. I mean, Comedy never done nothing like that, you know?'

I can't see any point in telling Darryl what I really think. It wouldn't change the outcome. It would feel like speaking ill of the dead.

'So you reckon Joel did something to his car?' Darryl's saying.

'No. Nobody did anything to his car. Someone ran him off the road.'

The senior constable said another set of fresh tyre marks was found at the scene. 'We believe the vehicle and a second car may have been drag racing. We're now appealing for the driver of the second car to come forward.'

Darryl says, 'I only ask because, is there someone I should go and see? I mean, it looks like I'm going to run the business now. I don't want to fuck it up like Comedy did.'

'Sell the business to SlapTickle. They'll make you a good offer.'

There's a silence like a lead weight falling through the air.

'Shit. They already did.'

Ted Boyle. A maestro.

'You should accept. I don't know how they feel about competition.'

'Yeah,' he says, breathing heavily.

'Goodbye, Darryl.'

The senior constable says, 'There are speed limits on the road because speed kills. No matter what sort of vehicle you drive, when you impact with a tree, usually the tree wins.'

There was a moment when I could have got through to Comedy, when he seemed genuinely vulnerable. Instead I called him names, scared him back into his shell, because suddenly I didn't think I could really work for someone like Comedy Johnson.

On TV, the senior constable is getting emotional. Out there in the dark with the media lights and the dead bodies, he says, 'You can imagine I get tired of coming to sites like this and telling your television cameras about the dangers of speeding. I feel like a stuck record. But *still* there are people who don't take our road rules seriously. Drivers of sports cars are just as vulnerable to speed as other road users.'

Chased out of town by his murderer, then scolded by the police for speeding.

That's what Comedy would have called *tragic irony*.

The senior constable says, 'These deaths were preventable.'

And through the walls of my flat, he's talking to me.

DARK DAY

BACK WHEN WE were engaged I used to tell Annie that living by yourself is like coming home every day to your own brain.

Well, that goes double for when you live in your office.

There's a shower at the end of the hall that doesn't get used by anyone else on this floor, and I've emptied out one of my filing-cabinet drawers to store my doona and pillows during office hours. Living in a place without a kitchenette isn't a major adjustment; I never cooked much when I had one. I don't miss television. About the biggest problem is that it's been raining most of the day.

All afternoon there was paint bulging out from the ceiling like a waxing yellow moon. I moved my couch-cum-bed to the other side of the office and, sure enough, about an hour ago the water burst through and left a splat on the carpet the shape of a goanna. There's a coffee tin on the goanna's head now, catching the water as it drips out so slowly.

The Chinese used to strap their victims beneath dripping taps; they'd keep you bound in place so the water landed bang on your forehead, drip drip drip. After long enough each drop becomes like a baseball bat to the face.

That's when you give up all your lovely Chinese secrets.

I don't want to go out. I just want to sit here and watch the roof.

The traffic noise is easing and it's fully dark now so I switch on the lamp. The newspaper on my desk is open to the announcements page. In the obituaries, everyone wants everyone to know that their mother or father died peacefully, or mercifully, or doing what they loved. Death gets such a polish here. The weddings column is more of the same: wondrous occasion, two become one, triumph of love, covenant before God.

My eyes come back to the same item:

ALL WELCOME to witness the union of Rodney Fisher and Kiara Morelli, who embark upon their glorious future together on Saturday, 3 p.m., Christ Church, Camberwell.

My eyes come back to the words:

...glorious future...

And I have to leave.

Annie would want me to leave. She'll be the kind of mother who takes her kid by the hand and leads them next door and makes them own up about the broken window.

We haven't spoken in more than two years. She doesn't play a big role in my decisions. But it's her fault I'm in this mess.

Before I leave I check the coffee tin. There's barely an inch of water in it so I leave it in place. Let the water keep coming and let this thing keep catching it. I switch off the lamp and pretty soon I'm in a cab, still thinking about Annie, still thinking about what it might be like to get dripped on to death.

Kiara Morelli lives in a flat in Coburg, which is a long way from Camberwell—in distance and, in her case, aroma. Kiara's balcony opens out over the fenced grotto where the residents of these flats dump their garbage. Summer here must be its own unique kind of torture. Although we've never met, I've come to know Kiara pretty well. She isn't likely to appreciate the convenience of tossing her trash bags out the window.

I duck quickly through the rain and up both flights and knock, try to piece together some kind of introduction. The pieces haven't gelled when the door opens just three inches. It's someone who must be Stephanie, Kiara's sister, with a look of pretend fear on her face.

'Hi?'

'Hi. My name's John. I'm here to see Kiara.'

She smirks with big eyes. She's prettier than her sister, a lot younger. I'd guess right on the brink of thirty.

'Are you sure you got the right night?'

'I rang this afternoon and left a message. She knows I'm coming.'

Now she scowls, disappears from the door but leaves it ajar. I hear her say, 'It's a man. He said he called you...'

Crockery hits crockery and a tap runs. I push open the front door. Stephanie is right there with her back to me, whispering urgently into the kitchen. 'I thought he was a stripper, like, on the wrong night.'

She lets go a spectacular giggle and Kiara appears, looking past her sister, looking at me for the first time ever. Stephanie doesn't turn around, doesn't know I can hear her when she whispers, 'Who is he?'

Kiara must be wondering the same thing herself. She peels off a pair of rubber gloves and says, 'Let's find out.'

She holds out a dry hand. 'Mister Dorn?'

I shake it. 'Miss Morelli.'

'This is my sister, Steph. She thought you were a stripper.'

Stephanie blushes with more red than you'd expect from someone her age. 'Sshhhhhh!' she urges, then giggles more, almost choking. To me she says, 'I didn't...ummm...'

Kiara says, 'I had my hens' night here last night. Someone

invited an exotic dancer...' Kiara looks wide-eyed at Steph and they both giggle. Kiara says, 'I'm getting married on Saturday.'

'To the dancer? That was fast...' I smile at Steph.

They laugh the same laugh, the way sisters do. Kiara says, 'So what can I do for you? You didn't say in your phone message. You work for Rodney?'

'In a way. But he doesn't know I'm here.'

'Okay...'

'I was trying to be discreet.'

'Right.' The smile has dropped from Kiara's face, but Steph is still beaming, waiting for us to joke around some more.

I say, 'If you'd rather I didn't come inside, we could go out...'

Kiara teaches primary school kids how to finger paint and add up small numbers. Right now she's giving me the face she must give her students all the time. The one where she squints at you, wants you to know she's figuring you out.

'Stephy, would you mind putting the kettle on?'

The younger sister turns and hurriedly disappears. Kiara keeps squinting. I know I don't look harmless.

She says, 'You can come in, but first I have to know what this is about.'

I nod slowly. 'Okay. Let me ask you...and forgive me for getting personal. Do you have a premarital financial agreement with Rodney?'

Her eyebrows rise. 'That is personal.'

'Rodney's a banker. He's in venture capital, right? His job is all about risk management, minimising loss and so on.'

'Yes, but—'

'So Rodney decides to get married. The smart move financially, and what would be in character for him, would be to have you sign a binding financial agreement that minimises his liability. That way, if the marriage failed, for whatever reason, you couldn't take him for half his assets. He'd hold on to everything that was his, you'd get back what was yours. Has he asked you to sign that kind of agreement?'

She doesn't answer. She doesn't even really react.

I say, 'Or is the one you signed surprisingly generous, to the point where your lawyer practically fell over himself to process it before Rodney could change his mind?'

Her eyes shift a little, but apart from that she gives nothing away.

'I still don't understand—'

'If you had to sign the kind of agreement you'd expect from a man like Rodney, then I'm wasting your time and I'll go. But if he caved in, if that agreement says that you get spousal maintenance and maybe a swag of property interests, and if you're wondering how come, then I can explain. That's all I want to do.'

There's energy in her that I sense but can't see. She tamps it down by clearing her throat. 'And who are you?'

'I'm John Dorn. I'm a private inquiry agent. I think there are some things about Rodney that you need to know.'

Her eyes drop. The face she makes now, I don't think it's one her students see very often.

'Oh God,' she says.

She glances back into the flat for Stephanie, who's in the kitchen making noise.

'Are you sure I need to know? I'm getting married on Saturday, for goodness sake.'

'It concerns you directly.'

She rubs a hand on her apron, pushes open the door and forces herself back against the wall to let me inside. I step through a short corridor and into a living area that's feminine, well kept considering the space is too cramped for a pair of adult women. One wall is a series of children's paintings, all big brushes and colours, most of them framed. In all of them there's a tall figure who I bet is supposed to be Kiara. On the shelf is a series of vegan cookbooks and the flat smells of the vegetables they had for dinner.

'Stephy, I'm having a talk with Mister Dorn in my room. No listening at the door, all right?'

Stephanie doesn't answer.

'All right?'

'All right,' comes back shrill. Something is thrown into the sink but it doesn't break.

'She doesn't like being kept out of things.' Kiara's voice cracks as she swings open a door and I step into a master bedroom that's barely big enough for the bed.

'Sit down,' she says.

I sit on the bed and slump, try to seem the least intimidating I can. The blinds in here are drawn but through them come the sounds of rain and Middle Eastern music from another flat.

On the table by her bed is a photo frame. It's a picture of Rodney and Kiara, pressed cheek to cheek, somewhere like a restaurant, posing obediently. It's a digital frame that dissolves right while I'm looking at it into a group of seven children at a school carnival, arms wrapped around each other, Kiara kneeling between them all, smiling so big you might think she was crying if it weren't for the grinning faces around her.

Kiara closes the door. She squeezes past me to the wardrobe and opens it only a few inches, which is as far as it will go with a bed in here. From a small wooden chest she draws a white stapled document.

'I didn't want this,' she says, holding it lightly between thumb and forefinger. 'It was Rodney who demanded a "pre-nup", as he called it. And he said that legally I had to get a lawyer. So I did. Barry was pretty tough apparently, but I wasn't involved at all. Then, like, two weeks ago, Rodney acquiesced to everything. Barry seems to think I should be extremely happy, but I haven't read it. I signed it, though. Shouldn't I have?'

'I don't think that makes any difference.'

She sits on the bed with her back straight and her hands folded in her lap, slightly neater, more refined in her movements than I'd imagined her.

'Please…let's not draw this out. What's happened?'

I lean forward, clasp my hands and bow my head, wanting to keep her calm. I gently clear my throat.

'Rodney paid me to do something bad. And I did it.'

From far off I hear his shoes, sharp cracks against the hot concrete that circles this motel, every step a cannon firing. I've never heard shoes this loud. Perhaps he gets them specially made.

I pour more gin into a tumbler that is scratched and dimpled from all the drinkers that have stayed in this room before me. I slosh in the tonic and swirl it with my finger, waiting for the shoes to reach my door.

A soft knock.

Heat and light come at me as I pull on the handle. I look down while my pupils adjust.

'Come inside quick,' I say.

The shoes are expensive leather, tasselled, a deep sunset colour. The rest of his outfit is carefully casual, true to whatever catalogue he bought it from, right down to the summer jacket tossed over one shoulder. It all contrasts with the ruddy, asymmetrical face that smiles as he steps inside. I close the door and my eyes have to adjust again.

'Nice to see you too,' he says.

He lays his jacket on the bed and glances around. There's the typical ugliness and stink of silverfish and this particular motel is built of concrete blocks, which makes the rooms like kilns this time of year. But also they're soundproof. No one next door can hear what we say, accidentally or not.

I needed our meeting place to surprise him. This dusty motel outside Kerang, where there are more people-sized rocks than people, where the sun shines hard on absolutely everything, it's a hard place to get followed to. Not that I expected him to get followed. But I could go to jail for what I've done, so I need the grand total of people who know about it to remain me and Rodney.

Through rimless glasses his eyes fall on the briefcase, closed and locked on the writing desk. He has the smallest mouth I've ever seen; even when he licks his lips it doesn't get any larger than a ten cent coin.

I say, 'I need to search you.'

'I'm sorry?'

'I can't run the risk of you copying the disks.'

'Are you drunk?'

'Turn around.'

'Do you think I'd have any idea how to copy these disks, even if I wanted to?'

'Turn the fuck around.'

'Goodness me. You are in a mood.' He turns slowly. I slip my fingers under his collar, down his chest. 'Last time you practically fell over yourself to get my business. Now you—'

Rodney giggles when I press his armpits, because he's ticklish and also because he thinks this is stupid. 'Hope the bloody maid doesn't walk in,' he quips. Then, because he wasn't sure if I got it: 'She'll think we're a couple of poofs.'

Roughly I raise his foot and tear off one of those fancy shoes and a sock. 'Christ.' He grabs hold of my head to keep his balance.

I raise the other foot and do the same. There's nothing there. I step away and let Rodney fall back onto the bed. I pick up his jacket, squeeze it all over.

'Happy?' He's less flippant now.

I reach for my drink, gulp some, wipe my mouth.

He asks, 'Is something wrong? You seem anxious. Has something happened that I should know about?'

I put the drink down slowly, running through the various answers to that question. Something has happened, hasn't it, John?

'Nothing that concerns you,' I say.

I open the briefcase and pull out a pack of cards, a laptop computer, a can of lighter fluid, a pack of matches, headphones and five CDs in clear sleeves. They're labelled *Fisher, one* through *five*.

'Sit down here,' I say, indicating the chair in front of the writing desk. 'And give me your phone.'

Rodney sneers, shakes his head. But he slaps the phone into my waiting palm.

'A tad paranoid, aren't we?'

'After what you hired me to do, you're going to accuse *me* of being paranoid?'

Rodney stiffens. He's used to being the rude one. 'I only did what any prudent man would do under the circumstances. I plan to have children with Kiara, do you understand? I have to be sure there are no skeletons in the proverbial.'

'There are other ways of doing a background check.'

'And I've done those. This was the last box to be ticked.'

Having made his point, he sits down in front of the laptop. The five disks perch primly beside it.

'One for each session,' I say. 'Forty-five to fifty minutes each. It's the last one, disk five, that's got what you're looking for. The others are less interesting.'

He picks up disk five and slides it into the laptop.

I reach out for the playing cards and refill my glass, give another finger-stir.

Rodney turns to me. 'I'd rather not listen to these in front of you.'

'That's a shame.'

I crash onto the bed.

He doesn't take his eyes off me. I lay out the cards and don't look up. Maybe he's thinking of something to make me leave the room. Maybe he's waiting for me to glance up so he can give me his expectant face. Finally he rotates his body to face the computer. Puts on the headphones. Clicks play.

Gustafson says, 'Come in, Kiara,' right at the moment I press record. Their voices get louder, fuller, so they must be moving to the centre of his office.

'Did you get caught in the rain?' he asks.

'I like the rain,' she says back.

I'm parked in a thin, forgotten kind of alley that's really an abyss between tall buildings, where it's still raining twenty minutes after it's stopped everywhere else. I can't hear the drains sluicing water over the dumpsters because there are headphones clamped around my ears, but I can see it drizzling across my windscreen. Which is good. Because if a pedestrian glances at my car from the street, they probably won't see me inside.

Gustafson says, 'How are the wedding plans coming?'

Still distant, rustling, maybe taking off a raincoat, Kiara says, 'We spent this morning sampling cakes.'

'What did you settle on?'

'Chocolate mud.'

'Ah…my weakness. But tell me, what does a vegan chocolate cake have in it?'

'Mostly avocado.'

'You're kidding.'

'I'll save you some.'

Five weeks ago I broke into Gustafson's office and found a single coffee table placed between two comfortable armchairs. On top of it sat a lonely box of tissues. I'd switched on one of four or five lamps despite it being daytime—his windows are heavily fogged, the walls a deep red. On his desk I saw a photograph of three men, brothers I would guess, wearing fly-fishing overalls, grinning like they'd just caught the biggest fish of their lives. One of them had blond hair, the one in the middle was a round man with a great Santa Claus face, his beard neat and trim. The third wore tinted prescription glasses.

I don't know what he looks like, I've never seen him in the flesh, but with clues such as the admiring talk of cake and the kind of subtle exhalation I hear now as he sits down, I've concluded over these past five weeks that Doctor Gustafson is the fat guy in the middle of that picture.

'How do you feel today?' he asks.

'I'm...' Kiara knows this isn't smalltalk. Her voice is on-mic and loud, so she must be sitting down too. 'I feel good. Getting nervous, I suppose.'

'About the wedding?'

'I suppose.'

There's a short silence.

'To tell the truth, I'm exhausted. I spent the night at Rodney's, and it wasn't all sleeping...' I hear the smile in her voice. 'And that makes me feel good. I like that we're like that.'

'It can indicate a healthy relationship.'

'Yeah...'

Gustafson says nothing.

She says, 'And also, Rodney's such a lad. I guess a part of me thinks, if I can satisfy him, he won't need to be with other women anymore.'

Gustafson says nothing to that, either. Dead air filters through my headphones.

'It's security, I suppose,' Kiara says. 'I haven't known him very long. Only a few months really, and there are times I wonder if I know him at all. But our sex life is…really good. And I know he wants children too. Those are the things that make me feel confident about getting married.'

For five weeks I've listened to her talk about Rodney's libido. As far as I can tell, she's trying to convince herself that she can change him. Or that marriage will change him. Despite how obvious it is, and despite all the money she must be paying Gustafson, he hasn't told her yet that she's lying to herself.

'How are the negotiations coming along?' His voice is distant, echoing, like someone talking at the far end of a church. Hearing him wasn't a priority when I taped the microphone in place.

'The financial agreement?'

'Yes.'

'I don't know. I try to have nothing to do with it. And I told Rodney that. I said, this was your idea, you and Barry figure it out. I know they haven't agreed on anything yet. And I know they both hate each other, but that's all I know.'

'What do you think will happen, if they don't reach an agreement?'

'They will. I'm really not worried about it.'

More silence. I've never been to a shrink, but I'm guessing all this silence is normal.

Gustafson says, 'I'm wondering if you're ready to talk about what happened. To your sister and her boyfriend. You gave me some broad strokes at our first meeting, but…Do you feel ready?'

'Ummmm…'

He says, 'You've been reluctant so far. And that's fine. There's no pressure.'

I wind up the levels on the receiver and on the laptop, but there's only hiss.

She isn't responding.

This morning I refilled a Jameson's whiskey bottle with cheap bourbon and stashed it beside the driver's seat. Now I reach for it and unscrew the lid and take a swig. These 'broad strokes' happened before I got this job, but Gustafson's been tapping her on the shoulder like this for all of the five weeks I've been listening. And every time he does I get a sick twist in my guts and I have to ease it with something. Then, every time she doesn't talk about it, I reward myself with a drink. And since she's never talked about it, every week I've been getting soused right here in my car.

She asks, 'What's the rule? With doctor–patient privilege?'

I drink.

'I'm bound by my professional code and by law not to break your confidence.'

'But is it really that clear cut? I mean, there must be exceptions.'

Drink.

'Not really.'

Silence. I hold the bottle ready.

She says, 'I know I've wasted a lot of time in here. I'm sorry.'

Drink.

'You don't need to apologise. The impression you gave me, when you first came here, was that you wanted to make a clean breast of things before your wedding. Would you say that's true?'

'Yes.'

And I take the opportunity to finish the bottle. Which is a shame, because what she says next makes me want a drink more than ever.

'You're right. I might as well get it over with. I just don't know how to tell it.'

'Let's start with what you remember about that night.'

Then she tells her story, and my laptop computer records every word in twenty-four-bit stereo. Clear and sharp and perfect.

The thing is, it wasn't self-defence. Glen was drunk and he came up the stairs at me and shouted something…I don't remember what. I could smell alcohol, not just on him but everywhere in the house, and I asked him if he'd been drinking. Stupid question. He shouted at me that it wasn't my business. Called me a slag and told me to piss off. He didn't hit me or even threaten me. He just stood there, on the top step, and I remember thinking he was waiting for me to do it. I thought he knew that's what I was going to do. Like he was daring me to, the way he was yelling. So I pushed him, just my palms against his chest, but I did it as hard as I could.

He lost his balance and reached for me. If he'd reached for the banister he'd have been fine. But he reached for my arm and I pulled it away and he went back and his legs…his legs folded up and he dropped and I screamed. I know I screamed because that's all I've thought about since it happened. Not because of the guilt. Just because…I didn't know for sure if anyone heard me. Like, if Glen's neighbours heard me then they'd know that someone was there.

He fell backwards and I screamed and covered my mouth to stop the noise and I turned away. I heard him go down the stairs and straight away I started crying. I think I was bawling before he reached the bottom. I think I'd been about to cry all that afternoon, since Steph had come over, and this was all it needed. He was at the bottom of the stairs, against the sideboard, and one of his arms was on a funny angle. It was pulled back sharply behind his head and when I saw it I thought he must be dead. No one's arm could look like that if they weren't dead. But I ran down the stairs and he was breathing, but not awake. His eyes were half-closed and I could only see the whites of them, like his eyeballs were turned all the way back into his head. That's how he looked. I didn't want to touch him. I didn't want to leave fingerprints on him. I thought, if I leave fingerprints, I'll go to prison. So I was thinking pretty clearly like that, I guess.

I thought about calling an ambulance, but then I thought, he'd tell the police I pushed him. And I'd go to prison for sure. You know, it's not that prison loomed that large in my head. It's just that, without me, Steph would be out in the world. With Glen, probably. She'd have nowhere else to go. All of this went through my mind in a few seconds.

I went back upstairs and got Steph's suitcase and packed it. Then I went room to room, getting everything I thought she'd need, which is what I'd come to do in the first place. The bathroom and everything. There were empty bottles all over the house, just beer bottles everywhere, like he was collecting them. For Steph to clean up, I suppose. She wasn't always such a doormat, but she got that way, living with him.

And I kept saying to myself, I must be in shock. I must be in shock. This is what it's like to be in shock. But I didn't feel sick or numb or anything. I stopped crying and I got her things, clothes, her diary. Then I took the suitcase down the stairs and I had to step over Glen. I kind of looked at him but only quickly. He hadn't moved. I couldn't tell if he was breathing then.

No one saw me leave. I mean, I have to assume that now. When I got home, Steph was watching TV, curled up on the couch. And I remembered how, earlier that day, I'd wanted her to move in, you know? I was so angry about what had happened, all I could think was that she had to get away. So what if my flat is too small? But then I got back home, lugging her suitcase into the loungeroom, and there she was with her eye all swollen up, and I thought, this is it. This is what my life is now. Every moment was going to be about Steph. And Glen. This was going to infect everything.

She looked at the suitcase and she asked me if I'd seen him and I said,

'No. He wasn't there.' And that was the end of it. She kept on watching TV. I sat down and watched it too.

In my rearview mirror I see it's raining again.

Gustafson says, 'What else can you tell me about how you felt?'

There's rustling and a moan, like Kiara is stretching, waking herself up.

'I felt terrible. I half-thought the police would be waiting for me when I got home. I expected it every day for three weeks. And then, one day, there they were.'

'What did they say?'

'They said Glen was dead. They said his partner at the bike shop had broken into the house. He found him. Glen had been there all that time, they said.'

'And during that period, only you knew what had happened to him?'

'Yes.'

'What was that like?'

'It was like…' I can hear Kiara reaching, trying to be truthful, 'It was like running in the dark. Knowing you're going to hit something and hurting with the anticipation. For all of those three weeks, Steph had been talking about going to see Glen, and I'd say no. Give him time. Let him know he's done wrong. Make him…' Kiara's voice breaks. She sniffs back tears. 'Make him come to you.'

She breaks down, muffles her sobs with something, probably her hands. Gustafson waits. I wait too.

In the rearview I can see all the way to the end of the lane and across the street to a shopfront, though I can't see what it sells. There's clothing on mannequins in the window, but it's strange-looking clothing. The mannequins look strange. The water splattering across the back windshield makes it difficult to see.

Kiara composes herself. 'So when the police came over... Helping her through that was the hardest part. The police said Glen had been alive for about twenty-four hours before he'd finally died. Steph blamed herself, for not being there.' Kiara honks mucus into a tissue. 'She has this thing where she cries so hard she starts to choke, and I have to slap her on the back to make her breathe. She's been like that since we were kids—'

'Okay,' Gustafson says. 'Let's keep talking about you, though. No one suspected that you were involved?'

'No. They said Glen had some ludicrous amount of alcohol in his blood when he died. It was like the police were trying to convince *me* it was an accident.'

'What about Stephanie? The police suspected her?'

'They asked her questions. She told them he'd hit her but she didn't know he'd fallen.'

'And they believed her? Just like that?'

Kiara inhales quickly so she can laugh. Which takes a few seconds. She's making a point.

'They took one look at Steph and knew she was the most truthful person any of them had ever met. She can't lie to anyone. She's...it's like this switch in her head that never got flicked. Like, she trips up on her words, speaks in noises...That's the beauty of Steph. I don't think for them there was ever a question of foul play.'

The shopfront I can see in my rearview has women coming and going. Some of them push prams. Others don't, but it's all women. I rotate my body and squint hard through the rain. I'd like to forget what I'm listening to and solve the puzzle of this store. But the rain's too heavy now.

'She felt responsible? For what she thought had happened to Glen?'

'Yes.'

'What about you?'

Kiara's voice is suddenly dried up. 'It comes and goes. Some days are really bad. The idea of leaving someone to die…It makes me sick. I want to ring up the detective and confess. I have this sense of wanting to be punished. Like, I want to pay the fine and go home.'

'Do you think you'd feel better if you told your sister the truth?'

Kiara takes in a big breath. 'I did. I told her…two or three months ago.'

'What prompted you to do that?'

'That was one of the bad days. I'd had a glass of wine. Steph had been having a bad day too. Talking about Glen. Wanting to visit his mum in Perth. I started to cry, and then she started crying. Then I told her.'

'How did she respond?'

'It took a long time for her to understand what I was saying. Once she did, she was so forgiving. Immediately she's telling me, don't worry, we'll keep it a secret. I think maybe she was relieved… Like, she didn't have to feel guilty anymore.'

In my rain-splashed mirror a hugely pregnant woman is looking at my car, then she turns and waddles through the shop's screen door and suddenly it's obvious what the store is selling. Maternity clothes. Those mannequins are pregnant mannequins. The woman who walked in looked like Annie. Or at least, how Annie would look if she were pregnant. Blood pumps into my head and I have to remind myself that it's not Annie. We only broke up a couple of years ago. She's not going to be settling down, having a family.

'You still have bad moments?'

'Since I told her? Yeah, of course.'

'Maybe telling your sister wasn't enough. Have you considered talking to your fiancé?'

My headphones fill with laughter. 'Nooooooo.'

'Why not?'

'I'd lose my triple-A rating.'

'What do you mean?'

'Rodney couldn't marry me if he knew about this. I love him, but he's two-dimensional in some ways.'

'You think he'd break it off?'

'Do you tell your wife everything?'

'Well...I won't tell her I had cannelloni for lunch today. But you're talking about something with real psychological implications.'

'It's not an option, doctor. Rodney's too conservative. It's just not an option.'

The woman I saw go into the store is coming back out now. The one who looks like Annie. I watch her slowly close the screen door and wait in the shelter of the portico, and now I see that she looks like Annie because she is Annie. About eight months pregnant. And she's standing there to stay dry and she looks over at my car again and then she steps out into the rain and she looks over again and then she's gone.

I take off the headphones.

The light in here has changed in the last fifty minutes, or maybe I've changed and so I'm noticing the light now. I'm on my back on the bed with my head pillowed forward, aimed at Rodney. He rubs a hand across his brow, pushing deep into the skin. He's about to get up out of the chair, then doesn't.

'Fucking well bugger me,' he says.

Without the light behind him he's smaller. His face has more lines in it than before, showing years I hadn't noticed—he's at least ten years older than Kiara. Even so, I don't remember his hair so thin or his neck so flabby. Listening to that disk has aged him.

'Do you think it would be suspicious if I broke it off immediately?'

'Uuuuuh.' I feel like I just woke from a coma. 'I don't know.'

I reach for the gin bottle and pour into my glass.

'Can I get one of those?' he asks. Like I'm going to get up and mix him a drink. I hold the bottle out and it hovers in the air until he comes and takes it.

'Christ...' he says, moving to the bar fridge. He seems oblivious to the state I'm in. 'Last month we thought she was pregnant. She wasn't, but we thought...Christ. Can you imagine if she was?'

Just that word prompts uncomfortable thoughts. To distract myself I finish my drink, heave myself forward and let the alcohol drain from my head. There's a stiff ache in my neck. I stand painfully, move to the computer and eject the disk.

Rodney sips his drink and sits back down, reclines, crosses his legs. He's already philosophical. 'Well, it was nice while it lasted. She was a good girl, Kiara. I tell you what, you wouldn't think it would be so hard for a bloke like me to find a wife.'

I carry the disks to the motel sink, drop them in and squirt the lighter fluid over them. Then I light a match and drop it on the disks. The smoke is thick and black and I push open the window, fan at the vapour. The blue fire peters out and the disks shrivel into black clumps. I look down at them for a long moment, then I turn and fold my arms. It takes a second for my eyes to focus properly on Rodney because the image of the flames seems to have burned into my retinas. I try not to slur.

'So...you're gonna break it off?'

'Of course. I mean, I don't like to be so predictable. But the fact is she's absolutely right about me.'

I adjust myself against the sink.

'It's just that you might be missing the most important...the most important angle.'

'What's that?'

'Well...' I shrug like what I'm saying is obvious. 'Isn't it ideal? Knowing her secret like this?'

'God, no. Don't be naive. This is a scandal waiting to happen. Banker's Wife Charged with Murder. My reputation. My livelihood. My mother, for Christ's sake.'

'But isn't it *ideal*. If she decides she doesn't want to be with you after all. If she starts up with another bloke. You make one phone call and she's had it.'

'She wouldn't start up with another bloke. She's not that kind of person.'

I snicker, loud. 'Now who's being naive? Take it from me, every relationship goes sour eventually. And then, when that happens, you threaten to call the cops and tell them she confessed to you and you just can't live with the knowledge. She won't hold up under questioning. Neither will her sister.'

'Come on,' Rodney rears, laughing. 'I'm saying to you that I couldn't bear that kind of upheaval—'

'But it would never come to that.' Something that might be an alarm is ringing softly in a corner of my brain. I pause, but it's nothing I can't douse with another swig of gin. I take several small steps to the fridge and pour some into my glass.

'When things get tough, you tell her what you know. That's enough to put her in jail. Then you lay down the law. You tell her how things are going to be.'

I add tonic to the glass, splashing some down the fridge door. When I turn back to Rodney he's calmly analysing me and maybe he knows that what I'm talking about is more than just him and Kiara.

But what he says is, 'You mean, like insurance?'

I say, 'Yes.'

I add a little more tonic, which requires a moment of intense focus.

'But if it came out. The stigma of it,' he shakes his head. 'My wife the murderer...People would say I was duped.'

'People would say you're a survivor.' I drink a long sip. 'But it would never come out because...You're gonna have kids, right? If she's got kids, she'll do anything to stay out of prison. No man could be better positioned for when his wife tries to dump him or just... you know...fuck him over.'

That alarm is ringing louder so I finish my drink and now the alarm is gone, leaving only the acrid stink of burnt plastic that's filled the room. I balance my way to the front door and open it. Light pours in and I take refuge on the far side of the bed, slump there cradling nothing.

Rodney is shaking his head. 'I see your point. But the risk is... It's professional suicide.'

He puts on his jacket. I pull his mobile phone from my pocket and toss it onto the bed and he picks it up and says, 'I guess this is goodbye. You'll forgive me for saying I hope I never see you again.'

I shrug, fall back onto the pillows, feel my head swim. Rodney sees me, seems to judge me, so I close my eyes.

He says, 'Did anything happen that might make her suspect anything?'

'Like what?'

'Did she see you? Did the doctor find the microphone?'

'I took the microphone out. No to all three questions.'

'So when I tell her it's over, and if she decides to investigate for herself to find out why, she's not going to find out why, is she?'

'Not unless she bugs *your* shrink's office.'

I laugh at my hilarious joke. There's no response from Rodney. I say, 'I hope I never see you again, too.'

No response to that either. After a moment I open my left eye. The door is still open and Rodney is gone. Even in those shoes, the war in the distance that they sound like, I didn't hear him creep away.

*

The electronic picture frame does what it's been doing all the while since I got here. The restaurant photo of Rodney and Kiara reappears, the two of them with their mindless, charming grins. Kiara's face in that picture is as different to the one that's next to me on the bed as a face can be.

Right now, she looks to have the worst kind of hangover, eyes bloody and swollen from crying and rubbing. She sits hunched, clutching the pillow which is all she's had to wipe her face on and now you can see tears and saliva and make-up smeared across the fabric.

She doesn't want to leave this room to get a tissue. She doesn't want Stephanie to see her like this.

'I can get you something.' I say. 'A towel or something.'

It's late now and we're lit by just a blue silk lampshade on the other side of her bed. I remember how dark it was in my car, when I first heard her tell her story. It's like that in this room.

'Why are you here?' She asks, sniffing back the mucus.

'I saw the announcement in the paper.' The folded premarital agreement lies on one of Kiara's pillows and I pick it up, flick through it. It's good to have something to focus on that isn't her. I find what I'm looking for on the last of the four pages. I read it out loud:

'*In the event that either party is convicted of an indictable offence, that party's rights under this agreement are void.* That's not an unusual clause, your solicitor probably didn't care much about it. But it sorts things out for Rodney. It means a court can't alter what the agreement says, and you have no rights under the agreement. You'd be lucky to come away with what you own now.'

She stares at the floor in front of her and I don't know if she's listening. I'm partly expecting her to deny this is happening and throw me out.

'No…' she says. 'That's not what I meant.'

Her hands shaking, she rubs her eyes with her wrist bone one more time. Her voice is just a chesty croak, slow and lifeless.

'You could easily have slipped an anonymous note under my door. But you chose to come and see me and sit through this.'

'I felt bad...'

'But you must have known you'd feel bad. Before you did it. And you did it anyway. And now here you are.'

This isn't exactly unfamiliar. People who get bad news, sometimes they like to make it about me. They want to make it that I'm the problem, that if it weren't for me they wouldn't be feeling this way. People like this, they might have a point.

'I needed the money,' I say. 'I hadn't had a paying job in weeks. Look—'

'Bullshit.' Despite her broken face her eyes flare with anger. 'I've got kids like you in my group. They play up just for the attention, then I sit them on my knee and tell them off, then they start crying and I give them a hug. Six-year-old catharsis junkies.'

'I didn't come here for a hug.'

'So why are you here?'

Her whole body is ragged and drained like she's been through an exorcism. I don't know where she's getting the energy to speak.

'Look...' I say. 'I don't feel bad about telling you the truth about Rodney Fisher. If what I did means you're not going to marry that prick, then you can analyse me all you like, but—'

'Who says I'm not going to marry him?'

Someone dumps a load of bottles into the recycling bin two storeys down. A guffaw made of glass.

'You still want to marry him?'

'I'm thirty-eight, for God's sake.'

'So what?'

She shrugs, wipes away more snot. 'I'm pregnant.'

God. Is there anyone who isn't?

'Does Rodney know?'

'Not yet.'

'It doesn't mean you have to marry him.'

'I'm a primary school teacher. How else would I raise a child? On hand-outs?'

That electronic photo frame, Kiara must have watched it dissolve a million times, from the picture of her and Rodney to the picture of her and all those children. Over and over and over.

She says, 'You have to leave now. I'm sorry I couldn't offer you the emotional purge you were looking for.'

'Hey, don't worry about it.' I stand up, pull on my jacket. 'I can hug myself without much trouble.'

'Maybe you're the one who needs to see Doctor Gustafson.' Her Italian eyes shine. 'You're the one with the real issues.'

She's genuinely baiting me, picking a fight in a room itself the size of a confessional. I don't say anything, open the bedroom door and step out.

Stephanie isn't there. When I reach the other side of the living room, I see that her bedroom door is ajar and inside she's lying on her single bed, in her underwear, big headphones around her head, reading a magazine. Her legs kick back and forth between the bed and her backside. She has no idea of there being anything else in the world.

I linger for a moment, wanting to say goodbye. But it feels like a lie, so I walk on and reach the front door.

'You might be wrong, you know.' It's Kiara's voice. She's come to her bedroom door, the document in her hand. She waves it gently. 'You said yourself that that clause is standard for these sorts of things. Rodney might have decided he wants to marry me because he loves me. Did that occur to you? That he just fucking loves me?'

'I know what people look like when they're in love. And when they're not.'

'You're what? The world's greatest detective?'

'It's got nothing to do with being a detective.'

It takes me half an hour to find a taxi in the rain.

I make a point of not looking at the coffee tin, the one that's catching the leaking water, until after I've sat down at my desk. When I do look, I see that it must have overflowed at least an hour ago. The shape on the floor is now a woman with a great big belly standing in the rain.

That's fine. Let her do that. Let me get back to watching the leak in the roof.

I wonder about the first drip, the first one to make the tin overflow, some time earlier tonight. At the moment it landed, when the water first crept out over the rim, maybe something coincided, like a car crash outside, or a thunderclap.

But what's more likely is there was nothing to announce it. And I wonder, even if I'd been sitting here watching, if I would even have realised it had happened.

DEATH AT LE SHACK

DEMETRI CALLS ME with a job.

One of his clients is sitting in a living room in Sandringham with a dead prostitute on his couch. When I get there I'm supposed to make sure the police don't cause problems.

I say, 'Isn't that what they're for?'

'This is just a drug overdose. Frank wasn't even there when it happened. But the cops know Frank. They could try anything.'

'What's his last name?'

'Tenant.'

'Haven't heard of him.'

'He's not a big fish. Maybe he thinks he is. Usually his bag is to be less than forthcoming with the ATO, though he's never been prosecuted. But there was an incident a few years ago...I helped him on a possession charge, which blossomed into a conviction, and he still maintains the police planted the coke on him.'

I have to ask. 'So did they?' I'm thinking of Vincenzo Gruppo, a carpet salesman the news has been all about lately. Cops set him up for possessing ecstasy and last week the Supreme Court apologised and freed him and now police integrity is the new bandwagon célèbre.

'I never saw the proof, but Frank's still ropable about it. He doesn't want it happening again.'

'He thinks they'll fix him up for *murder*?'

'To hear Frank tell it, the entire police force is champing at the bit to fix him up for murder. I've tried explaining that they couldn't care less. His business is taking off, it's *legal*, they're not interested in him anymore. But Frank's got this…victim mentality.'

'And the customer is always right…'

'I don't mind sending someone over to make sure what isn't going to happen doesn't happen.'

'Was she alone when she died?'

'Seems so. But I've had all of a two-minute conversation with him that ended ten seconds ago, so I don't know much. He and some friends picked her up last night and took her back to his house in Sandringham. Today they go out for lunch, leave her behind, come back and there she is, hypodermic right there on the floor. They didn't even know she had the stuff with her. No foul play suspected.'

'By Frank.'

'Honestly, the only thing he's worried about is that the cops are going to do to him what he did to her the night before. And if he says it's cut and dried, then I don't need to bugger up my Saturday when I can bugger up yours.'

'So I go over there and, what? Look tough?'

'That's right. They won't call triple zero until you arrive. If Frank flips out you can give me a bell, but I don't expect him to be a problem. Frank doesn't use heroin and he doesn't kill prostitutes. This is just bad luck.'

'Poor guy. Just when business is taking off.'

'And watch your mouth with him. Frank's been good for me and he can be good for you. Don't butcher the cash cow.'

*

Lining the gravel path to the front door is a row of tropical plants and there's a manicured lawn around a massive concrete fountain. The place feels like those expensive resorts in Fiji you see on travel shows but could never afford to actually visit. It has an hilariously ironic name, *Le Shack*, written out in a collage of bathroom tiles at the entrance to the driveway and again on the patio wall. At the base of the fountain there's a life-size mermaid carved into the cement, her tail dipping into the rustling pool as water rains around her, and the expression on her face is like this mermaid thing is getting stale.

Someone who must be Frank Tenant opens the door wearing nothing but a pair of slippers and bright orange speedos. He says, 'It's about bloody time. Let's get this done before she stinks up the place.'

You can tell Frank's from London, though most of his accent has faded. He turns and strides ahead of me into the living room, hairy skin glistening with sunscreen. He's like a fifty-year-old teapot, short and stout, and he parades proudly before me as well as his two extant guests, Trevor and Nancy.

Franks introduces them and says, 'Trevor's my lawyer.'

Trevor wears black clothes and gold jewellery, his grey hair is expertly maintained. I've met his type before—the rock and roll lawyer. He nods to me and goes back to his magazine.

'If he's your lawyer then why did you call Demetri?'

Frank grins, puts on a gangster's voice: 'Trevor don't do *this* kinda law.'

I'm guessing that Nancy is Trevor's wife, but Frank doesn't bother to say so. She's ten years younger than both of them and sits in an armchair by the window, dressed in a fur coat and maybe nothing else. She seems to watch me indifferently, but I can't see her eyes through those enormous sunglasses.

Next to her are french doors leading to a balcony overlooking

Red Bluff and, further along, Sandringham beach. It's a calm, sunny afternoon. Two people on kayaks are splashing each other with their paddles. There's a cruise ship out on the horizon, as airy and opulent as the room where I'm standing. Only in here there's a dead girl on the couch.

She's stretched out on her side, facing away from me, one hand drooped over the armrest. Her skin is pale but you wouldn't say deathly. Not yet. You might think she'd fallen asleep in her expensive evening gown if it weren't for how she's not breathing.

Frank says, 'Demetri told you what I need you for?'

'I'm supposed to keep an eye on the cops.'

'Exactly. Some chick ODs on my couch, it's not an invitation for the pigs to waltz in here and turn this place into their own playground-by-the-sea. They stitched me up once before, and now they're making a habit of it. That dago on the news? That is some corrupt shit. So they need to get the message that I'm onto them. Are you up to that?'

I lean over to look at the dead girl.

'Are you up to it?' Frank insists.

Her dress is small and revealing, but leaves enough to the imagination to mean she was good at her job. Probably a thousand, twelve hundred a night. She's pretty enough.

'John, I'm talking to you.'

The pretty ones make me the saddest. I know that shouldn't make a difference.

I ask, 'What name did she use?'

Frank pouts, annoyed, looks over at Nancy to see if she'll reciprocate. She gives him nothing. He says, 'Cindy.'

On the coffee table next to Cindy is a used ashtray, a lighter and a foil satchel, probably with more heroin in it. The needle is on the floor.

'Do you know where she got the gear from?'

'No idea.'

'You weren't with her when she bought it?'

'God, no. Why on earth would...We didn't even know she *had* the stuff, your Honour.'

'Frank never has anything to do with drugs. I can vouch for that.'

This is Trevor, not looking up from his magazine, mechanically reciting his talking points.

To Frank I say, 'And you weren't here when it happened?'

'Nope. She was watching TV when we left.'

'After you came back, did you touch anything? Move her in any way?'

'We turned off the TV.'

'How did you know she was dead?'

Frank scoffs. 'People don't usually sleep with their fucking eyes open...'

'I felt for a pulse,' Trevor offers, still reading. 'There wasn't one. Ergo...' he turns a page for emphasis, 'she was dead.'

'So where were you when it happened?' I ask.

Frank says, 'We met some friends for lunch.'

'Where?'

'Silvio's.'

'You went to Silvio's dressed like that?'

'No, no. I've been on the deck catching some sun. I had time to kill, waiting for you to show up. You know I called Demetri over an hour ago?'

'Who did you meet there?'

'It was a business meeting,' he nods gently with his eyes closed, the international sign for That's All You Need to Know. 'They'll corroborate, if it gets to that.'

'You left a prostitute here, in your home, alone?'

'Top shelf girls don't rip off your TV. She wasn't a streetwalker, she was expensive and I was good business for her. Besides, I hadn't paid her yet. I knew she'd be here when we got back.'

'Where did you book her from?'

'Executive Pleasure. I've got their card around somewhere.'

'Is this her purse?'

'Yeah.'

'Have you gone through it?'

'Why would I?' Frank's forehead and belly glimmer at me. He looks to his companions for back-up. 'Why the fuck does any of this matter?'

I open the purse. There's not much inside. A fifty-dollar note. Condoms. A driver's licence in the name of Angela Curzon.

'Her real name's Angela,' I say.

'That's useful.'

'You can call the police now.'

Frank sighs and moves to the phone, his face showing the world what a burden Angela's death has become. Picking up the receiver, he says, 'I was supposed to get my hair cut today.' He raises a hand above his head and, half-laughing, shouts, 'I cannot *believe* this fucking bitch!'

While he gives the details into the phone I sit on an antique chair adjacent to Nancy. There's a summery cocktail on a coaster beside her and I look around for the bar but I don't see one. I glimpse a stringy bathing suit underneath the fur coat.

I say, 'You been sunbathing too, huh?'

She turns to face me like I can't possibly be talking to her. She says, 'No,' and turns away again. In profile she resembles the mermaid outside. Languid. Over it.

Frank hangs up and shrugs at nobody. 'They're on their way.' He steps past Trevor and into an easy chair, sipping a glass of whisky I hadn't noticed until now. Now that I've noticed it I can smell it, from all the way across the living room. Through the french doors the ocean has changed colour and the kayakers are gone. As we sit in the bright silence my hopes of being offered a drink die a thirsty death; I figure Demetri would hear about it if I asked for one so soon after getting here. I'm taking in the crass details of the room— the wallclock in the shape of a woman's breast, the stool by the front door with a bull's head printed on its seat—when Trevor drops his magazine theatrically to the floor.

'Is this *really* going to take the rest of the day?'

I say, 'It might. They have to search the house. Take statements. They won't be in a hurry.'

He turns up his nose and looks away, and in this moment I see Trevor flinch, like a small electric charge sparking in his brain. He asks me now, suddenly less bored, 'Will they search the whole house?'

'Probably a lot of it. Photograph it.'

'Will they search us? Our personal things?'

Frank laughs, but there's no humour in it. 'We've got a corpse in here, Trevor. They'll do whatever the fuck they want. What do you think John is here for?'

Trevor's eyes are growing fearful. Frank hasn't noticed yet.

'Will they go through my things? My briefcase?'

I say, 'Definitely.'

Frank's still laughing. 'Trevor, there better not be a kilo of coke in there.'

'No, Frank, it's just…'

He doesn't finish, tries to imply the thing without saying it. Frank leans into Trevor and makes a face.

'What?'

Trevor mutters, '…in the briefcase.'

'What are you talking about?'

Trevor says, 'What Alex gave us at lunch…'

Frank stuffs even more derision into his face.

'So what? It's a contract.'

'It proves that we're promoting his tax scheme.'

'Right…'

'And if that scheme is deemed abusive…'

Trevor's still not saying it. Frank's still not getting it.

'*What?*'

Trevor's mouth quivers. 'The civil penalties alone could send you bankrupt…'

Frank's eyes close. His head lolls back and a groan that starts in his belly comes out as: 'Fuuuuuuuuuuuck.'

Trevor says, 'That's right.'

'We have to get rid of it.'

'We *can't.*'

'We have to *burn* it before they get here.'

'We can't burn it. We *need* it.'

'We can get another copy from Alex.'

'With a dead girl on your couch? After he's been questioned and asked to corroborate that we met him for lunch? He used to be the mayor, for Christ's sake. He's not going to want anything to do with this. If we destroyed the contract he could cancel the whole deal.'

Both of them are panicked, but I don't know what they're talking about so I can't tell if they're overreacting. This Alex person is presumably Alex Mills, who I knew indirectly when he was running the City of Port Phillip, who I believe was pimping out members of his staff at the time to campaign contributors. I've heard rumours about his shady GST schemes, but everything I know about tax offences wouldn't rouse a chihuahua from its beauty sleep, so all I can do is sit back and watch the show.

Frank gets to his feet and paces across the Persian rug, turns back the other way. He continues like this for a while, distressed, wearing nothing but orange bathers.

'We have to *hide* it. Somewhere in the house where they won't find it.'

Trevor's the calm one now, watching Frank. 'Do we really? I mean, it's got nothing to do with this.' His hands go out to indicate Angela. 'It's a piece of paper. They'd only seize it if the search was conducted by the ATO.'

'Who knows *what* they'll walk in here with? They can seize my *underwear* if they want to. For God's sake, Trevor. How could you leave this until now? That contract's enough to sink me. It's the *whole bloody show, Trevor!*'

He strikes out at the telephone, the closest thing to hand. It arcs across the room but doesn't break, just rolls along the rug past Nancy's feet.

She's staring out the window, doesn't appear to be listening. She's either stoned or so jaded that she actually finds this boring.

In the silence Frank breathes deeply with his hands on his flabby hips. Trevor stares at the floor.

'I'm a successful man,' Frank says, softly. 'And I got that way by being a paranoid bastard. We know the Tax Commissioner's got it in for me. If she, or anyone in her office, or anyone who wants to crawl up the arse of anyone in her office, were to find out that a search of Frank Tenant's home is about to take place...'

Trevor picks up the briefcase from behind the couch, nodding. From inside he takes out a thin red folder and cradles it in his lap. The way the sun hits it through the french doors, it's the brightest thing in the room.

'I could just leave with it...' Trevor says. But even as he speaks, an engine none of us had noticed shuts off and now we notice it. Nancy, glancing out the window, gurgles, 'They're here.'

Frank takes several steps towards me. 'Okay, John. This is where you come in. Where can we put it that they won't find it?'

'I can't advise you on how to dupe the police force.'

'Come on, it's a contract, not a blood-smeared knife. Do what you're paid for.'

'That's not what I'm paid for. And as Demetri's representative, I can only advise you to cooperate with law enforcement to the best of your ability.' I offer him the words like a chocolate I picked up off the floor.

Frank curses under his breath, turns to Trevor.

'The private investigator has to say that, I suppose.' He takes the red folder from Trevor. As he does, there's a rapping on the front door.

'Okay, Mister Pussy,' Frank points at me. 'You *are* here to manage the police, so go manage. I'll take care of this.'

With the folder in his greasy, sunburnt hands, Franks slips out of the living room and into the hallway.

I take Frank's house keys from the mantel and open the front door.

First in are the paramedics, not hurrying like they never do. They lean over the girl and start slapping her face and calling out for her to wake up. Nobody's told them she's been dead for three hours.

A plainclothesman and two uniforms are crossing the lawn, eyeballing me as they approach, and behind them there's a patrol car. All four doors are opening. I step onto the patio tiles and lock the front door behind me, hold up a palm to the detective.

'Can you show me some ID, please?'

He's a fatherly type with a standalone moustache and serious eyes set deep in his head, dark enough to be almost indiscernible from his black monobrow. It's an Easter Island face, moulded by the weather of a thousand years.

He flips out his wallet: Detective Steven Carney.

He says, 'You Tenant's lawyer?'

'What's a homicide detective doing here when no one's been pronounced dead yet?'

The uniforms, six of them now, all glare at me—pleased, probably, to have found someone to hate so early in the game. I don't mind if they think I'm a lawyer.

Carney says, 'Can we get past, please?'

He steps towards the door. As delicately as I can, I get in the way.

'I'm John Dorn. I represent Demetri Sfakiakopoulos, Mister Tenant's solicitor. Mister Tenant is concerned for his privacy and for his personal well-being should the police conduct a search of his home. He'll agree to a search only if the officers, all of them, submit themselves to a pat down, by me, before they enter.'

They look at each other with a kind of wonder. Though it didn't seem possible, Carney's monobrow plunges deeper into his eye sockets.

'Sorry, son, that's not how it works. We've got reasonable grounds to kick down that door if we need to. Now get out of the road—'

Carney reaches for the handle but I grab it first, hide it with my torso, both hands clasping it behind my back.

'You *don't* have reasonable grounds. This is a private residence, and Mister Tenant wasn't here when Angela Curzon died. There's no emergency that requires you to gain entry, and there's no reason for you to think that Frank is destroying evidence. Now, he *wants* to help you do your job, but if you came to play pin-the-crime-on-the-donkey, then you can trundle off back to St Kilda Road and get yourselves a warrant.'

'For goodness sake—'

'I know it's unorthodox,' I say, lowering my voice, inches from Carney's face. 'But I'm not asking much, given what you fellows have been up to lately.'

This is where it's useful that they think I'm a lawyer, since it was lawyers who pulled back the curtain on the Gruppo scandal. It might even make them think I have a legal leg to stand on. But my gambit really depends on Carney, on his ego. Half the cops I've ever met would already have kicked down the door. Just because they can.

Carney cocks his head, looks at me sideways, his eyes small glints of light in those black recesses. The other cops shift from foot to foot, impatient. Then Carney screws up his face and laughs, and the uniforms join in like a studio audience.

He says, through giggles, 'I hope getting touched up by a lawyer is what I always dreamed about.'

'I'll be gentle,' I say.

He smirks while I frisk him, then gives me a mocking nod when I unlock the door to the house.

I pat down the uniforms. They're not used to being on this side of a body search but they've got nothing to hide. Demetri was right. They're not interested in setting up Frank. A couple of them glare at me and give me their cop face, but no one has to make a quick trip back to the patrol car.

One of them is a lanky telephone pole with *Jason Regander, Constable* pinned to his breast and a small gold band on his wedding finger. He's younger than the others by two or three years, quiet, but he holds my eyes as I search him, makes a point of it, then steps past me into the house. He's the last of them. I follow him inside.

Frank's wearing a shirt now, getting questioned by Carney. Someone is taking photos of Angela, who hasn't been moved since the paramedics gave up their attempts. She's face up, washed out like maybe she drowned in really cold water. There are transparent plastic bags taped around her wrists, trapping in what evidence there might be on her skin, under her nails. The photographer moves around the couch—shoots a picture, takes a step to his left, shoots a picture. A boxer circling a heavy bag.

I hear Frank say, 'The needle on the floor is what cost her her life, Detective.'

In separate corners of the living room are Trevor and Nancy, at the mercy of two officers and their notebooks. Nancy has removed her sunglasses and I'm struck now by her appearance: a sandy toughness that glows with vitamin D and freckles. Eyes that know everything skip across the room to meet mine. So bored. Challenging me to show her something new.

Frank says, 'Because people don't usually sleep with their eyes open...'

Regander, the telephone pole, he's stooped over the couch, peering down at Angela. He doesn't know I'm watching. He stares at the girl, takes a step towards her, keeps staring. There's no way this is his first real-world corpse. Maybe the pretty ones get to him, too.

Frank says, 'I suppose I have more faith in people than you do, Detective.'

Regander would keep on staring, I suppose, if he weren't snapped out of it by Carney, who turns now to face the room and hollers, 'Okay. Singh, Regander, Tan, do the house. Johan, Miller, the grounds. Get a move on.'

As soon as our numbers thin, the paramedics return and heave Angela onto a stretcher. One of them pulls a blue sheet over her face and they wheel her out. Frank examines his couch and appears satisfied that it's back to normal, no stains or scuff marks. He fluffs the cushions while Carney talks to him.

Frank replies, 'It rests squarely with her, Detective. Squarely with her.'

Nancy surveys the living room and yawns.

Trevor sees her and catches the yawn, shrugging with his mouth agape at the officer who gestures to him with the notebook, asking him another question.

I step into the hallway.

The house opens into several bedrooms, an equal number of bathrooms and another deck where you could watch all the bikinis you wanted with the telescope that's propped against the rail. The Spanishness of the place doesn't let up—the doorways are all curved, the walls are a messy white stucco and there are ceiling fans everywhere. Some rooms have more than one.

A smear of grease is just visible on the door to the study and I'm looking at it when Regander emerges from a bathroom at the end of the hall. His palpable decision is to ignore me as he enters the study, even as I follow him in and close the door.

He continues to ignore me as he starts through the drawers of a stained oak writing desk. Behind it is a series of windows with a view out to the garden and to its left is a wall of coloured file folders, every make and shade, rising from floor to ceiling. Frank's life in documents.

Once I've taken in the sheer tonnage of paper, I say to Regander, 'So you know Cindy?'

Regander doesn't look up. Doesn't react at all.

'Constable?'

'What?'

'You met Cindy before?'

Still he doesn't look up. He sifts through the desk drawers, chewing his bottom lip with that massive policeman's jaw.

'Nope. No. I don't know her.'

'You recognised her when you saw her.'

'Whatever you say, sunshine.'

I nod. The policeman keeps rifling.

But then the silence gets too much for me and I say, 'You didn't recognise her real name, Angela Curzon, when I said it outside on the porch. You wouldn't have been so surprised to see her if you knew her as Angela. So I'm pretty sure you don't know her from an arrest.'

Without looking at me, Regander claws at the back of his neck, scratching an itch there.

I say, 'You knew her by her working name. Cindy.'

'That right?' he says.

'That's right. Just then when I asked if you'd met Cindy, you knew I was talking about the dead girl. How did you know that?'

Regander smirks but keeps his eyes on what he's doing. He opens a tin of thumbtacks and examines them closely.

'I didn't know who you were talking about. I just wanted you to piss off.'

'I don't think so. I think you know her working name because you know her the way a client knows her.'

He doesn't react. Instead he replaces the thumbtacks, keeps scratching his neck.

I say, 'But it seems to me that she's out of your price range. A thousand dollars a night? My guess is she was a pay-off. From Executive Pleasure to you. They comped you because you did them a favour. What was it? A client acting up? One of the girls mistreated? A quick round of we-don't-want-any-trouble-officer and you were on your way, am I right?'

'Piss off.'

'You don't have to tell me. Your service log will show any visits to Executive Pleasure. Or do you think I can't get access to those?'

He's forgotten to stop scratching at his neck and I can see the edge of a red blotch that's formed back there. The steady smirk has become a grimace. His eyes search the room, finally rest on me.

'You making a threat?' he grunts.

'No.'

'If you want to make threats, I can get you kicked out of here. I *can*, you know. I don't give a shit who you are—'

'Don't get tough. Let's drop it.'

He nods deliberately. Triumphant. In the last of the drawers he finds nothing, moves on to the mantel of tourist ornaments behind him.

I swivel to address the wall of folders, squinting. I can't believe there's a system to this nightmare. On the edge of the third shelf down I spot another greasy smear of sunscreen. I look close.

It's slotted in there, innocuous and almost completely hidden. Frank's needle-in-the-haystack approach.

I say, 'Can you see the tip of a red folder just here along this shelf?'

Regander doesn't answer. I wait. He doesn't look back.

I say, 'This is important. You'll want to see this.'

Regander forces a smile, tries to seem casual, looks up with those young eyes. I point again.

'The red folder there. You see it?'

'Yeah.'

I say, 'Pull it out.'

'Why?'

'Because you are going to want to take it with you.'

'Why don't *you* pull it out?'

'I don't want to get my prints on it.'

'What is it?'

'I don't know.'

'Piss off.'

'Look, I could open it and *read* it and I still wouldn't know what it is. It's in tax language. You may not know Frank, but the tax office does. And they'd do more than just shout you a beer if you were the man who seized this particular red folder during a homicide investigation, only to discover that it was a fraudulent licence application or a dodgy insurance claim.'

His face is confused. 'Why don't *you* take it?'

'If I do, it's theft. If you do, it's in the throes of a perfectly legal criminal investigation.'

'I don't get it...You're trying to screw your own client?'

'He's not my client. My client is a man who gets paid the most when Tenant's in the most trouble. You've got to take it out of here under your jacket, because you don't want the fuss you'll kick up if Frank sees you with it. Later on you say there were some crystals on it you thought might be cocaine, turned out to be baking soda...But you're a cop, I don't need to tell *you* how to manufacture evidence. Meanwhile, your cunning as a criminal investigator led you to question the contents of the folder and send it to the ATO. Open and shut.'

'Not interested.'

'Then I'll have to refer you to the earlier part of this conversation.'

'What?'

'If you don't do it, or if you do it wrong or associate my name with it, I'll offer my services to your wife. I'm sure she'll be interested to know what kind of business relationship you had with Cindy. And she'll pay me with *your* money, understand?'

Regander doesn't say anything. Looks at the red folder.

I say, 'The alternative is to enjoy with her the half-price movie vouchers the commissioner will send you when you bring down Frank Tenant. It's up to you.'

Regander scowls, shakes his head. But at least we've connected. I thought maybe I'd have to go through this whole spiel with him still searching the desk.

He says, 'That could get me sacked.'

'So don't let it.'

I stare at him, try to think of another good point to make. I can't think of one, so I leave the study.

Back in the living room, Carney is talking in the corner with Trevor. Frank sits alone on the couch, skimming the same magazine Trevor had earlier and there's something sparkling and golden in a glass tumbler next to him. I wish I knew where these drinks were coming from. Another uniform is going through Trevor's briefcase.

I set myself on the stool by the front door and Frank sees me. He nods, victorious. I ape it back to him.

Nancy is in her big armchair, the sunglasses back on her face. She is turned mournfully to the french doors, watching the ocean, the ennui turned up to eleven. I wish she could have seen what I just did.

When Regander comes out I can't tell if he's got the folder under his jacket. But he makes straight for the door and as he passes he gives me the same kind of nod Frank did, gets nothing in return.

Pretty soon I'm going to have to think of a way to explain to Frank and Trevor why the folder isn't there. Something convincing that will keep Demetri retained. But I'm not going to think about that for another few seconds. I'm going to rest on this stool for a moment.

I didn't have much doubt that Regander would take it. His instinct is to save himself, and cops make decisions on instinct. I'm the opposite. I can stare at the ceiling in my office and overthink what to have for dinner.

Not that I thought hard about this.

It's something I've been doing lately: Comedy Johnson, Rodney Fisher. I can't seem to find a client I want to help. I can't seem to find a client I don't want to undermine. What's funny is, my *big* failure, the one at the Pioneer Hotel, the one I'll be almost-famous for forever, that's still a couple of weeks away. And when that all unfolds, I won't be undermining anybody. Not even myself. I'll just be trying to do my job.

THE CRYBABY TECHNIQUE

WHAT I'M DOING in the lobby of the Pioneer Hotel is waiting for a guaranteed no-show. A martini and a few hands of blackjack must be the last things on Billy Benedict's mind. But here I am anyway.

Waiting.

The lobby is like a well-lit aeroplane hangar where a rich man stores all his good couches. I'm sitting in one of them now, facing the entrance, waiting for a security guard to question me or nudge me with a nightstick. There are dozens of these uniforms hovering confidently around the entrance, more than you'd normally see in a hotel like this, and something's got them frisking and wanding everyone who comes in. Suitcases pass through metal detectors, handbags are opened and rifled. The front wall of the building is a window, tinted and big like God's sunglasses, and beyond it are more security officers peering into the taxis and limos that motor along the driveway and brake to a smooth professional stop. These guards carry mirrors on broom handles they use to see if something's attached to the vehicle's undercarriage, like a bomb or a machine gun, I guess. No one's panicked, it's business as usual, but a sunny afternoon at the Pioneer surely can't always be like this.

Patrons get searched at the entrance, giggle about it, come in, look up and gawk at the sheer size of the hotel lobby. At one end is an open-plan piano bar the size of an ordinary city block. It's so far away I can't hear the piano, but I can see the stick figure in the tuxedo running his fingers along the keys. At this end is me, and behind me the walkway to the casino. I've chosen this couch because of that—no one gets into the hotel, or from the hotel into the casino, without me seeing.

The man I'm waiting for, the one who isn't coming, he likes casinos.

Billy Benedict was a financial planner in Sydney, handling hundreds of small-time investors, four point three million of whose dollars he vaporised at plush casinos like the Pioneer. This was over the three years when the gambling got *really* bad, and it meant the total life savings of several dozen families, as well as most of the life savings of about a hundred more.

His method was to poach the small-timers from his colleagues at ANR, who were more than happy to hand over the low-commission accounts and never bothered to ask what good they were to Billy. He skimmed a little off each at a time, juggling money from one to the next, pleading uncertainty in the market when anyone asked why their nest egg was getting *smaller*. According to the papers, he got the royal treatment at casinos in Brisbane and Sydney: drinks, canapés, naked croupiers, whatever. How that made him feel might have been more of an addiction than the gambling; either way it cost the same. Sometimes, when Billy had a big win, he'd pour a few dollars back into the accounts he'd fleeced.

Most of the time, Billy didn't have a big win.

So he got creative. He recycled receipts and analysis certificates, drew up fake stock charts, even forged trading tickets on his home

PC. With the kinds of methods available to a crafty accountant, I'm surprised it took them only three years to catch him.

It was a group effort featuring the Casino Squad, the Fraud Squad, the Australian Securities and Investments Commission, even the Stock Exchange had a hand in it. Everybody loves a bad guy like Billy Benedict. He's the lone gunman of financial impropriety—purge him and you can claim to have purged everything that's wrong, so then you don't have to wonder if the problem goes deeper, if deregulation and corporate cults and the free-market mantras might all be tricking mum-and-dad investors into believing the playing field is actually level. The New South Wales Minister for Finance held a press conference and said the defalcations of Benedict shouldn't be allowed to reflect badly on the industry as a whole. He said we should all sleep better knowing he's behind bars.

Not that he ever got there. Benedict was released on bail and for ten months now he's been saturating the news. His lawyers had him sign a self-exclusion agreement with the Mercury Casino in Queensland, to shore up evidence of his gambling addiction and maybe win some clemency from the sentencing judge. I don't know why anyone would need *more* evidence that he's a gambling addict.

Most of the investors got their money back through ANR's guaranteed account. But all the attention must have cost ANR more than just money, so they've been lobbying for Benedict to be prosecuted to the full extent of every available law. Nothing was going to save their reputation, the newspapers said, but the total destruction of William Benedict.

Today it's in the papers that the trial begins in a fortnight.

What isn't in the papers is that William Benedict has vanished.

The firm who called me, Linehan and Tillman, the ones representing Benedict, they said he went out for breakfast this morning, came home, quickly packed some things and, as far as they could tell, jumped off the face of the earth. Now they've got two days before he's due to show up at his local police station, which he has to do every few days, which is one of his bail conditions. Meantime, if the police or the court or worst of all the press get hold of the fact that Benedict has disappeared and not even his lawyers know where he is, then Linehan and Tillman's case, especially the not guilty part, is dead in the egg. Absconding is taken, rightly or wrongly, to be evidence of guilt. Not to mention a default on the bail money. Which, in Benedict's case, was exactly one million dollars.

I asked Terry Linehan, when he called me, who posted Benedict's bail. At first he wouldn't say. Through a subtle use of tone he implied that it was none of my business.

The job, Linehan said, was to wait at the Pioneer Hotel here in Melbourne, on the off chance Benedict shows up. They've got PIs like me posted at every legal and illegal casino in the country. They figure a gambler like Benedict can't keep away for long.

Linehan used to be a Supreme Court judge here in Melbourne; he's the one who sent down Spiros Angelis for eleven years. But he must have got tired of umpiring instead of playing, so he stepped down from the bench and started up his own firm in Sydney, which is where he called me from. I don't imagine he usually makes these kinds of calls, but it's more intimidating when the big guns call you themselves. You're more willing to do stuff for someone you've seen on TV about a billion times. You're less likely to sell your story to the press.

I asked Linehan, 'He's on the run and you think he's going to play cards? He can't be that dumb.'

'We have to cover our bases.'

'Expensive bases.'

'There's a million-dollar surety at stake.'

'It was your firm who put the money up, right?' I'm not proud of it, but this is me trying to show a hotshot lawyer how smart I am. 'Or someone close to you? Someone who's feeling pretty silly right now?'

There was silence. Then Linehan breathed into the receiver, said, 'It would be a breach of ethical standards for our firm to act as Benedict's surety.'

Lawyers aren't supposed to do it. Unofficially, it happens all the time.

Linehan said, 'But hypothetically, *if* we were to have done so, my reasons would have been the same as those the judge had for granting bail in the first place. Benedict's high profile, he's surrendered his passport and the whole country knows what he looks like. I said to myself, *he can't be that dumb.*'

In my mind, in a conference room at Linehan and Tillman's office in Sydney, there's a clamour of lawyers flailing with telephones and laptops, panicking to find their missing asset.

'Do you know for sure that he's fled? He hasn't officially skipped until the day after tomorrow when he fails to report. Maybe he's planning to be back in time?'

Linehan breathed into the phone again. 'Call it thirty-five years of dealing with white collars like Benedict. They get petrified of jail, tie themselves up in knots about it. His answering machine picked up this morning and I knew he'd absconded.'

'Okay. So long as you're happy for me to sit in the Pioneer lobby and do nothing for fifty dollars an hour.'

'That's the deal. Unless you spot him.'

'And if I do?'

'Bring him back to Sydney.'

'How?'

'I'll leave that up to you.'

Even though he couldn't see me, I shook my head.

'If you want him clubbed and dragged back to Sydney, Mister

Linehan, I'm not sure I'm your man. You should look up Leo Spaske. He loves the jobs where he gets to hurt people.'

'We tried him,' Linehan said. 'He's not available.'

I checked my pride: a little pinched.

'And I mentioned nothing about hurting the man,' Linehan said, ever the lawyer. 'We of course encourage our agents to operate within the bounds of what is legal.'

I said, 'All right. I'll consider myself retained.'

'Good. We'll fax through a picture of Benedict. You'll have to be in place for at least forty-eight hours, or until you hear from us, starting now.'

'Tell me, of all the men you've got working on this, is there a bonus for the guy who brings him in? A percentage of the surety, maybe?'

'Nope.'

'Good,' I said. 'Because there's no way Billy Benedict is coming to the Pioneer.'

The magic wand at the revolving front door arcs up over people's jewellery, their belts and boot buckles. Two teenagers are giggling at their mother, whose earrings have set off the metal detector.

This is what I have to entertain me for the next two days.

At the couch adjacent to mine are three men in well-cut suits with their ties tugged loose and heavy drinks in their hands. One of them, the one with no hair, he's looking around the lobby, trying to kill the lull in conversation.

'That waitress…' he says, indicating a short-haired woman wearing a cravat. 'I'd go her.'

The other two moan their approval.

And I'm sitting here listening to these brain surgeons when the mystery of the beefed-up security is solved. Over my shoulder appears a man in a black suit. Black shirt, black tie. His hair is black. The blackness of it all is what draws my attention, but then, after a moment, I know him. He's Neil Bighuty, formerly Constable Bighuty stationed in Moorabbin, 'Big' to anyone he didn't arrest. He was kicked off the force a year ago, which is the last I saw of him.

I remember the night itself. Him, freshly fired and red-faced from crying, asleep on the planks of the St Kilda pier while I watched the sunrise.

If he clocks me it doesn't show. He hardly moves, hardly seems to be breathing, surveying the room like he's looking for someone. Then he touches a hand to his sleeve and I hear one of the businessmen next to me say, 'Jesus Christ...'

From out of the casino walkway emerge four more men in black, flanking a woman with the blondest hair I've ever seen, who would still be considered tall even without the skyscraper heels. Her outfit fits snugly like a wax she's been dipped in. Her sunglasses cover most of her face.

Another one says, 'Is that...?'

She strides quickly to the elevator bank where Bighuty has a lift waiting. Then she and all the men are gone.

I turn to the trio of businessmen. 'Who was that?'

'Wasn't it Hannah Delaney?' This is the short one.

'Hannah Delaney, the actress?' I ask.

'Wasn't it?' he says.

'Of course it was.' This is the bald one. 'She's engaged to Adrian Krewz, so the security is, like, crazy here.'

'She's engaged to Adrian Krewz?' I ask.

'Yeah, dude.'

'The football player?'

'Dude...' This is the third one now. 'Where have you been living?'

The other two laugh. I end it there, decide I'm going to order a drink and raise a private toast to Neil Bighuty, who in twelve months has risen from disgraced police officer to VIP security detail, the kind of job for which most of the force would disgrace themselves on purpose. Money, travel, authority and, when your charge is eternally pursued by stalkers and photographers, the possibility of actual violence. It's a meathead's wet dream.

I hear the bald man say, 'I would definitely go Hannah Delaney.' Simultaneous, the other two say, '*Duh.*'

Right now, security officers are wanding a couple of tourists in white trousers and golf hats. The more I look at these guards, the more I see it's a bluff. They're mostly teenagers, goofing around; sizing up the cars, the women, each other. The uniforms and machinery are here to scare off a potential threat to Hannah Delaney, not to foil one. I guess, most of the time, that's what a security service is for.

I'm thinking this, and also about that drink, when I first see Freckles through the tinted windows of the hotel lobby. I call him Freckles because I don't find out his name until later and he's got freckles and I have to call him something. His hairline's receding but it doesn't make him look old; he has the face of a child, one that's scowling because his team just lost, and he stands at the far end of the driveway, frozen there, making that face at the security procedures that have turned the front entrance into Checkpoint Charlie.

Something's bulging under his suit jacket, under his left arm. When a security person glances over he u-turns, overacting casual, then he walks away quickly with a self-conscious bobbing motion. From this, it's easy enough to tell that he's drunk, so I stop thinking about him as he scurries off down the street and out of sight.

I ask a waiter in a cravat for a scotch on ice and when it comes I hold off on sipping it, even as an appetiser. Instead I let the ice melt for a minute, let it water down the scotch just enough, watch it swirl like a tiny supernova that's been captured and placed lovingly in a glass tumbler just for me.

I don't know it yet, but this is the calm before the storm. It will be this moment I look back on later when I'm careening down the hotel stairs, blood pouring out of everywhere, cursing the name of everyone I've ever known. It's right now that I'll think about in a few weeks when I'm answering journalists' questions, the same ones over and over about how much I'd had to drink, how long I'd been here, how responsible did I feel. This is the moment I'll wish I could go back to, the last one today when things are actually as boring as they seem. Because right when the scotch is ready, right when it's evolved from hotel beverage into perfect thing, about twenty minutes after I saw him the first time, there's Freckles again.

He's in the lobby, coming from the outdoor pool with that same deliberate gait, careful steps across the marble floor so as not to draw attention. There are small dark blotches on his collar and his eyes are wide, like he's just as surprised by his appearance here as I am. He makes a beeline for the reception desk and I see that the bulge is still there under his arm; his hand covers it awkwardly while he talks to the receptionist. I suppose he's checking into a room. He shows her a driver's licence and she gives him a passkey, not at all fazed by the stains on his collar. Maybe it looks like tomato sauce from where she is.

With another furtive look around the lobby, he heads for an elevator, gets on board. His eyes scan the room again and maybe they come to rest on mine for a instant. Then the doors close.

I take a hit of scotch and feel it soak in deep, loosening the knot in my stomach. I belch my gratitude. Beside me the three businessguys are in agreement that they would each do the girl at reception, and I think about moving couches. Then I think about spending the next two days moving couches to get away from people like this, waiting for someone who isn't coming, and then I think about Freckles, what a mess he was. I wonder if I should do anything about him, wonder if I should have another drink before I do. I finish the scotch and catch the waiter's eye.

I'm letting the ice melt again when Neil Bighuty steps into my line of sight, grinning. He's heading over from the elevators, strolling coolly in his black suit and salon haircut, scratching his nose and trying to hide a giggle like we've been busted by the teacher. I smile back, give a big nod as he reaches me.

'JD,' he says. 'It's been bloody ages.'

'It has.'

'Are you staying at the hotel?'

'I'm on a job.'

Big looks at my scotch. 'Working hard?'

'You want one?'

'I quit.'

He tugs up his trouser legs and sits beside me on the couch. 'Geez,' he says. 'The last time I saw you must have been...'

Before thinking I say, 'That night in St Kilda.'

'Yeah...' A sudden cool in his demeanour. 'I guess I looked pretty funny to you.'

'I was pissed. I don't recall a lot of it.'

Big's eyes look like they have more to say. Whatever it is I try to steer past.

'Was that Hannah Delaney I saw you with? I figured you blokes were either her security detail or her strippers...'

'We're security, John,' Big clarifies, without even a courtesy laugh. Something else I remember about him is that he only appreciates jokes about other people.

'All this...' I point to the army of security personnel. They've formed a thicket around a group of four Asian men in matching tracksuits. 'This is your doing?'

Big rolls his eyes. 'For what they're worth.'

'Has something happened?'

'Her fiancé, Adrian Krewz. Been getting some weird mail. There are fucking crackpots out there, JD. Let me tell you. You wouldn't believe some of the stuff they write. You wouldn't believe some of the stuff they write *with*.'

Big cranes his neck and watches the four men in tracksuits as they move through security. He gives them a piercing analytical stare, then turns back to me.

'You still a detective? No...what was that fancy name you gave yourself? Private inquiry agent?'

'Yep. Still doing that. But look at you, you're going well.'

Big smiles. 'Things are good, things are good. This is my dream job. Did you know I make more than two hundred k a year?'

Big raises his fat, bushy eyebrows like he's really wondering if somehow I knew that. I do my best to look impressed as he crosses his legs and throws his arm casually back over the couch.

He says, 'And the perks, let me tell you...'

Big keeps talking, about his suit, about his hi-tech cufflinks, and I'm seeing that he isn't the Neil Bighuty I remember. Clothes weren't a big part of his world back then. When you brawled as much as he did, clothes couldn't be important to you. He wasn't the sharpest cop on the force, but he was the toughest, the thug they called in to break the other thugs. They sent him out to bust the bogans in the west and the bikies in the north and, for fun, the South Yarra posers dealing coke out of their shiny cars, the ones who thought they were above the law because they were white and rich and smiled a lot. It occurs to me now, as I watch his mouth savour his words and sneer them out, that Big has become one of those guys: well dressed, keen to talk about being well dressed. He's not a thug anymore. I wonder if he misses it.

He sees my gaze linger on his hairdo and he says, 'I get it cut for free at Givaani. Miss Delaney is one of their regulars.'

I'm about to fake an urgent phone call, apologise repeatedly so Big doesn't get too offended, when Freckles appears in the lobby again, stepping out of the elevator and heading away from us to the piano bar. There's no bulge under his jacket but that's the only thing that's different. He murmurs quickly to the barman and gets a neat bourbon in return, smells it pointlessly then carries it through the maze of empty tables to the bar's entrance, trying to appear sober and controlled. He falls into a chair that faces the lobby and takes a long sip. I take a long sip too.

'Miss Delaney is literally the best actress in the world,' Big is saying. 'For her hair and body type. That's my opinion anyway.'

I'm guessing Freckles has come back down to brandish himself in front of hotel security, make sure no one's onto him. And no one is. One uniform is telling a story to four others now, which involves punching gestures and his own uncontrollable laughter. Freckles watches them, expressionless. He orders another drink.

Big says, 'You haven't changed a bit, JD.'

'Really?'

'Mister Too-Cool-for-School-Private-Dick.'

He comes down hard on that last word.

'All right...'

Big shrugs. 'Whatever, right? But you always had to be so fucking special. So *aloof.* I read that word the other day and I thought, that's a good word for my old friend, John Dorn. Always walked a perfect line. Never got his feet wet.'

'All right...'

'Yep. And now I'm making the money, doing the kind of work you can only dream about, but you look at me like I'm still just another bogan copper for you to treat like shit.'

I'm glad he didn't have that drink.

'I'm working, Neil. Dazzle me with your insecurities another time. There's something going on here, something you should be interested in. It might be to do with Hannah Delaney.'

The trio of businessmen get up from the couch next to ours, brush my shoulder with their thighs as they pass. I watch them walk away, wait for them to be properly gone.

Big raises his eyebrows.

I say, 'See the guy with the brown hair and long forehead, sitting at the entrance to the bar?'

Big's glance is smooth, professional.

'What about him?'

'He was at the far end of the driveway about an hour ago with something under his coat. The metal detectors scared him off, so he walked round the back and came in over the fence between the freeway and the pool.'

'*That* guy did?'

'He must have had trouble, there was blood on his shirt when he came in, but he's hammered so he hasn't noticed or doesn't care. And there was something hidden under his jacket. He checked into a room, went up in the lift, and now he's come back down and there's nothing under his jacket anymore and he's sitting at the bar, drinking. He's waiting for something.'

Big blinks at me.

I open my hands. 'That's the story so far.'

He grinds through the gear change from listener to thinker and grimaces like it's painful. 'Do you reckon it's anything?'

'I reckon he's brought in something he's not supposed to, and whatever it is he's left it up there in his room. He wasn't here when you brought Delaney through, but he might be waiting for her...'

I take a drink. Still pained, Big looks at my scotch as I put it down. 'Maybe. Maybe you were busy reading the drinks menu when he walked in the front door, and that thing under his jacket was the bottle *he's* been drinking from.'

'Maybe.'

'Where would a guy like him get a firearm?'

'I don't know.'

'And if he does want to shoot Miss Delaney, what's he doing waiting for her *without* it?'

'We could argue, or you could just go up to his room. Either there's a gun there or there isn't.'

'I can't break into someone's room, with or without a good reason.'

'Hotel security can't get in?'

'On your say-so? 'Fraid not. They'd get sued.'

I don't remember Neil Bighuty being this kind of stickler. I should drop it and let Freckles shoot whoever he wants. I have no love for movie stars. And then I could tell the world that I warned Bighuty and he didn't listen.

I say, 'I'll go up and take a look.'

Big smirks. 'In his room?'

'If you can get me the room number.'

'How are you going to get in?'

'Well...' I say, swivelling on the couch to face him directly. 'Hotels like the Pioneer only get business like Hannah Delaney if they agree on certain procedures. Like her personal security staff holding universal passkeys, in case of emergency.'

Still smirking, he rolls his eyes back in his head like I'm electrocuting him. 'There's fucking *no way* I'm giving that to you. Are you out of your mind? That would be my job.'

'Then I'll get in some other way.'

'How?'

'Some other way.'

Big's smirk turns into sceptical laughter. He stares at me a moment, giving me a chance to take it back. When I don't he turns and points to reception. 'Is that the girl who checked him in?'

'Yeah.'

Big saunters over, shows her his ID.

With his back turned, I suck down the rest of the scotch in one long hit.

Big returns smiling. 'Room 1504, and for the record, his name's Rene Mush.' Then he cocks his head to look at Mush, who's watching the lobby while he drinks.

'I *do* want to know if he's a credible threat to the principal...' Big must love lines like that. 'But you're not armed, you're not authorised and you've got no way of getting into his room. Why bother trying?'

'The rooms up there are supposed to have superb views. I was thinking of breaking into one anyway, just to take a look.'

He doesn't find that funny either.

I stand up and take the photo out of my pocket. 'I need you to cover for me while I'm gone. Do you recognise him?'

Big stares at the picture. 'Nope.'

'His name's William Benedict.'

Big shakes his head vacantly. I think to myself, *Where have you been living?*

'You're looking for him?' he asks.

'Yeah. He won't show up, but if he does, call me.'

I write my mobile number on the back of the photograph. 'And call me if Rene Mush starts back to his room.'

Big can't think of a reason to say no. He says, 'If anyone asks, JD, I've got nothing to do with this.'

'Okay.'

'As far as I'm concerned, we never met.'

'Okay.'

I knew Neil Bighuty for the six months between when I was introduced to him by Detective Senior Constable Dennis Burke and when he was booted off the force for killing a teenager in the backyard of Moorabbin Police Headquarters. We drank a few times, Dennis being the only reason either of us was there. We traded stories and performed for each other our worn-out histories. Then he and Dennis would head to the strip clubs.

I'd go home. I guess that's what Big meant by aloof.

Something else I remember is how he used to pull out this picture of his ex-girlfriend from his wallet, hand it around to people and talk about her like they were still an item. Her name was Sotiria and the picture was taken on the Greek island where she was born. 'Sotiria' was written on the back of the photograph, like you'd ever forget that name, and Big said that it meant 'tragedy' or 'salvation', he couldn't remember which. Dennis told me that Sotiria was married now to a sergeant in the armed robbery squad and hadn't spoken to Big in the two years since she dumped him. But for some reason, Big hadn't given up hope.

Then came Willie Somers.

It began with a smash-and-grab at a mini-mall on Swanston Street, the ordinary kind you see on *Crime Stoppers*. At two in the morning the thieves drove a stolen Subaru through the front glass wall, filled the car full of sports gear, shoes, clothes, backed it out and drove north.

A cleaner across the road saw it happen. He stood on the balcony of a Flaming Galah Steak House restaurant, puffed on a cigarette as he watched the thieves below, and when he finished he rang triple zero and told them he'd heard one of the kids laugh and call another kid 'Willie'.

When Willie Somers, the owner of the stolen Subaru, turned out to bear a certain resemblance to one of the thieves on the CCTV recording, they brought him in to meet Constable Neil Bighuty.

Surveillance tapes are worthless on their own. Businesses and security agencies are eternally reluctant to shell out for a camera system that can provide actual evidence. Usually the store records over the same tape again and again, which means officers have to analyse fuzzy black and white images so distorted that not even the culprit's own mother could give a positive ID. They knew they didn't have enough on Somers, not for a conviction, but they also knew they had the whole thing figured out: uptown kids get bored of tennis and computer games, want to try something edgy and dangerous like a robbery. They don't know how to steal a car, so they report one of their own stolen and send it through a plate glass window because, hey, it's insured. And what do the police know about investigating stuff?

Big used to brag that he could get anyone to confess to anything, usually by way of intimidation and doom-saying. That's the approach he took with Willie Somers; the goal was to sweat out of Willie the names of the other guys on the tape. But Willie wasn't talking. Even with Bighuty standing over him and pulling faces, Willie just snarled and stroked his straight blond hair. The officers observing noticed that Willie looked pale, but that's just what people looked like with Neil Bighuty interrogating them, so at first they didn't care. After a while the kid said he wasn't feeling well and asked to go outside for some air. Big escorted him, and the rest of the investigators took lunch.

In the courtyard behind the police station, where the officers usually hold their Christmas party and give their retirement speeches, Willie and Big were all alone. Willie told Big he was thirsty and Big offered him a drink from the garden hose. They were out there not for ten minutes, according to the rest of the station, before Big ran back inside, ashen-faced, carrying Willie like a groom carrying his bride across the threshold. Only faster.

Willie had suffered a heart aneurysm, which is basically a stroke, which happens to people with weak hearts, which Willie had, which he hadn't mentioned when they brought him in. All the medical examiner could say was that he had probably suffered palpitations during the interrogation, had therefore appeared pale and dazed to everyone observing. This also explained why he drank more than two litres of water in the courtyard, which is how much they found in his stomach. And it also explained why he was dead. There were no bruises or marks on him, and Big told the press he'd interrogated the boy using textbook procedures. He told the press he'd just been unlucky. Then someone said that Willie had been more unlucky. Then Big got fired.

'Willie Somers was a cocky little shit who played with fire,' Dennis phoned me that afternoon. 'But they won't say that on the TV. No, they just say, *Look at this white kid the cops killed.*'

It's not just Big. As long as I've known him, Dennis has had a weakness for police thugs. He sees them the way the rest of us see endangered gorillas: dumb and lethal and in need of our protection. Dennis didn't hate Willie, he just hated what was happening to Big.

'And I tell you what else, the little prick did it,' he said, like that mattered anymore. 'Everybody knows that's him on that tape. But without a confession we couldn't take it to court. Everybody knows *that*, too. The press *know* this is the kind of fluke accident that only makes people hate the police, and they know sacking Big is just more public relations for the commissioner. But they don't *give* a shit.'

Dennis was having trouble finding cops to come out that night with Big. No one wanted to get tagged by the police brutality brush, so when I got there Dennis and Big were already plastered and it was clearly going to be just the three of us. Big looked up at me, smiled like I'd just delivered a fantastic eulogy at his mother's funeral, then he told me a joke about a hooker with dysentery.

What I remember most about that night is Big not talking about it. Not about the smash-and-grab or Willie Somers or his own bad luck. The closest he came was when we wound up on

St Kilda pier with Dennis asleep on the beach behind us. Dennis's clothes were all torn up from a fight with a pimp at Omar's Lounge. After that he'd guided us to the beach with the promise of something spectacular. He wouldn't say what, and now he no longer could because he'd passed out. There on the pier, Big and I passed a bottle of pear-flavoured vodka back and forth, which was all that Big could swipe from the bar while everyone was watching Dennis and the pimp.

It was dark without the streetlights to help me see. It took a few moments, but I eventually figured out that Big was weeping, not making much noise, not saying anything to me, not caring I was there. His body shuddered and the tears fell silently down into the black water beneath us. Then he took from his wallet the photograph of Sotiria and tore it up ceremoniously.

He tossed the pieces into the lapping water and sobbed until he fell asleep.

It was a little dramatic, like it was something he'd seen someone do on TV. But that doesn't change that he meant it.

I watched the sunrise alone. I guess that's what Dennis took us out there for. It's the kind of thing he'd have done for Big, like it symbolised something. But I'm not sure.

The elevator opens out into a hallway lined with antique lamps. The lamps give out almost no light and portraits of sad people hang on the walls, silent and tasteful. At room 1504, I try the handle.

Locked.

Plan B is to move further down the hall to 1503. I knock.

The doors at the Pioneer have no peepholes, but they do have chains. This one opens as far as the chain will allow and a wide, bubbly face looks out.

'Hi. My name's John Dorn. I'm head of security for Miss

Hannah Delaney. Did you know Miss Delaney was a guest here in the hotel?'

Her hair's an expensive caramel blonde and she wears so much make-up it's like she's in disguise. I show her my private investigator licence and she blinks at it.

'Yes. I saw her downstairs.' She rolls her eyes, giggles. 'I mean, I only *thought* I did. But I suppose I *really* did.'

She's beaming and I lower my voice, confidential.

'I'm sorry to ask you this, but I'm staying in the room next to yours, and I've *locked* myself out, and it wouldn't be such a big deal, except that it's the *third* time I've done it today, and I'm just *too* embarrassed to go back to Miss Delaney and have her sign out *another* passkey for me. Now, I think I can get there from your balcony. Would you mind if I gave it a try?'

She giggles again and unchains the door, pulls it open. She's wearing a paisley dress that covers a large, rounded body.

'Come on then. But you're *not* allowed to look at the mess. I'm still unpacking, you know.'

She giggles and I giggle back as I step into a big room with a big bed and a big suitcase open on top of it. There isn't any mess. You'd have to work pretty hard to make a mess out of this kind of luxury.

Inside the suitcase is more paisley, some magazines and a couple of bottles of wine. The labels are old and papery and in French, but I don't make her for an expert. She's travelling alone, but by the way the tissue paper neatly divides everything in her suitcase, you can tell she doesn't travel often. I'd guess she's recently divorced from someone who knows wine. And she's taking a trip. Celebrating.

I say, 'Thank you *so* much. I feel like such a *klutz*.'

'Don't be silly. It's not a problem at *all*.' She closes the door and follows me into the room. 'But you have to tell me what it's like working for a superstar like Hannah Delaney.'

Her eyes open expectantly wide.

I say, 'I get my hair cut at a *really* good place.'

Her mouth drops open and she grabs my wrist dramatically. '*Givaani*?'

'That's right.'

She says, 'Oh,' and squints at my hair, trying to see the art in it. I point across the room. 'This is the balcony?'

'Yes. Go ahead.'

When I open the door the wind reminds me that I'm fifteen storeys up. Afternoon is slowly turning the world orange and the shadows of the railing are long, thick. Between this railing and the one on Mush's balcony is a gap one metre wide and one thousand metres deep.

I look down into that gap, see the ants that are security officers with their mirrors on broomsticks. I try to pinpoint where I'd land if I fell.

The woman, she comes out and stands next to me, holding her dress down against the wind. She frowns at Mush's balcony, the one she thinks is mine.

'How...?' That's all she says for it to be clear what we're both thinking. Either I hire a helicopter and a reliable pilot, or I jump.

'I'll have to jump,' I say.

'No. You *can't*.'

'It's not *that* far,' I say. 'I leap further than this every day at *security* training.'

Then she nods, understanding. Then something occurs to her. '*Wait*,' she says, and darts back into her suite. She returns instantly with a Pioneer Hotel postcard.

'I don't usually do this sort of thing, but do you think you might ask Hannah for her autograph? She's getting married in a few days, and this could be the last autograph she gives with her maiden name. I imagine it might be wonderfully *valuable* one day.'

She hands me the postcard. 'You'll have to ask her to date it as well.'

'Love to,' I say, and stuff the postcard inside my jacket. I give myself as much run-up as there's room for. It's a metre up over the first railing, a metre across the gap, then a metre back down onto the safety of Mush's balcony. Like jumping over a school desk.

I push off. I'm running.

But then she yelps, a cry like I've trodden on her toe. There's enough panic in it to make me panic and I abort the jump a split second before it happens. My knees give way, I trip into the railing, grip onto it and hang there, drop onto the tiles.

I get up and walk back to my starting point.

She's blushing. 'I'm sorry. It's just...This is like something from a Hannah Delaney *movie*.'

I start running again. This time when she cries out, I ignore it. I'm airborne.

With both my feet off the ground, and with the ground hundreds of feet away, time slows down and it's like I'm jumping between planets. Suspended here, a number of things go through my mind, but most of all I realise that I'm doing this, putting my life at risk, because of Neil Bighuty. Some guy boasts about how much money he makes and my response is to leap off a building. Maybe if I'd recognised this five seconds earlier, I wouldn't have jumped. I would have gone downstairs, bought another drink and told Big that this is his problem.

I hit the ground on Mush's balcony. It's an awkward landing because of my fear of not making it and my ankle twists beneath my weight, the knuckle dragged across the tiles as momentum carries me into the outdoor furniture set that scatters when I push my hand through it and it all ends with me curled in a protective ball beneath a plastic chair.

A voice says, 'Are you *okay*?'

I don't want to answer, don't want to stand up. But I do both. '*Yeah*. Yeah, I'm *good*.'

The sun is setting and making her glow. The wind is pulling back her blonde hair like the fingers of some invisible Givaani stylist. For the first time, she looks beautiful.

'Thanks for your help,' I say, pushing at the door to Mush's room. Thank God it opens.

'That's *no* trouble,' she waves. 'Tell Miss Delaney I *love* her films.'

'I *will* tell her that.' I wave back, then limp inside.

It's luxurious and minimal despite the busy floral wallpaper. It's the mirror image of the room next door, only instead of an open suitcase on the bed, there's an ancient Arnold point-three-eight automatic.

I hop past the bed to the minibar and crack open the largest bottle of the group, then slump against the fridge, recovering.

For anything other than a point blank killing, an old gun like the Arnold would be useless. It's only accurate up to about a foot. But it's small and powerful and just what you'd want if you were planning to walk up and shoot someone dead in a hotel corridor. Either Mush is more proficient at this than I gave him credit for, or he's had help. Someone who knows guns.

The liquor hits and my head swims faster. I put the bottle in my pocket and take out a handkerchief, wipe the beads from my forehead and pick up the gun. It's fully loaded and the serial number has been filed off.

My phone rings. 'Yeah?'

'Where are you?'

'I just got into Mush's room.'

'How?'

'I shimmied down the chimney.'

'Bullshit you did.'

'And guess what. There was a loaded thirty-eight waiting for me on the bed.'

'No shit?'

'No shit.'

Big is less impressed than I'd hoped. 'Listen, that guy you were waiting for, the one in the photo…I forgot his name. He's here. He's at reception.'

'Benedict's here?'

'Yeah. He's dressed down, got a few days' growth and sunglasses and a hat, but it's definitely your guy. He's checking into a room.'

'Where are you?' I ask.

'I'm still on the couch, chatting nonchalantly to an old friend on my mobile telephone.'

'Okay. Well…it's been a pleasure. You get your boys onto Mush, I'll come down and meet Benedict.'

'Wait…' There's silence. I can hear the low roar of the lobby around him, soft and vibrant. 'Mush is getting up. He's paying his bill at the bar. I think I'm about to introduce myself.'

'Well, you better hurry if you want to—'

Now there's an even louder roar, in my head.

I say, 'Wait a moment.'

I say, 'Benedict just walked in, and Mush is paying his tab?'

'Yeah. He's in a hurry too.'

'Did Mush see Benedict?'

'Couldn't miss him. He walked right across the lobby.'

I was so sure Benedict wouldn't come to the Pioneer.

I say, 'Mush isn't here for Hannah Delaney.'

There must be a line around the block for revenge on Billy Benedict. And all of them are harmless-looking small-time investors who'd have to drink themselves stupid before going through with it.

'He's here for Benedict.'

There's doubt in the silence from Big. 'How did Mush know he was coming here if *you* didn't know?'

'That'll be my first question too. What's he doing now?'

'Wait...' Another silence. I listen. Everything else in Mush's room is so quiet.

'He's headed for reception. He's headed straight for Benedict. I'm going to intercept.'

'*No.* Don't hold him up. Don't let him see you. He's not armed.'

'But you said he's here for Benedict...'

'He'll come back up for his gun first. *Tell me what's happening.*'

'He's at reception now...He's standing next to Benedict... Benedict has seen him...Is he supposed to recognise him?'

'Maybe not.'

'Well, he hasn't. Mush is right next to him, reading a brochure on the desk.'

'Benedict's still checking in?'

'Yeah, the girl's just given him a passkey.'

'Is he getting the room number? Is Mush listening in for the room number?'

Another silence. Big says, 'I think that's right.'

'I need you to do me one more favour. I need *you* to get that room number for me.'

'Okay. And as soon as Benedict leaves, I detain Mush, right?'

'No. Let him be.'

'*Why?*'

'You're outside of your job description now, Neil. But thanks for your help—'

'Fuck *you*. This is the most fun I've had since I left the force. Benedict is headed for the elevators...Mush is hanging back at the desk, watching.'

I scan Mush's room, looking for something small, made of metal.

I say, 'Did they search Benedict at the door?'

'Affirmative. They didn't find anything.'

'What's his luggage?'

'Just a gym bag. Not heavy. He's getting in the elevator... Mush is watching...The girl at the desk is asking Mush if he needs anything...' Big guffaws, forces himself to keep his voice down. 'He freaked out, just walked away from her.' I hear rustling. Big is crossing the lobby, fast and quiet. 'Benedict's gone...Mush is headed for the elevators now...He's waiting for one.'

Inside the fridge I find an ice bucket. Inside the ice bucket I find a small metal ice scoop.

Big holds the phone away from his mouth. 'The man you just checked in, what room's he in?'

The girl squeaks back, 'Four-twelve.'

'What name?' Big asks.

'The reservation was under Bernardo, Aaron.' She says.

Big speaks into the phone. 'Room 412, under the name Aaron Bernardo. Mush is still waiting for the elevator.'

'I have to go. If you're offering help, I could use it.'

'I'm too juiced to stop now.'

'Meet me in the stairwell on the fourth floor. Don't let Mush see you.'

Big starts to speak, but I end the call.

They manufacture Arnold handguns with the screws welded loose because their customers like to open the casings and get busy altering the trigger's sensitivity or enlarging the calibre or drilling holes for a half-arsed silencer.

I've got about thirty seconds before Mush gets back.

Inside most automatic handguns are two inch-long pins called vaulting wires that lever back the hammer and snap it free. Without them, you might as well throw the bullets at people.

I use the pointed edge of the ice scoop like one half of a

Phillips-head screwdriver, scraping and scratching at the grip screws, hacking at them to get them loose. The first one comes, but I'm so frantic with the second that I take a chip out of the bottom of the grip.

I'm sure Mush won't notice.

I wedge the handle of the ice scoop underneath the vaulting wires and wrench at it with everything I've got, clamping the gun between my legs and twisting the scoop clockwise.

Very softly, from along the corridor, comes the tone of the elevator.

With my last effort I tear open the webbing in my left hand and with it the vaulting wires come free. As I jam the casing back together there's a noise outside the door: Mush looking for his passkey.

I wind back the screws by hand, just enough for the gun not to rattle like a broken toy when he picks it up. I hear the relaxed sound of the hotel door unlocking and I drop the gun onto the bed and step over it into the en suite, into the bathtub, press myself against the tiles behind the fogged window that ordinarily you'd slide closed. There's blood trickling down my hand and maybe Mush won't notice whatever I splashed onto his bed and carpet.

I hold my breath to keep quiet, listen hard.

What happens first is that Mush tears into the bathroom.

After all those bourbons it shouldn't be a surprise, but when Mush bursts in, pulling open his fly, I almost cry out in shock. I feel my pulse in my head as Mush moans like I've moaned so often, alone and uninhibited, projecting a steady stream into the toilet bowl. I'm not well-hidden this side of the shower screen. All it will take is one sober glance for Mush to see there's some bloke standing behind it.

He flushes and turns to the basin, belches. He doesn't wash his hands, just stands there, listens to the filling of the cistern. Again I panic, thinking he's seen me, that he's trying to make sense of my black silhouette in the bathtub, but gradually the sound of gushing water fades and reveals the sound of him, Mush, sniffling and coughing, weeping at his own reflection in the bathroom mirror.

And it builds. What begins as a subtle sob becomes a big cat giving birth, growls pumped out in sharp bursts between sharp inhalations. It keeps building, Mush becoming the Incredible Hulk, spitting words at the mirror:

'You *fuck*...*You* fuck...Loser...You fucking *loser*...'

I look down to see blood dripping from my hand onto the white of the bathtub.

'Pissweak faggot loser...Pissweak arsehole...You're a fucking pissweak fucking loser...'

Sobs take over, loud and mighty, amplified by the bathroom tiles. Through the shower screen I can see his body slump, his head hanging below his shoulders, arms gripping the sides of the basin.

He takes two deep breaths, turns and he's gone.

After the shortest of moments there's the cracking open of what I suppose is the mini-bourbon, then silence when I suppose he's drinking it. There's more growling and deliberate moaning, more abuse directed at himself, as well as quiet moments when he drinks.

Then I hear the room door open and close, and I listen to that silence for about a second.

When I rush out of the en suite with a white towel wrapped around my hand, the gun is gone from the bed, replaced by the empty bourbon bottle. There are three drops of blood on the carpet that Mush either didn't notice or thought were his own.

I move to the door and listen.

DING—the elevator tone. I give Mush three seconds to get on board, then I'm out the door, limping to the stairwell as fast as my ankle will let me, pain cutting through my shin. Down the stairs I have to hop three at a time and more than once I stumble and crash, unable to save myself because my good hand is on the other side from the handrail.

An hour ago I was watching the ice melt into my drink, not even licking my lips for fear of spoiling the liquor's touch. Now there's blood trickling into my eye from a graze on my forehead and when I think I'm wiping it away I'm actually just wiping blood across my face.

And I'm thinking, *I wasn't even the first choice for this job.*

The stairwell doors in the Pioneer feature small, 1950s-style fire windows and Big is peering out the one on the fourth floor when I get there. Without glancing back at me he says, 'Don't worry, he hasn't gone in yet. He's getting into the zone.'

Then he turns and sees me and laughs.

'Jesus...What have you done to yourself?'

Peeking through the fire window, I see Mush in another dim corridor lined with doors. He's running a hand through his hair and taking the same deep breaths as before, only quieter. The lump is back there under his jacket and he's decided that the least suspicious thing to do is to walk back and forth along the corridor, holding his hand to the lump and talking to himself.

'He's been there about a minute,' says Big. 'He's acting *all* fucked up.'

'He has to get himself raw before he can go through with it.' I grunt, getting my breath back.

'If he doesn't get a move on he'll sober up.'

Big leans against the concrete wall, grinning. Either because what he said was funny or because that's the only outlet he's got at this moment.

'Are you going to tell me now why the fuck we're not stopping him?'

Now Mush is turning circles on the carpet, slapping his hands against his hips, a few metres down from the closed and unsuspecting door of room 412. His fly is still undone after his trip to the bathroom.

'Benedict's skipped bail, right? Or at least he will have, about forty-eight hours from now.'

Big doesn't respond, just taps his foot on the floor, full of nervous energy.

I wipe the blood from my forehead with the towel. 'His legal team wants me to take him back to Sydney before that happens. But I'm guessing Billy doesn't want to go back to Sydney because he doesn't want to find out that everything he ever heard about jail is true. So my theory is that Mush and a gun can help scare him into it.' I shrug at Big and say, 'That's what we're doing here.'

Behind his knitted brow and his fat eyebrows, he's working through it, tapping away with his foot and nodding. Then he looks back at me. 'And who's Mush?'

'Benedict ripped off a lot of people. I'm guessing Mush is one of them.'

Mush is wiping the sweat from his palms on his pants leg, right outside Benedict's door.

I say, 'Get ready.'

Big smooths back his hair and cracks his neck. 'What's happening?'

'Mush is about to knock.'

'So then what? Benedict opens the door and Mush shoots him?'

'Maybe. Maybe Mush will want to talk first. He's never shot anyone before. To do that, he'll have to get into the room.'

'How are *we* going to get in?'

I look Big in the eye and make a face, which he understands, even though my face in this condition must look ridiculous.

'Fuck you,' he shakes his head. 'Fuck *you*. It shows up on their database whenever I use it. They'll want to know why.'

'We'll figure out something to tell them.'

Big is about to protest more, but I say, 'Here we go.'

Mush knocks. And waits, shaking his hands, trying to loosen them up, swaying from foot to foot.

Big says, 'What if he just shoots him?'

'He won't. His gun doesn't work.'

The door to 412 opens.

From this angle I can't see inside the room or who is there, only that Mush is talking, probably having trouble because he's hammered. Something's said back to him and he listens, then speaks again, then gives up and out comes the Arnold. He holds it low and close to his body, gestures like there's water dripping out of the barrel and he's splashing the doorway with it. Then he steps into the room, closes the door quickly behind him.

We move out of the stairwell and quickly down the hall. Or at least Big does; I'm still hobbling. There's no one else in sight, which is good, because if anyone saw me with this much blood smeared on my clothes they might call the police. We park outside Benedict's room, listening.

'How long before we go in?' Big whispers.

'Just long enough for him to see that Mush is for real.'

Through the door comes a slamming sound, which could be violence, or it could just be someone closing a dresser drawer. Big reaches into his pocket for what I expect is the passkey. What he brings out is his own revolver.

'You won't need that.'

'I know. It isn't loaded.' He lifts his eyebrows like I'm in on the joke and stuffs the gun in his waistband.

When the voices start to carry through the door there's anger in them, in the dynamic of highs and lows that combine to make a roar, and Big knows this is it. He swipes the passkey and we go in.

I feel as though there's something I should say, something to announce our entrance, but nothing comes. There's nothing that would have any effect or reason behind it. And no one would hear anything over Benedict anyway. He's cowering on the bed in a hotel robe, his arms up over his face, hollering a stream of nonsense:

No no no wait wait wait no please wait wait no.

Mush stands over the bed, the Arnold hanging lazily in his right hand, like he's about to deliver a warning shot into the doona. This is the first time I've seen Mush up close and he's more like a child than ever, a child saying to his parents, *this is my angry face*. As we enter he whirls around, his freckles exploding with surprise.

The Arnold rises, levels at Big, who stops his approach. His arms come up in surrender.

I move for Mush. His mouth gapes. He swings the gun to point at me. As I get close his jaw juts sideways.

He pulls the trigger. The weapon makes no sound at all.

A man with a gun, soaked in booze and sweat and blood and hatred, he might do that if you surprised him. The shock reacts before he does. He doesn't know who I am, so Mush trying to kill me isn't something I should take personally.

I don't take it personally, but I do pull the gun from his hand and get a fistful of hair.

'Take him back to his room,' I growl at Big, pushing Mush at him. The angry face opens to let out a squeal of panic.

I say to Big, 'Find out who he is, and who else knows he's here.'

Looking at Benedict, there's concentration in his eyes, like he's willing me to really be saving him.

Mush flails against Big's grip. 'Wait, I…I didden do anything!' He says it to me as Big takes hold of his collar, hauls him in close. 'What're you doing? I didden do *anything*!'

Big raises his jacket to show Mush the revolver.

'Don't fuck me about, understand? This gun works.'

Big muscles Mush out the door and when they're gone it's quiet and I have to say I'm happy with how quickly that happened.

Benedict's still concentrating on me, caught up in the crumpled bedsheets that glisten with moisture. He's wet the bed, but the adrenaline has kept him from noticing. He tries to speak, but can't seem to summon any words.

I limp to the mini-bar and make a drink. Vodka, why not? Mixing my drinks isn't going to make tomorrow's hangover any worse. I pour in tonic water.

'You want one?'

He doesn't answer, doesn't seem to hear the question.

Leaning against the bar fridge, sipping gratefully, I'm suddenly very impressed with Neil Bighuty. Benedict is unkempt and unshaven, looks like he hasn't slept for weeks. Even behind a hat and sunglasses, Big recognised him from a distance of ten metres, with only a small black and white photo as a reference. I've seen Benedict in the papers for most of the last year and I doubt I'd pick this messy Caucasian out of a line-up. But it's Billy Benedict all right. Not looking much like an accountant, looking more like a fugitive who thought he was about to die.

'How do you feel, Billy?'

Benedict doesn't answer, stares at the ceiling. A silver crucifix hangs in the vee of his robe. He must have been about to take a shower.

'You feel like you want to throw up?'

Groggy-eyed and slow, he looks back at me and says, 'No.'

'Well, that's on its way, I guess.'

He looks around the room like he just woke up and doesn't recognise it. Then something rational occurs to him.

'How do you know who I am?'

'Well…That's the *big* surprise.'

'Are you a cop?'

'If I were a cop you'd be under arrest for using a fake ID. But the cops don't need to know about that.'

This is too much information. He says 'What' and 'Huh' both at once and it comes out, 'Whuh?'

'Terry Linehan hired me. I'm here to take you back to Sydney.'

The blood drains from his face and wherever it goes, it makes him angry.

'Fuck it. I fucking knew it. Tell Linehan to go fuck himself.'

'I don't think he'll accept that.'

'You can't make me go back,' he says, rising to his knees. '*You* can't *make* me do *anything*. And neither can Linehan. Who are you, anyway? Another fucking *lawyer*?'

There's blood smeared on my trousers and on my face and on the towel that's wrapped around my left hand. My right foot can't take any weight. I don't know what about me looks like I'm a lawyer.

'Awwww shit,' Benedict moans, holding up his wet hand. He's discovered the wet patch all over himself and on the bed. Rather than crawl off, though, he falls back into the mess, sobbing, then springs back onto his knees. Wanting me to see how upset he is.

'*I'm not going back to Sydney*,' he splutters. '*I just want everybody to leave me alone. Why can't everybody just leave me*—'

My slap catches him more on the ear than the cheek, but it quiets him down. 'Look at me.'

He clasps his ear, stunned. Shies away in case I hit him again.

I say, 'Look at me.'

His eyes come up.

Poor Billy. He's used to a different kind of treatment at hotels like this. He's used to betting the highest hand limits in Australia, and everything that brings with it: free meals and show tickets and escorts.

I say, 'I didn't go through what I've been through today so you could *opt out*.'

He's used to chocolate boxes full of 'lucky money' and genuflecting staff.

I say, 'If you come back with me now, no one but Linehan's people will know you ran.'

He's used to private jets and penthouse suites.

I say, 'That's the only way you'll be safe from people like Mush.' And look at him now. Vomiting.

It splatters across the doona cover which is already a mix of tears, sweat and piss. With it comes that retching sound you can't fake, the one that comes straight from your stomach, so I step away, make another drink and sit down by the balcony door.

On the small writing desk I put down Mush's weapon and find a brown wallet. Inside are forty-five dollars and a driver's licence for Aaron Bernardo. The photo looks something like Benedict, but it isn't him.

Outside has become night. Little lights blink back at me, twitching at the sounds of Benedict's muffled sobs. I want to go upstairs and bring Mush down here, show him this weeping mess on the bed.

Then Billy speaks, more throat than voice, 'I'm sick…'

He comes out from under his arms. There's an impossible length of saliva stretched from his mouth to the bed that he wipes away on the pillowslip. 'I'm sick…I'd like to go to the bathroom please.'

'Go ahead.'

Benedict stumbles delicately to the en suite and runs the tap, leaving the door open. I strip the bed and wrap the soiled sheets into a ball that's going to be a fine discovery for housekeeping tomorrow. Then I call the trains, watch Benedict splash water over his face and gargle a miniature bottle of hotel mouthwash. There's a train for Sydney two hours from now. I'm about to call Linehan when I stop myself—we can do that from the station. If there's a dozen other men around the country looking for Benedict, getting an hourly rate, they'll probably appreciate the extra couple of hours before Linehan calls it off.

Benedict comes back in a fresh robe and sprawls headlong across the naked mattress. I pour him a glass of water. When I give it to him, he says, 'So Linehan knew I'd done a runner?'

'Reckons he's got a sixth sense for it.'

Benedict smirks and shakes his head. 'He's one arsehole, that Linehan...'

'Do you know Rene Mush?'

'Not his face. When he told me his name, yeah, I knew who he was.'

'Someone you fleeced?'

'Superannuation, insurance bonds, I can't remember. He lost a lot.'

'I thought they all got their money back.'

'Not all of them. I was never authorised by ANR to accept clients online. Which means the clients who came to me independently and never came in the door of ANR weren't covered. Fucking small print, right? Fucking ANR. They're the ones who fucked him. But I guess he sees it differently.'

'How did he know where to find you?'

'How the fuck should I know?'

'When was the last time you had contact with him?'

'I can't fucking remember.'

He waves me off, like thinking is too hard for him right now. Then he stares vacantly at his water glass, thinking. 'Did he really want to kill me?'

'Looked like it to me.'

He stares at the water.

I ask, 'Why did you come to the Pioneer?'

'It's the only casino on the east coast I've never been to,' he shrugs. 'No one to recognise me.'

'But to a casino. To somewhere as open as that...'

'My money's been frozen. I had to get cash somehow.'

I blow a sigh at the obviousness of it. 'Who's Aaron Bernardo?'

Benedict grins. 'A lawyer with Linehan and Tillman. I swiped his wallet last week because I kind of look like him. I needed some ID to get me on the train.'

'That's how you got to Melbourne?'

'Yeah. Is that how we're getting back?'

I don't answer, think about that question. Draining my glass is the subtlest way of celebrating I can think of.

I hold out my hand. 'My name's John.'

But before Benedict can shake it, a phone rings somewhere. My mobile.

Big says through it, in a loud and hollow voice, 'How are you going?'

'All right,' I say. 'You?'

'Good. Good. Shall I tell you about what I found out?' He sounds more polite than usual.

'Sure.'

'So...Mush loses all his money to your boy, and there's this clause in the small print that says ANR doesn't have to pay it back because Benedict—'

'Skip that part. I heard it already.'

'Okay...His marriage breaks up, the bank turns down his loan, his wife gets a new boyfriend, nothing to live for, fuck the world, I'm going to kill Billy Benedict. So...he hires a private dick in Melbourne to find out where Benedict lives. He says this guy's name is—'

'Leo Spaske,' I say, nodding at nothing in particular.

'You know him?'

'Yeah.'

There's the shortest of silences. 'Really?'

I don't know why this should surprise him. 'Yeah. Tall. Nordic. Obsessed with knives. He was a standover for Lex Shortman once upon a time. Linehan offered him this job, but he turned it down. I guess now we know why.'

'All right, well...' Big hesitates. Seems to be gathering his thoughts. 'Spaske called Rene this afternoon saying, "Benedict's on his way to the Pioneer, just thought you might like to know... Nudge nudge." So Rene gets plastered and hails a cab.'

'All right. I'm coming up to see him—'

'I can take care of Mush,' Big clears his throat. 'Help him see the error of his ways. I'll get right up in his face.'

'I'm going to give him back his gun. And we've got to find a way to keep him from telling anyone about this.'

'You've got to get your bloke back to Sydney. Let me look after Mush,' Big says. Then he says, 'Trust me.'

I'm squinting at the wall above Benedict, who's sitting on the bed, squinting back at me. He can see that I can see something's wrong.

'What's happened?' I ask Big, turning away from Benedict.

'Nothing,' Big says quickly.

'What's...?' Then there's no point talking. I end the call.

Holding Benedict's dressing gown closed is a fluffy white rope. I wrench it loose and the gown falls open.

'*What the fuck are you doing, man?*' Benedict goes into a panic again, which makes two of us.

'Sorry,' I say, wrestling the rope free and winding it around Benedict's hands and tying them to the bed post. 'I won't be gone long. I need you to wait here.'

My whole body has a nervous energy shaking it up as I pull the bind tight, twisting Benedict's wrists. 'Fuck *you*, man,' he says.

I take his passkey from his wallet. Then I'm out the door.

It seems an age before I reach the fifteenth floor. And all the while what I'm not thinking about is how nice it is to take the elevator this time.

I knock hard on Mush's door and call out Big's name. He comes straight away, was waiting for me, pulls open the door slow and knowing. I push past him, don't look him in the eye. There's something he's going to say but doesn't because there's nothing that's going to stop me finding Mush.

Where Mush is is in the bathroom. In the bathtub. On his back. Hands pinned behind him. A rubber shower hose extends from the tap in a rambling loop and ends on Mush's chest where his cheap white shirt is wet through. The tap isn't running, as far as I can tell.

But Mush is dead. I can tell that.

For a moment, like a fist to the face, I sense that I'm about to cry. I feel the sting rush up from my stomach to my eyes and pool there, ready to leap out, so I twist my face into a shape and force it down. Remembering that only minutes ago Mush tried to shoot me doesn't help. The only thing that helps, staring down at him, is knowing that I shouldn't be surprised. That really, when you think about it, John, really, there wasn't any other way that this could end.

At the trial, where Big was eventually sent down for killing Rene Mush, Big explained all about the crybaby technique. You restrain the subject and clamp the end of the hose into his mouth using bulldog clips or gaffer tape or just your hands will do. You run the tap fast, but not too fast, and at first the subject will swallow as much of it as they can. That's why Willie and Mush both had so much water in their stomachs. Pretty soon, though, they can't swallow any more and they hold their breath and that's when you turn the tap on as hard as it will go so that water comes surging out their nose, ears, eyes. It's clear, then, why they call it the crybaby.

Among other things, what it does to the subject is it makes them feel like their head is exploding.

The best part is, the crybaby doesn't leave a mark.

Except when the subject dies.

Mush's childlike features make him all the more hard to look at, but I keep looking. Patches of his clothes and his hair are soaked, his face is shiny green and his eyes are bugging out of his head, vaguely cross-eyed. Maybe he just went and choked on the shower hose before Big could get started. Or maybe this is another heart attack.

The bathtub he's lying in is where I hid about an hour ago, blood dripping from my hand onto the white porcelain, listening to Mush provoke himself. Somewhere beneath Mush's body my blood is still there and my first instinct is to heave him aside and wash the blood away. But I don't. I dig my hands into my pockets, keep looking at the dead man, like I'm in some way paying my respects. But that feels stupid because his fly is still undone.

Terry Linehan came down from Sydney to pick up Benedict himself. He couldn't get anyone to believe that Benedict always meant to go back to Sydney in time to meet the reporting condition, but he got Benedict's excursion to Melbourne disallowed at the trial. By then, though, with the kind of attention that followed the death of Rene Mush, there was no way the jury didn't know he'd made a run for it. Benedict was remanded in custody during the course of the trial, and on the third day, playing cards in a holding cell with another prisoner, an argument broke out. They were only playing for matchsticks, but still he was beaten unconscious and lost part of an ear and had a bite taken out of his nose. When he got up to give evidence, his head was swollen red like an apple.

Benedict changed his plea and got a non-parole period of two years. His injuries weighed heavily at his sentencing.

And Linehan got his million dollars back.

Big comes to the doorway behind me, his hands in his pockets, too. 'You should have gone. I could have taken care of this.'

I don't take my eyes off Mush, so it must look like I'm lashing out at a dead body. '*How*? My fingerprints are everywhere, not to mention my *blood*. The woman in the next room knows my *name*. How could you have taken care of this?'

Big says nothing. I can't look at him, but I imagine he's biting his lip, trying to think of an answer that makes him sound more like a professional and less like a maniac.

'Leo Spaske, I mean, it had to be a fake name, you know? I didn't…I thought, if this bloke really existed, it had to be a fake name. So I wanted to know the real name, so…' His voice cracks as he speaks. 'I only wanted to give him a scare. Just make him a little uncomfortable, you know? I just…It was unlucky. I was just unlucky.'

I turn to look at him, to show him my disbelief. His head is such a sweaty ball of denial and fear that he is almost unrecognisable.

He says, 'Most of the time, you only have to turn the tap on and they—'

'For your own sake, Neil, stop talking.'

I saw Leo Spaske give evidence at Big's trial but I never spoke to him directly. He denied selling Mush the gun, said he'd never owned or dealt in firearms in his life. No other theory was ever proposed for who provided it to Mush, but Spaske's firearms charge was dropped for lack of evidence and, officially, the mystery of Mush's thirty-eight Arnold goes unsolved.

Up there on the stand, impossibly tall and blond and flashing enormous Scandinavian teeth, Spaske claimed that Mush had paid him ten thousand dollars to tap Benedict's phone in Surry Hills. Mind you, the plan wasn't that Mush should track down Benedict and kill him. Rather, Spaske said, they wanted to monitor Benedict in case he attempted to skip bail. It was all in the interest of justice, he said. They were going to listen in on Benedict's phone calls to make sure he stayed in Sydney and then went to trial and then went to jail. Spaske had no idea of what Mush was planning. If you believe Spaske.

When he heard Benedict make a reservation at the Pioneer Hotel under the name Bernardo, he called Mush. Spaske assumed Mush would dutifully call the police, didn't worry for a moment that his wiretap was illegal, figured he'd earned his ten thousand dollars and forgot about the whole thing. There wasn't enough evidence to prove that Spaske knew what Mush was planning or why he really called Mush that day. But he'd breached the *Listening Devices Act*, and if you break the law they can take your licence away. Which is what they did. To Spaske and to me.

My evidence at Big's trial was a marathon. Every possible thing about me and Big was a conversation subject, since I was the only person who knew all about what had happened at the Pioneer Hotel and was still alive and wasn't on trial for murder. The prosecutor painted me as a cowboy with no sense of blah blah blah and I didn't argue. By then my licence hearing had been and gone and I didn't care enough to fight. I'd already lost what I had to lose.

Scrawled on the summons to that hearing was *unprofessional conduct of a serious nature* and *infamous conduct in a professional respect*. But really, unlawful entry was their only card. The one rule for a private investigator is *don't break the law* and that's what I'd done;

it didn't matter that I hadn't knowingly put Mush's life in danger when I sent him off with Big. With the kind of attention I was getting in the press they had to take me down for something. The cowboy PI. The loose cannon. At the hearing the woman in the paisley dress, from the room next to Mush, got up and called me a parasite. I guess she was angry at me for what I'd said to her at the elevators. But I'd just found Mush's body and I was overcome. I would have apologised but I never got the chance.

At my hearing I told them what Linehan had hired me for and that giving Benedict a scare seemed like the best way to go about it, then I listened to them tell me all the reasons why it wasn't. They didn't even let me have a lawyer going in. Coming out I was unemployed.

'I'm calling the police.'

'Yeah,' Big says. 'Fuck it.'

But both of us keep standing there in the bathroom, staring down at Mush like he might come back to life. My mind is searching for angles, of which there are exactly none.

'Could we...' Big tries, 'Could we tell them everything, only leave out your friend Benedict?'

'Why?'

'If people think Mush was here to shoot Miss Delaney, which remember is what *you* thought, then at least...'

'At least you look like a hero.'

'You take Benedict back to Sydney, nobody knows he ever left, and then...'

'How do we explain my fingerprints?'

'We tell it just how it happened, only without Benedict.'

I shake my head.

'The girl downstairs checked in a guy named Aaron Bernardo.

You used your passkey to get into his room and ten minutes later Mush is dead. What happens when they can't find Bernardo? The CCTV footage will show he looks a lot like William Benedict.'

'We'll figure out something to tell them. You said so yourself.'

'What happens when they find out Mush is a former client of Benedict's?'

'Coincidence.'

'What happens when they track down the *real* Aaron Bernardo, who turns out to be one of Benedict's lawyers?'

'That's easy. We say—'

'*I'm not lying to the cops, Neil.*' I have to yell this to make him shut up. 'Anyone who gets away with it is just lucky, and I don't want to rely on luck when there's a dead man in the bathtub.'

I step past Big to the telephone by the bed, keep my eyes on my shoes.

'If I were you I'd do up his fly before they get here.'

I pick up the receiver, put it to my ear. But Big's finger comes down on the phone prong.

'Do you think…' Big says softly. 'Could we keep Miss Delaney's name out of this?'

I look at him. His eyes drop, glassy and bloodshot. After accidentally killing Mush he must have run his hands through his hair a thousand times before calling me. The stylishness is gone.

I say, 'No.'

'She'll be crucified in the press.'

'She'll love the publicity.'

'But she's getting married.'

I don't answer. Big leaps at the silence: '*I won't go down as the man who ruined Hannah Delaney's wedding.*'

'You'll go down as worse things than that.'

Then Big hits me.

His fist collides with my left eye in a final act of denial and I'm in no condition to take a punch so it sends me to the ground arse-first.

Big puts his hands on his hips and walks away, maybe scared that if he doesn't he'll keep beating me. He reaches the window and runs his hand through his hair again, then sighs and says to the city at night, 'I've wanted to do that for a long time.'

My eye is numb but I feel it swelling. The pain in my ankle shoots up my leg. 'Feel better?'

He doesn't answer.

Delicately, I hook the telephone cord and draw the dangling receiver towards me, try to figure out how I'm going to dial without standing up.

The Medical Examiner gave evidence that the cause of death was drowning, and Big's prosecutor made the argument that although Big hadn't intended to kill anybody, he was nonetheless a dangerous psychopath, out of practice in the ways of torturing subjects. Big himself agreed that he'd let the tap run a few seconds too long, and that that was all it took for Rene Mush. Mush's ex-wife gave evidence too, which the prosecution snuck in there as a kind of victim impact statement, but about the kindest thing she had to say about Mush was that he only became a *manic* depressive after they lost their retirement fund. Then they divorced and she hadn't seen Mush since the day they signed the papers. I've worked on a bunch of divorce proceedings for pathological gamblers—they're usually over quickly because there are no assets left to divide. I guess the same goes for the defrauded victims of pathological gamblers.

More than half the trial was devoted to the tale of Willie Somers, former bored teenager and newly reinstated poster boy for cop-haters all over the world. On the stand Big let it all hang out. He said he'd taken Willie outside and told him how he was going to use the garden hose and where. Willie was pinned down, the garden hose jammed in his mouth, but he hadn't swallowed more than a few mouthfuls before he went into a kind of seizure and blacked out. Big spent precious minutes trying to revive the boy with slaps to the face and yelling in his ear, but none of that worked. Even if he'd tried regular CPR, with the kind of condition Willie had, the Medical Examiner said that that wouldn't have worked either.

His defence counsel asked if the crybaby is what he'd been ordered to do. Big said no. Making him just another lone gunman. The Police Commissioner made a statement, said there was no culture of violence in law enforcement and the actions of one man shouldn't be allowed to reflect badly on the police, in Moorabbin or anywhere else. Problem purged. We should all sleep better knowing he's behind bars.

He'll be behind bars for twenty years with a minimum of fifteen.

At the sentencing he wept, uninhibited, like he did that night on St Kilda pier. The press latched onto that and, with his unique method of torture already notorious, Big was written up as The Crybaby Killer, the label glued to him before he even left the dock. Forever, I guess.

There was a lot of talk about whether Hannah Delaney would be called to give evidence. Big must have been relieved when she wasn't. Her wedding to the football player went ahead as planned. Later they successfully sued a tabloid for publishing photos of the wedding when the wedding was supposed to be private. As a reprisal, that publication interviewed Big in his prison cell, then published it with the headline: *Crybaby Killer Delaney's No. 1 Fan.*

Dennis Burke was there for the sentencing, the first time I'd seen him in months. He took me outside so he could smoke a cigarette in the rain, away from the crowd.

'You remember Sotiria?' he asked me.

'I remember the photograph.'

Dennis took a drag and the wind whipped away a plume of smoke. 'She left her hubby.'

'He's a cop too, right?'

'Yeah. And a coke dealer. Total fucking arsehole.'

Disgust showed on his face, then the wind whipped that away too. The rain stayed put.

Dennis said, 'When Big heard they'd split up, he called her. They were supposed to meet up for coffee, but then he pulled that shift at the Pioneer and postponed the meet. How about that, hey?'

I blew a drip of water off the tip of my nose. 'Are you seriously trying to make me feel sorry for Neil Bighuty?'

Dennis seemed to think that was a fair question. He concentrated so as to answer properly.

'Fifteen and twenty. That's what they give to psychos who massacre their families. He's not just a sick fuck, John. He's not. I think *you* need to understand that more than anyone.'

'Why me?'

Dennis finished his cigarette and said, 'Because he hated your guts.'

He didn't want to go on. His face showed embarrassment, which he shook off and then he laughed in that way he has.

If I could have felt anything, I might have laughed too. But he did it for both of us, the rain on his jacket becoming a clean blanket of wet.

'The police are on their way,' I tell Big as I head for the door. 'I've got to go bring Benedict up here.'

His expression doesn't change, like he's wondering where I'm really going.

I limp past the bathroom, which I don't look inside, through the door and stagger as best I can along the hallway.

My left hand, with the towel wrapped around it, I see it's started bleeding again. I get hit in the face but it's my hand that bleeds.

Under my eye is red and sweaty, swelling at the point of impact. There's dried blood on my clothes, my forehead. So when I reach the elevator and it opens, and there's the paisley dress from 1503, she doesn't know it's me at first.

After a moment, recognition.

'Hello,' she stammers.

'Good evening.'

'Goodness…What happened?'

There's no point in lying to her anymore. The police will talk to her. Tell her I'm a liar. That I don't work for Hannah Delaney and I can't get her an autograph. That I humiliated her. That she was duped and she let a stranger into her hotel room.

I say, 'There was an incident…'

She's suddenly horrified, comes to me, pinches my sleeve. 'Is *Hannah* all right?'

I hobble into the elevator, turn around, feel a trickle of blood behind my ear. Then I look at her with all the hate and blame of what happened today.

'No,' I say. 'She's *dead*.'

The woman puts a hand to her mouth, distraught.

We keep those looks on our faces and I'm waiting for the elevator doors to close.

The doors close.

GRANDMA'S HOUSE

OF ALL THE things they did to Joanna, the one I don't stop thinking about is this:

Nathan urinated into a plastic container, put the tip of a syringe into it, filled the syringe. They had these things just lying around, according to Joanna. She saw them shoot up at least twice in the five days she was held there, though what the stuff was she couldn't say. Something that made them twitchy and wild-eyed—she wondered why they took the stuff when it made them so anxious. She couldn't say if they were high when they did this.

While Dale masturbated, Nathan injected Joanna with his urine. Into a vein in her arm. She was tied to the chair and there was a football sock stuffed in her mouth and taped in place. Nathan hesitated at first, let Dale work himself up and Joanna thought he wasn't going to do it, that it was just the anticipation that was going to get Dale off. But he did it. Joanna doesn't remember what happened after that.

Doctor Richter said it was likely that, at this point, Joanna fell into a 'malaise'.

At that same sentencing hearing, another doctor said that

Nathan Money had been physically abused by his father when he was a boy. Maybe the judge believed him, but he didn't really care. He sentenced Nathan Money and Dale Craig to a non-parole period of sixteen years apiece.

I don't know what Joanna Maddur has planned for the next sixteen years. I'm happy not knowing. I'm happy for my imagination to fill that in.

The taxi driver is an Indian man with a big turban and I ask him to wait. It's all sunshine heat today and we drove for so long I fell asleep with the window open, the air drying out the sweat on my face. Where we've stopped is Ferntree Gully, at the foot of the Dandenong Ranges that watch over Melbourne. I take the envelope out of my jacket, leave my jacket on the seat and step out to a row of old, worthless homes.

They aspired to more. Some of them are half-renovated, the skeletons of granny flats and extensions abandoned years ago, rotting in the sun. Some are half-painted, like the job was going well until they ran out of paint and they never got around to buying more. Some of the lawns are mown. There are people pushing prams who stop and look at me in the taxi. They don't get a lot of taxis out here; this is car-driving territory. But I don't have a car anymore.

The house I'm walking to is at the bottom of the hill. The gully of Ferntree Gully. I'm wearing a shirt that has a stain on it and halfway to the house I regret leaving my jacket in the cab. I brought it with me today specifically so it would hide the stain on my shirt, but I don't have the energy to turn back to the car, not in this heat. And I'm taking the day slow. I drank more than usual last night and my face wears that special look, like someone just whispered to me a story I found particularly boring. If this job takes more than ten seconds, I may need to sit down.

After I lost my licence six months ago I guess I went a little funny for a while. Demetri found me holed up in my office, sitting around listening to the ringing in my ears, spying on the people out my window, drinking to make my dreams less vivid. He took pity and offered me work as a trumped-up errand boy. I like it about as much as I liked doing the old stuff, which doesn't mean much. It pays less, but even if it paid the same or even more, I don't do enough of it for that to make a difference. Demetri just wants to keep me busy until I can reapply for my licence a few months from now. I haven't told him yet that I'm not going to do that. And until he finds out, whenever he needs someone in a suit to deliver an important piece of paper somewhere, this is me.

The front yard is overgrown and the sign that says BEWARE OF THE DOG has also grown over. I prick up my ears anyway, listen for the sound of padding feet, but instead, well before I reach the front door, I hear a television, and before I knock I can tell the voice is speaking a thick Asian language. The Japanese TV news. I knock hard to be heard over those officious, sober tones.

Demetri can't have a lot of paying clients living on streets like this, in houses like this. But he gets a guilty twinge sometimes because he makes so much money keeping sociopaths and criminals out of prison. He compensates by working free of charge for sociopaths and criminals who otherwise can't afford him. Every now and then the gamble pays off and one of them turns out to be innocent, or at least innocent of whatever they're charged with. Their plights have become very public crusades at times, garnering for him social justice awards and a lot of television appearances. I remember I used to admire him for it.

Demetri says I've become cynical.

The door opens just an inch. With the brightness of the day outside it takes a while for me to see the old woman inside there, and in that time she doesn't speak. She's not remotely Japanese, despite the television blaring behind her. Through fat-rimmed glasses her eyes offer me all the fear that old people reserve for the outside world and probably she would have chained the door before opening it except that where the chain used to be there's just a weathered patch of splintered wood. This door was kicked in a long time ago.

'Hi...' I say with an oaf's smile. I fumble with the envelope, pull out the stapled document from inside and read the heading. It's a summons for a sentencing hearing next week. I find the address.

'This is 29 Weston Crescent? Is that right?'

She has a tiny face, densely freckled, and her hair is like wild white straw but it's maintained. There's no Alzheimer's in the way she examines me, no dementia in the clothes she wears or the ribbon pinned to her collar. She's over eighty, but she can glare cautiously at a stranger like a woman half her age.

She says, 'Yes, that's right.'

'I'm supposed to deliver this thing to...' I check the name in the top corner of the summons. 'Nathan Money.'

Yeah. This is just the kind of street where a family called Money would live.

Nathan and Dale knew Joanna from around the neighbourhood. Ferntree Gully is the kind of place people are constantly escaping from, so anyone who grows up there and doesn't leave becomes a kind of legend, even young women barely out of their teens. She'd worked in the Belgrave Arcade instead of finishing her VCE, sold lipstick and eye shadow and rouge to single mums, got hooked on methylamphetamine somewhere along the way and then she got sacked. To pay for the habit she wound up selling drugs and that's how Nathan and Dale got her into the car and all the way to the basement where they tied her up.

That room, going by Joanna's description, was my idea of a bogan hellpit. Essendon football posters coated the walls alongside explicit pornography printed off the internet and at least one picture of Nathan groping a german shepherd and laughing. Nathan's favourite place to sit was his Pamela Anderson beanbag. Over the five days they didn't eat often because of the drugs but when they did it was Kentucky Fried Chicken. Half their meal usually wound up smeared across Joanna's face and body because the boys found it entertaining. There was a hatch leading up to a laneway where the boys went to the toilet and there was another door leading up to the house proper and the boys never *ever* went in there. At one point Dale tried, but Nathan stopped him and the pair fought violently. A razor blade was produced.

When the plea was over, and when the judge announced their sentence, and when he asked Nathan and Dale if they understood their sentence, and when Nathan said, 'Yeah,' and Dale said nothing at all, Dale still had the scar across his face where Nathan had cut him.

That fight is what first gave Joanna the idea that someone was living beyond that door.

She looks at me blankly and I raise my voice. 'Is Nathan at home?'

She stares at me for another moment, then shakes her head urgently and disappears. While she's gone the door relaxes open to reveal the typical living room in the typical old woman's house. There's a doily on a carved coffee table, a doona and pillow folded there on the couch and a collection of painted ceramic birds attached to the wall beside a small picture of the Virgin Mary. It's dark and dusty and tidy.

The television volume drops but it stays on. She comes back to the door and squints at me through those glasses.

'What did you say? I didn't hear you because of the television.'

The way I'm feeling, I can't stand up for much longer. I steady myself against the brickwork beside the door, wonder how long it's going to take to have this simplest of conversations.

'I work for Nathan's solicitor. Is Nathan in?'

'Oh no. Here's not here now.'

'But he lives here, is that right?'

'Pardon?'

'Does Nathan live here?'

'Y-yes. You're…um…?'

'I work for Nathan's solicitor. I have a summons for Nathan.'

'Nathan is my grandson.'

'Yes, and your grandson committed a crime of some kind and he's getting sentenced, in a courtroom, next week. This piece of paper will tell him where to be and what happens if he's not there. But I have to give it to him personally. Do you know when he'll be home?'

'Oh, no.'

'Do you know where he is? Who he might have gone out with?'

'No…no.'

Her eyes are way more intelligent than the words she's speaking. It's as though she's waiting for me to ask another question, the one she'll answer properly and in detail. I glance behind me to the street, turn back to her.

'Is your name Mrs Money?'

'Yes, I'm Mrs Money.'

'Look, I've got a taxi waiting, and really…I don't want to come back to Ferntree Gully unless I absolutely have to. Are you sure your grandson isn't home?'

'Well…I've got rheumatism, you see.'

'Where does your grandson sleep?' I point to the doona and pillow. 'Does he sleep there on the couch?'

'Oh, no. Sometimes I sleep out here. In the rumpus room. When my leg's bad and I can't get down the hall.'

'Where does Nathan sleep?'

Adjusting the glasses on her head, she slowly turns and indicates a closed wooden door in the corner of the rumpus room. 'In the basement,' she says.

'He lives in the basement?'

'Yes. I don't know if he's there now.'

'So he *might* be here.'

'I don't feel very well, you see. I've got rheumatism and I should be lying down.'

'Do you think you could check to see if he's here?'

'Um...'

'Or I could. I could knock on that door there...'

'Um, well...He's not there now.'

'He's *not* there?'

'No...He went out earlier on.'

'Right. You're sure?'

'Oh, yes.'

I roll my eyes as obviously as I can. I don't know what Nathan's done, but if I have to come back out to Ferntree Gully, I hope they throw the book at him.

Nathan and Dale didn't give evidence at the plea. Partly because that's not the practice in sentencing hearings these days, and also because letting them speak for themselves would have done them more harm than good: they are not powerful intellects. For example, Dale wrote his name, *DALE*, in cigarette burns across Joanna's left foot. This was useful when it came to identifying Joanna's assailants.

Another example is, they fell asleep and Joanna almost escaped. She told that story when she gave evidence herself, how for two days she'd watched the boys drink themselves into a funk, kept awake by the drugs they'd mainlined. Finally they passed out, drooling, face down on the threadbare carpet.

It was like a furnace in that basement, and the sweat from Joanna's body helped her to gradually work free of the cable ties that bound her to the chair and to creep slowly over the litter of junk food stained with tomato sauce and semen and blood. She made it to the stairs leading up to the laneway but the door was locked. She snuck across the room to the other door, also locked. She tapped gently against it.

'Hello?' She whispered. 'Hello? Is anybody there?'

An old woman's voice said, 'Pardon?'

Joanna said, 'Help me. Please help me.'

The old woman said, 'Pardon?'

'Open the door. Quickly. Please please open the door.'

'You leave me alone,' came back the voice. 'I'm trying to sleep.'

Joanna began sobbing. She was sobbing in the courtroom also, as she told this story.

'Please. They're hurting me.'

'No, they're not. I can't hear you.'

'Please—'

Suddenly there was a cracking of knuckles against the door.

'*Nathan!*' The old woman was shouting. '*Nathan! Are you in there?*'

Nathan stirred. Joanna's sobbing overwhelmed her.

'*Nathan! Are you awake?*'

Nathan grabbed Joanna and she screamed, which woke up Dale, and the two of them tied her back to the chair and got the football sock back into her mouth. Nathan yelled abuse at the door and the old woman went quiet.

But the best example of how smart these boys were is that they let her go. As if, after five days, she'd just go home and sleep it off.

*

It's really the heat that decides for me. And the small waves of nausea as I slouch here. And the prospect of a bloody mary in front of the desk fan in my office. With a muted belch I push myself off the wall and shake my head.

'Can you tell Nathan I'll be back on Thursday afternoon? He really needs to be here to see me. Can you tell him that?'

'I don't hear anything, you see. I have the TV on.'

'You have to give Nathan that message. Can you do that?'

'On Thursday, yes.'

She doesn't seem to have trouble hearing me. God knows why she needs the TV so loud, even if she does speak Japanese.

'I'll be back on Thursday, in the afternoon. He needs to be here.'

'Nathan doesn't tell me anything.'

'Okay, but—'

'He protects me, you see.'

I stop what I was about to say. 'He protects you?'

'I have the TV on. I can't hear anything.'

'Are you going to tell Nathan to be here Thursday afternoon?'

'Yes. I'll write it down.'

'Okay. Sorry to disturb you, Mrs Money.' I edge back towards the taxi.

'That's all right.' She smiles. For the first time.

The door closes.

I pass back through the gate with its redundant dog warning and stop and turn and look at the house. I'm wondering if Nathan will peek through the window for a read on the stranger who came looking for him. There's something about the house, like a white noise pitched too high for me to hear but that still makes my ears hurt. That gets louder the further I move away from it.

I get in the car and the driver says, 'Back now?'

I'm about to answer but I don't. I open the summons that's

folded up in my hand and search for the box that names the offence, the thing that Nathan did, that he'll be sentenced for next week.

It seems an eternity before I find it. I flip between the two pages a dozen times. But there it is, at the top of the first page.

Offence: Possession of a small quantity of a controlled substance, being cannabis.

I stare into the words like doing that might help me understand the old woman and my sense of unease. Possessing cannabis isn't exactly high treason. A 'small' quantity means less than two hundred and fifty grams. There's no mention of traffic or attempt to traffic. If Nathan doesn't have any prior convictions then the judge probably won't even record a conviction. Especially with Demetri on the job.

Today is so bright and hot the sky seems more white than blue. I toss the summons onto the seat next to me and roll down the window.

I say, 'Yeah, back, thanks.'

Goodbye, Ferntree Gully. See you again on Thursday. Maybe. Nathan won't be here anyway and half my pay will go to the driver.

We nose around the corner, headed west. I look forward to sleeping like I did on the way here.

It was the Thursday morning and I was trying to get myself off the couch when Demetri called.

'Don't bother,' he said. 'Nathan's been arrested.'

'What for?'

'I'm not sure yet, but the whole thing sounds too unbelievable to be true. He's up on false imprisonment and aggravated assault, but I expect the plod are just trying to scare him a little.'

'Who did he imprison?'

'Some girl. I don't know. I don't believe a word of it. The way it was told to me over the phone…You'd think Nathan was the devil himself.'

Something in my brain fired, crystallised. I sat up on the couch.

'When was this supposed to have happened?'

'Just this week. Nathan was only charged this morning.'

'Did it happen at his grandma's house?'

'I don't know. I haven't got any details. Listen, the last thing you need is another job to freak out about. I'm just calling to say you're off the hook. This cannabis business that was supposed to be next week has been adjourned, so the summons you've got is void. Don't worry, you'll get a cancellation fee.'

'Are you staying on as Nathan's solicitor?'

'Yeah, for now.'

'Do me a favour?'

'What?'

'Find an excuse and dump him.'

'Why?'

I didn't want to say why. Didn't want to *freak out*. 'I just think he's a waste of your talents.'

'I've got that Chapel Street thing coming up anyway, so I probably *will* have to give it a pass. Not that I like to leave clients in the lurch.'

'Good,' I said. Then I changed the subject.

I went along to the plea. The one for false imprisonment and aggravated assault. I sat there with a pounding headache and took notes on a notepad and made small mental calculations and listened to Joanna tell her stories. Like how she was literally kicked out the door to the laneway behind Nathan's home, wearing burnt clothes and no shoes.

She didn't go home. She went to the police.

Nathan's Legal Aid lawyer hammered away at Nathan's psychiatric evaluation because it was the only card she had to play.

From the bar table she reminded the court a good half-dozen times that Nathan as a six-year-old was abused by his father with a vacuum cleaner pipe and, according to Nathan, live spiders. But none of that mattered to the judge. You could see it in the way he slouched at the bench, in the way he never looked at Nathan or Dale. No one who heard Joanna's stories could possibly think that Nathan's problems were fixable. The court wasn't going to show mercy in the hope that Nathan could somehow be redeemed. He couldn't. Neither could Dale.

I didn't see Nathan's grandmother at the court. I suppose she was at home with the ordinary news playing at a perfectly reasonable volume.

According to the timeline in my notepad, if I'd listened to my instinct on the day I visited, if I'd gone to the back lane to see if there was another entry to the basement, if I'd insisted on going to Nathan's room, if I'd asked Elizabeth Money what it was she couldn't hear over the television, then Joanna might not have had Nathan's urine injected into her arm.

So that's the thing I don't stop thinking about.

All during the plea I wanted to stand up and scream at them all and tell them that I was there. That it was my fault. That I'd heard the Japanese news playing too loud.

What I did instead is I went home, closed the blinds and drank a bottle. But my head still ached. And my dreams were still vivid.

LEAVING THE FOUNTAINHEAD

THE RAIN HAS kept people away. I'm planted on a stool at the end of the bar and I'm halfway drunk on bourbon that burns in my lungs and in my throat, but it's cheap and this place is across the street from my office, so checkmate.

My office which is also my residence.

Or my residence which was once my office.

For all the nights I've slept there, and all the days I just sat around there before that, I must have come to the Fountainhead Hotel on only half a dozen occasions. It's always so peopled. I'm usually peopled enough.

But tonight the rain has kept them away. The stools stand empty and the barman has nothing to do but polish glasses, slowly, taking pride. Most nights there'd be seven or eight men seated here, lungs burning, flushing the day away. Tonight it's just me.

Way off in the lounge there's a couple of kids, barely old enough to drink, talking in hushed voices, ignoring their beers. Breaking up maybe. Or getting back together.

But that's it. I've been easing into the quiet for about half an hour, keeping my weight on the points of my elbows, looking up only to watch the water cascade down the front windows like there's an actual fountain on the roof of this place, true to its name.

I'm doing this, watching the water, when the barman speaks.

I say, 'What?'

Tiny pineapples and bananas decorate his shirt, which is easily the happiest thing in the room. The pores on his big friendly nose look like they've been drawn on, and his big friendly face smiles at me with an openness that must earn him a nice tip from anyone who comes in here alone and lonely. He's got the kind of moustache you don't see much anymore and beneath it there's a whiff of smugness, like he's immune to what affects his moping clients and he knows it. Or just thinks it. Or maybe I just think it. I can't read people the way I used to.

He says again, louder, 'Why the long face?'

And I force a grin. Bartender humour.

He snorts pleasantly, puts the glass he's been wiping on the shelf behind him, draws another from the dishwasher.

'You okay, bloke?' he asks, polishing again.

'I'm fine.'

'You don't look fine.' With an elegant swoop of his arm he pours a shot of bourbon into that freshly shined tumbler and puts it on the mat in front of me. 'This one's on the house.'

It's a throaty voice, comforting, like a lawnmower when you finally get it to start. I don't say, 'Thanks.' I say, 'Thank you.'

His shoulders push back against my gratitude. 'I can tell when someone's having a bad day.'

I neck the bourbon I've already got and clutch at the new drink, feel the glass still warm from the dishwasher, just as friendly as the man who poured it. It makes me turn back to the window, the rain outside.

He follows my gaze. 'It's a wet one, hey.'

'Yeah.'

'My word,' he says. 'What do you do, bloke?'

I look back at my glass. 'I'm a delivery boy.'

'What do you deliver?'

'Legal papers, mostly. Financial records.'

'You enjoy it?'

Maybe the answer is inside my drink somewhere. I peer in. 'I don't think so.'

'Yeah...' He pulls another glass from the dishwasher and says, 'What are you going to do?' Only it's rhetorical, so it comes out: 'Waddayagunnadoo.' And I'm hoping this is his way of ending the conversation.

But then he shelves that glass and says, 'Where you from?'

'You're used to a lot of people sitting here, talking to you... right?'

'My word.'

The way he keeps saying that, it's like his catchphrase. He delivers it with stern conviction.

I say, 'Well, I guess I don't really feel like talking.'

The barman nods, arches his mouth like a Chinese businessman agreeing on a price, turns his big round body away to the stack of ashtrays behind him and puts one on top with just enough delicacy to give me a rush of guilt.

I say, 'But thanks for the drink...'

He goes back to the dishwasher, pulls out another glass without looking at me, and I sigh at the awkwardness. There's a distant rumble of thunder. Beyond the window, headlights and neon signs flash at each other, and I don't want to go out there, so I figure it's good when a silhouette crosses the window and comes into the bar, ringing the bell above the door, splashing water from his umbrella onto the linoleum and giving the barman something to think about apart from how I'm an arsehole.

But seeing who it is gives me something to think about too.

Our contact was so brief and so long ago that he won't recognise me, which I'm thankful for. I almost didn't recognise him in that well-cut suit and those polished black shoes, his grey beard and hair trimmed to imply someone corporate. The last time I saw him he didn't imply someone *bathed*. As he approaches the bar, glancing at me with those fat black eyes and looking around the place to see how empty it is, I'm thinking it's like his face has been cut-and-pasted onto the body of an effete city executive, complete with a strawberry-red umbrella. Also, I'm thinking he could come in here dressed as an air hostess and anyone in Melbourne who isn't brain-damaged would still recognise Kevin Tomlinson.

But then the barman says, 'What can I do you for?' with that same good-natured smile and there's no hesitation in his voice or eyes. So what do I know.

'I'm looking for the Boatswain's Club,' says Tomlinson. 'Isn't it around here?'

The barman scratches his nose. 'The what, sorry?'

'The Boatswain's Club. Do you know where it is?' It's a voice like he was raised by foghorns.

'My word,' says the barman. 'You're on foot, are you?'

'Yes.'

'No problem.' He points emphatically, stretching his hand as far back and away from his body as it will go and waving a finger out there. 'You go six blocks along Russell Street until you hit Victoria Parade. You go two streets west along that until you come to Locust Lane, where you take a right. Go all the way to the end. The Boatswain's Club is on the corner there, next to the Parkway-Spruce Hotel.'

Tomlinson squints. His eyes twitch, one at a time.

'So...six blocks along Russell, left onto Victoria, right onto Locust.'

'It's a popular place. You can't miss it.'

'All right. Thank you.'

'No probs, bloke.'

The exchange is over in all of thirty seconds, then the bell above the door rings again and Tomlinson is gone. Back into the rain. I watch his umbrella open and float away past the window.

Then I look to the barman, waiting for him to look back.

When he does, he misinterprets my face. 'You want another?'

'Why did...' I'm about to ask the obvious question, but then I don't. Instead, I say, 'Sure.'

He pours me another. There's silence while he does it. Then he goes back to drying the glasses from the dishwasher.

In this rain, walking that distance, it'll take Tomlinson about twenty-one, twenty-two minutes to get where he's going. The barman, he's not doing these calculations. Even as I watch him, serenely shelving mugs, he might already have forgotten about the stranger who just came and went, carrying a red umbrella.

I ask, 'Do you know who that was?'

'Who? That bloke?'

'Yeah.'

'Is he famous?'

'Kevin Tomlinson?'

He doesn't recognise the name either.

'Spack Attack Tomlinson?' I offer.

This time he scowls and his gaze drifts past my ears. 'Sounds familiar...' he says. 'What's he famous for?'

'He's a psychopath.'

'You mean, like, a footy player?'

'No, he's a real-life psychopath. And a thief.' I take a sip, glance back to the door. 'And it looks as though he's doing well for himself.'

The barman slows the polishing of the glass, comes almost to a stop. His eyes search the floor. After two seconds of thinking, he snaps out of it, looks back at me.

I say, 'He stabbed his home economics teacher in high school, spent five years in a youth prison, got out and made a career robbing houses, and somewhere along the way he blowtorched his own nipples off. He's got a tattoo on his left arm that says *Rebecca*. He's also got hepatitis C, mild narcolepsy and once he won twenty-seven thousand dollars on a horse named Rent Arrears...'

I drink. The barman doesn't move.

'...which is what it says on his right arm.' The bourbon roars in my throat.

'How come you know so much about him?'

'I used to know this kind of stuff for a living.'

'Were you a cop?'

'No, I worked privately. The first client I ever had was someone Tomlinson robbed. At least, the police said it was Tomlinson. We never found out for sure. This was a long time ago.' I laugh to myself, feel the passage of time in my stomach the way a boat feels rust.

The barman keeps polishing, pretending he isn't worried about what's just happened. I'll let him pretend for a while.

'They invited me along to a raid on Tomlinson's flat. I was supposed to identify a stereo and TV belonging to my client. But I never got to do that.'

I expect stealth, but they just walk up to the door and knock. It's about as not like the movies as it can be. Seven uniforms plod along the second-storey catwalk, one of them's even whistling, and when they get to his door they knock politely and wait, in the midday sun, for it to open.

I'm at the back of the group, hanging so far behind you'd think I lived in this block of flats and I was just curious. The raiding party eye me with indifference. Some of them smirk at the distance I'm keeping, some of them don't try to hide that they're smirking. Some of them, I can tell by the way they chew their gum, are freaking out just the same as me.

We all know whose home this is.

The door opens and it's a woman, her hair pulled back tight, and there's lots of green shadow around her eyes. It's obvious she hadn't bothered looking through the peephole because she makes a face when she sees who's out here.

'Oh, *fuck off.*'

The sergeant at the head of the group, the name on his pin reads *Gant*. He offers her a folded sheet of paper and says, 'Becky, we've got a warrant to search this flat. Is Spacka at home?'

'No, he's not here,' she says back, louder than she needs to.

'You're going to have to let us in.'

Already other officers have their hands on the door, ready to push it open.

Her lower jaw is stuck out in thought, like she's actually wondering whether to take on these men hand-to-hand. It's a perfect, fraught moment. Then she rolls her eyes, drops her hand from the door and disappears.

The uniforms pour into the flat. As I creep towards the doorway I take a final look around to make sure Kevin Tomlinson isn't coming up behind me with an axe. This catwalk is one side of a courtyard, and the doors and windows of the other three sides are peppered with faces, craning at doorways, peeking through half-drawn curtains. They've come out to see the cops finally catch up with the madman who lives next door.

It's a dim, barely furnished place and I'm at the entrance to a short corridor. At the other end, Tomlinson is sitting on a torn-up couch, drawing on a water pipe. Two officers approach and he draws harder, sucking back as much smoke as he can before they reach him. When they do, and when they wrench the bong from his grasp, he exhales up into their faces. The big bad wolf blowing down a house.

I stay right here at the door.

I don't know what makes me look over, but when I do I see that the couple in the far corner of the lounge are kissing. They can't hear what I'm saying. They're caught up in their own story.

'So what happened then?' the bartender asks, watching me. He's still drying that same glass.

'Well...' I say, scratching my head. 'What happened then I had to piece together after the fact. I saw it, but I couldn't hear it. I only found out later what was actually said. And it got recounted at the trial. But I don't know if what was said really matters in the end.'

'So...he went on trial?'

'Yep.'

'But you said they didn't find the stolen stuff.'

'They didn't,' I say, sipping frugally from my glass. I look up at the ornate wooden clock above the bar. Beside it there are two bottles of Old Forester. One of them is half empty, the other unopened. A bottle like that, he and I could get to be good friends.

'There was nothing there. And I mean, apart from a few of Tomlinson's things, the place was outright empty. There was a quarter ounce of marijuana on the coffee table but, as it turns out, Tomlinson didn't go on trial for that either.'

It's been seven minutes since he left the Fountainhead.

Sergeant Gant is trying to hide his disappointment, angling the bowl one way, then the other, like it contains an unimpressive stool sample. Around him the other uniforms would be turning the place upside down if there was anything here to do that to. They wander aimlessly, checking behind furniture and under loose flaps of carpet, trying to seem busy.

'It's a hell of a parole violation, Spacka.'

'Big whoops.' Tomlinson is still on the couch, his eyes stained red by the drug. He wears a flimsy tattered singlet showing the words on his arms. His shorts are shiny green and gold, crowning skinny, impossibly hairy legs. The choppy fuzz that grows out of his face is caked with food and it's wet from who knows what. Becky sits next to him, marginally more clothed, eyes still green.

She says, 'It's not his mull, it's mine.'

'No kidding.' Gant is barely listening. He puts the bowl back on the table.

'Yep,' says Becky.

'Yep,' says Tomlinson, grinning.

Becky adds, 'I bought it and I own it, which makes it mine, right?' She knows the script.

'I'll go down for less than a month if it's not my gear,' Tomlinson taunts.

Gant sighs. 'It's on your coffee table in your flat and you're smoking it, Spacka, so we'll just see…'

He catches the eyes of several other uniforms, who shake their heads, shrug. They've found nothing.

'All right,' he grunts, waving at one of the officers, then pointing to the pair on the couch. 'Get them out of here. Everyone else, five more minutes.'

The cop who strides to the couch has black hair and a crooked nose and he's the one who was whistling on the way to Tomlinson's door. Fast as he can he's got his handcuffs out. He gestures at Tomlinson and says, 'Up.'

Tomlinson stands, achingly slowly, still grinning at Gant. Not even looking at the cop with the black hair though they're face to face. The name on the officer's pin is *Correll*, and he's handcuffing Tomlinson, hands in front.

What makes Tomlinson look at Correll is Correll whispering, 'A month is long enough to make a special friend inside, isn't it, Spacka?'

No one else hears it. Not Spacka's girlfriend, not Sergeant Gant, who's turning away now, looking mournfully at his watch. Not me, standing at the door, trying to keep hidden from even the police because I'm just a reminder of what they've failed to find.

Tomlinson stops grinning. He blinks twice and his eyes go dead. Correll stares back into those eyes and says, 'I've heard that's what you're into.'

None of us hears that either.

But Tomlinson does.

His face spasms, like those uninhibited moments right before you belch. His lips and eyes squeeze shut and his head jerks back and forth in tiny chicken pecks. But all his preparation is over in an instant and he lunges forward, not at Correll but at a sandy-haired giant who isn't looking when Tomlinson rips his name pin from his breast and wheels it into Correll's left eye.

He might be handcuffed, but Tomlinson stabs Correll twice in that eye and once in the nose before anyone turns to look.

Correll screams and Becky screams, but over the two of them Tomlinson screams the loudest, a throaty cackle with the psychopath right there inside it. The giant and Gant grab hold of him but he stabs Correll two or three times in the other eye before they get control of the arm holding the pin and blood is spouting like spring water from Correll's face but he's not making any noise now because the shock has overwhelmed him and he hits the floor and Tomlinson's trying to get down there to hurt him some more but six uniforms are holding him up and Gant has got Tomlinson's hair and everyone's shouting for an ambulance or for help and Becky's shouting that they're all bastards.

The way Gant pulls on Tomlinson's hair, Tomlinson's face is

angled at me. Amid the storm of struggling and shouting, his body tense with fight, Tomlinson locks eyes with me, this little person all the way over here. For a moment.

Me, who's not a cop, who's peeking around the door from outside the flat.

Me with my boggle-eyes. Me with my myth of Kevin Tomlinson that's been proved violently true.

And he smiles at me, hungry and jubilant, like he knows everything that's going to happen to me from this day on. And he's going to enjoy it.

'Crikey,' says the barman, softly. 'How was the cop?'

'Blind. Both eyes. And apparently he went a little nuts. I suppose you would.'

'My word,' he says, distracted. He's been polishing that glass right through my story. But not because I'm a spellbinding storyteller.

'Didn't this Tomlinson bloke go to jail?'

'Sure. He got eight years. But this all happened a long time ago. He's back out again.'

It's been fifteen minutes since Tomlinson left the Fountainhead. He'd have reached Victoria Parade by now.

'A lot of criminals act like they're crazy,' I say, getting ready to ask the obvious question. Properly this time. 'Then it turns out they're just ordinary people, only they want you to *think* they're crazy. But Spack Attack Tomlinson is the real deal. A genuine maniac.'

The barman's wrinkled brow furrows deeper.

I watch him now, with his big happy shirt and his big friendly nose. This big man with his big pores, he's wiping the same glass like he'll get three wishes if he does that for long enough. I bet I know what one of those wishes would be.

I say, 'So?' And rest my face on my hand, propped on the bar.

He looks up from the floor, glares back. 'What?'

I have to raise my head from my hand to speak. 'Why did you give him the wrong directions to the Boatswain's Club?'

'Hey?'

'You sent him to the Blue Fandango.'

'No.' He shakes his head urgently, laughs. 'I didn't.'

'The Boatswain's Club is on Elizabeth Street, not Locust Lane.'

He laughs again, shakes his head. Shrugs, shakes his head again, shrugs again. 'That's what I told him. I told him Elizabeth—'

'You sent him to the Blue Fandango. A bondage club. A bondage club that's got a sign right there on the street that says: *No Women, No Straight Men.*'

'No...'

'All right,' I grunt. My elbow slips off the bar and I sit up a little straighter. 'But when Tomlinson comes back and stabs you in the neck with that umbrella of his, don't go telling me *then* you didn't—'

'I used to work at the Boatswain's Club,' he blurts, gripping the wooden edge of the counter, staring at it.

That cuts my annoyance short.

He's finally stopped polishing that clean, clean glass. He says, 'It's one of those pretentious joints, right? Like when you buy a pack of cigarettes and the bartender opens them for you and pulls one out of the pack. I was always shit at sucking up to patrons...I hated it. And they sacked me. Some teenager with big tits got my job and now I'm stuck pouring drinks in this shithole.'

A car horn bleats right outside and a pained voice responds, *'Fuck off.'*

The barman doesn't seem to hear them. He says, 'People come in here all the time looking for the Boatswain's Club, but I send them to that faggot bar instead because...Just to get my own back, you know?'

His words hang there, glued to the air around us.

He says, 'I guess I've made a mistake.'

'My word,' I say.

I take another sip, then another small one, and I shake my head, try to change gear.

'It's no big deal. He'll get lost in the rain. Someone will give him directions. He'll find his way to the Boatswain's Club.'

The bartender nods, trying to believe it. His tongue works back and forth across his bottom lip, seeking reassurance. He says, 'Maybe he isn't that crazy anymore.'

'Maybe not.'

He waves the glass in the air as he speaks. 'Maybe prison sorted him out. Maybe he got treatment. He looked good, yeah? Well dressed. Maybe he's a normal person now.'

'Sure,' I say.

'Like you said, all that...that stuff...' And he points at me. 'That was a long time ago, right?' But even as he speaks, his eyes skip over to the door, wondering if it's about to open.

I say, 'A long time ago. Yes.'

He nods, satisfied, then turns to shelve that glass with the rest. He reaches it up to the wooden mantel above the register.

The girl over in the dining area laughs, a shrill giggle, not that loud—but it's enough to make the bartender flinch and he drops the glass.

It smashes on the floor.

For a moment he doesn't move, paralysed but still standing. Then he lowers his hands to his knees and he stays like that for several moments.

The rain isn't getting any lighter. If anything it's more intense. The noise of the street is like a meteor approaching.

I finish the last of my drink. 'I can go find him for you.'

At first he doesn't respond, still bent over like there's something on the floor that's more interesting.

Then, softly, he says, 'Really?'

'Yes.'

'What will you do if you find him?'

'Spin him a line. Get him to the Boatswain's Club. Make sure he forgets all about you.'

Slowly, he straightens up and rests himself on the bar. 'You can do that?'

Not being able to hadn't occurred to me. I say, 'Yes.'

'You'd do that for me?'

I try not to smirk. 'I'll do it for that bottle of Old Forester up there on your top shelf.' I point.

He turns to look. When he turns back he's thinking. 'Will you find him in time?'

'That red umbrella of his should stand out well enough.'

The barman tries to see through to my deeper layers. 'How do I know you'll really do it? How do I know you won't just take the bottle and go home?'

I lean forward on the bar. 'I've got a better one. How do you know the story I told you is even true? Perhaps I made it up to shake a bottle of whiskey out of you and I've never seen that guy before and I don't even know his name.'

'Is that what this is? Are you having me on?'

'Nope.'

He sifts through it all in his head—the clock, the Old Forester on the shelf, the half-drunk stranger who, as it turns out, isn't the one having the bad day. Then the tension evaporates, and there's nothing in his eyes but cool acceptance.

He goes back to the shelf and, tiptoeing briefly, brings down a bottle of Old Forester whiskey. I'm trying to show him my disapproval, but again he can't interpret it, so I tell him, 'The sealed bottle.'

I can imagine he wouldn't last long at the Boatswain's Club.

He's a man who doesn't like to be at a disadvantage. Now, as he swaps the half-empty bottle for the full one, he exhales, gentle and long, like I'm testing his patience. Like this is the last favour he does for me and I should stop asking.

Before he offers me the bottle he says, 'You *are* going to find him, right?'

The bell rings, and the fear is back in his face. His eyes bug out at the door like it's a horde of Indians come to ransack the camp. But it's two businessmen fresh from the office, dripping wet. They trot to the counter and one of them says, 'Two Johnnies, rocks.'

I yank the bottle from the bartender's grip, don't say anything. I feel his eyes on my back as I reach the door.

The man says, 'Hey barman, two Johnnies, on the rocks, please.'

As I step out into the rain, I hear him say, 'Hey barman, why the long face?'

Leaving the Fountainhead, I hear the two men laugh.

TROY

APART FROM THE chains and the dumbbells and stripped-back style of a prison rec room, the first thing you notice is the mirrors. They cover each of the walls, all of each wall and the ceiling, so you'd have to lie face down on the floor if you didn't want to look at yourself.

Not that these guys have that problem.

The mirrors multiply everything a thousand times over. When I first step in the door I don't see three topless men lifting weights and bulking up, I see a whole army doing that, reflected dimly against the makeshift gymnasium, all of them focused hard on what part of their body they're making bigger.

So focused that they don't see me. This is a big shed at the end of George's driveway, and George didn't invite me here tonight, so we'll probably get off to a bad start, me and these beefcakes, if only one of them will take their attention off themselves for a moment. They grunt and sometimes yelp with exertion, then smack the weights down with a metallic *thunk*. Everywhere is the stink of sweat and supermarket baby oil and there's eurotrash house music playing softly on a small tape deck. They could play it a whole lot louder if they wanted to—it's not like George's neighbours are going to come and complain.

Jimmy, the one with the thickest neck, is the first to see me. He's working his forearms, kneeling at a wooden bench with two massive black dumbbells, when he catches one of my reflections. Even when he sees me, his face full of angry suffering, the one like he's passing a kidney stone, he doesn't seem to care. He's got a good burn going. He doesn't stop his reps *or* his sets.

Ross is an anglo who wants to be Greek. He swings his leg back and forth from a metal frame, raising and lowering an impossible stack of black tiles using a cable that's hooked around his ankle. Each one of these weightlifters wears a loose-fitting singlet, tiny, tight shorts and sandals, but Ross's pale skin doesn't set off the outfit like the olive brawn of his companions. When Ross sees me, he does a double-take and blurts a cry of disapproval.

'*Oi!*'

George looks up from where he's changing weights on the bench press. There's no recognition, just a startled kind of curiosity at how a stranger could so brazenly wander onto his property. He opens those black eyes wide, waiting for me to say who I am. I don't.

So George says, 'Who the fuck are you?'

George took up bodybuilding at high school because the other kids used to tease him. Also because he was scrawny and hairless and hated himself. Only, you start pumping weights at a young age and all that protein that should be making you taller is instead making your pectorals bulge out in big circles. And look at the result: George is only four and a half feet tall.

Jimmy lets out a roar and drops the dumbbells. They thud against each other on the padded mat beneath him. His eyes roll back in his head, then his head rolls forward, his arms outstretched on the wooden bench like he's worshipping the nearby rowing machine.

'This is a nice set-up you've got, George. Good and big,' I say, smiling the best I can. 'Do with a few more mirrors, though...'

'I think you might be in the wrong place, mate.' George says this loud. Thin lips sneer unpleasantly, lined by dark fluff that's the fashion in Greek nightclubs, and this seems to be the only place on his body he's willing to grow hair. Everywhere else, including the top of his head, is waxed and shiny.

I say, 'No, George. I'm looking for some black.'

This rouses Jimmy from his stretching. He's just as built as George, with a golden hue, even under these ticking fluoros, that might be a spray tan. I've spoken a magic word. Suddenly I have his attention.

Ross's eyes flick to George. George offers nothing. He stares into me. The music has stopped and in the silence the sweet chirp of suburban crickets trickles in from the night outside.

Slowly, George steps over the bench press and approaches, swinging his arms out from his body like his muscles are just too damn big. He stops well out of reach, giving me the look: confusion tinged with a distant sense of relish because I might be someone he can get angry at. The leather weight belt that's tight around his waist emphasises his triangular frame, but his height invites comparisons not with the winners of bodybuilding contests, but with the trophies those winners take home.

Before I can properly formulate the wisecrack, George says, 'I think you definitely got the wrong place, mate. We don't got none of that shit.'

'I heard you do.'

'From who?' He juts his chin at me. 'Who says?'

'Everybody says, don't they?'

Spend any time around bodybuilders and you'll hear about

blaxitarine, dubbed *black*, a superhormone designed to grow the cells in your muscles and bones and to do it faster than any other anabolic steroid. Nastier, too.

It used to be that the side effects of steroid abuse were innocent enough: acne, infertility, premature baldness. But the way a mean-spirited cartoonist would draw you arguing with the supermarket cashier, that's you when you're on black.

If you were buried in a mineshaft and your only hope was to punch your way out, black could help you do it.

If you had to fight off a zombie invasion all by yourself, black might be just the charge you need.

Or you could end up like the guy in California, who levelled his neighbour's home, a whole weatherboard house, using just a baseball bat.

'You better fuck off, mate,' George says. His eyes are bugging out at me like he's using voodoo. 'We don't want no skip cunts in here.'

I point to Ross. 'What about that skip cunt?'

Ross flinches at my words, but a smile draws across his chin. He's excited too, I suppose, because I'm asking for it. With his eyebrows raised he takes two steps towards me and intends to take more but he's forgotten his ankle is still chained to the machine and he goes down hard on one knee.

George doesn't take his eyes off me. He whispers slowly, 'What did you fucking say?'

Ross unhooks the chain and rises quickly to his feet, humiliation radiating from his round face.

I say to George, 'I think he heard me.'

The energy in George is building. He scans me from my feet to my head, searching for a reason not to decapitate me with a single punch.

'You a pig?' He laughs like he's figured it out. 'You're a pig, hey...'

'I'm not a pig. I'm just an ordinary bloke looking to improve his muscle tone.'

Black is the only substance they test for at the International Federation of Bodybuilders. Not because it's dangerous. They just got tired of competitors stepping up on stage with blood pouring out of their nose. That's another side effect—the membrane in your nose breaks open when your heartbeat speeds up.

Ross is two feet taller than George. I can tell because he's standing next to George now, cross-armed and vacant even as he's concentrating. Jimmy's watching, chewing on his bottom lip like it's gum. Ross is an orphan who never had anyone to look up to until he met George, but all I could find out about Jimmy is that he owns the '73 Charger parked outside in the driveway and he loves it like a son. He doesn't let people wear shoes when they're inside it.

'Shit,' says George, grinning. His teeth have been straightened since the last time I saw him. 'You don't need black, mate. You need a good diet, you know? Lots of amino acids and that. Don't they teach you nothing at police school?'

He laughs, turns to Ross and Jimmy, who laugh in turn. It's an outlet for the energy pulsing through the veins in their foreheads, in the reds of their eyes.

I say, 'Why don't you shut your wog mouth and get me the black.'

I've never called anyone a wog before. It's kind of thrilling.

Another story going around is, a guy on black drew a picture of his wife on a concrete wall and bashed it until his arms were bloody stumps.

Subtly, Ross hops from foot to foot with excitement. 'Awww, mate.'

He speaks like a Greek, with George's same rhythms and drones. George is still glaring at me, chomping down on his lower lip just like Jimmy, trying to figure me out. He takes another step closer.

'You better watch your mouth, skippy. The last cunt who spoke shit to me got no fucking teeth left.' He steps closer again. 'We don't got no fucking black. So you better *fuck off*. Dumb cunt. 'Fore I kick your cunt face in.'

An acrid odour is drifting into the shed from outside. I take a big sniff out of the air and furrow my brow, distracted. 'Something smells funny…' I say this loud so Jimmy will hear me clearly. Ross's nose twitches sideways.

'He fucking stinks of booze,' Ross says. 'He's fucking pissed, hey.'

George's right hand slaps absently against his thigh as he thinks. Now Jimmy tips forward, alert. 'Yeah, I smell it.' He says. 'Phwoooh, it fucking stinks, hey. What the fuck is that?'

Another story about black is, it generates so much testosterone that your testicles stop working and shrivel up like raisins. One guy had prosthetics implanted because his real ones disappeared altogether.

I wait, try to give George a knowing smile, but my lips are trembling. I bite down and raise my eyebrows.

'You wondering what that smell is, George?'

George tries to know what I mean.

Dramatically, I glance around the room. In the mirrors, everywhere I look, there's me looking back.

'Yeah,' he says. 'You fucking stink, man.'

'Yeah. Sorry. I had a little accident. Outside. With your cars.'

That's all it takes to get Jimmy on his feet.

'What did he fucking say?'

'On my way up the drive, I tripped and accidentally stupidly spilled sulphuric acid over the Pontiac and the Charger out there…'

George's body starts to clench and spasm, as well as his face. His lips make a number of different shapes but he can't speak.

Jimmy's gone, running to the door. He steps out into the dark.

I glare at George glaring at me.

Just knowing Jimmy is out there, I can hear all the sounds of the suburbs. The crickets, dogs barking, a distant highway.

Then Jimmy saying, '*Shit*.'

George keeps glaring, shiny body twitching, his foot tapping the floor. He breathes even deeper.

I whisper to him, 'I'm *really* sorry.'

Jimmy's voice: '...*Fucking shit, man*...'

George's eyes close.

Now is when his nose starts to bleed.

I whisper to George, 'You don't remember me, do you?'

Another rumour about black is, it makes you forget stuff. One guy at an ATM got so frustrated trying to remember his pin number, he punched himself repeatedly in the temple and gave himself a haemorrhage, right there on the footpath.

The first blow doesn't come from George. It comes from Jimmy, who re-enters George's shed, makes an angry beeline from the door to the back of my head. I make a beeline to the floor.

The alcohol in my system makes my head swim more than it otherwise would. I rise onto my elbows. Jimmy can barely speak.

'The duco's...the duco's fucking melted off...off both them. This cunt's fucking wrecked them, man. They're fucking *wrecked*.'

On that last word he stamps down on my face with his sandal.

'Let's pour acid over *him*,' says Ross. 'That's what we should do. We should pour acid over this cunt.'

'Is he a cop or what?' Jimmy asks.

George doesn't answer. He's staring at me, trying to remember who I am. He wipes a trickle of blood from his nose and I realise my nose is bleeding too. Because of Jimmy's sandal.

Eventually he murmurs, 'How come I know this cunt?'

'You know him?' Jimmy asks.

'He's not a cop...' George scowls. 'I can't fucking...' He comes down over me with both hands on my collar, raises me to his face. Some of his blood splashes across my cheek and the rest of it he sniffs back.

Face to face, it's only him holding me up.

'Who the fuck *are* you?' he says. 'How come I know you?'

My right eye is swelling already. I know that feeling. There's blood running into my ear.

'Miresha Yusedich was my client.' With as much fake pride as I can muster, I say, 'I'm the guy who put Spiros away for eleven years.'

The scowl disappears from his face, then his hands loosen and I'm on the floor again.

Jimmy nods vigorously. 'Yeah. I remember. His name's John something. He's a fucking *arsehole*.'

I slowly rise back to my feet.

'Not anymore,' I say. 'I lost my licence.'

'*He* came *here*, right?' Jimmy's voice rises to a shriek. His excitement merges with the black in his system. 'He's fucking trespassing. We can do whatever we want.'

'Yeah,' says Ross. 'It's *trespassing*, George? Isn't it?'

Jimmy says, 'Yeah, it *is*. Let's fucking…Let's fucking…'

George slowly nods. We hold each other's eyes and he's squinting, as if there's something inside me he can't see properly.

I say, 'Do these fellas know it was you who killed Osman Yusedich? Do they know you let your brother go to jail for it?'

On my way here tonight, I thought *that* comment would be what finally tipped George over the edge. He screws his mouth into a ball and I can hear his teeth grinding together.

Judging by Ross and Jimmy's reaction, they either knew the truth about George or they're so high on black that nothing can distract them from the prospect of destroying me with their bare, giant hands.

George's whole body is ticking energy. I wink at it.

'I hear your brother's good in the showers. If you know what I mean.'

George sucks in a long stream of air through his nose.

I say, 'They love him in there. They've got him doing all kinds of stuff.'

For all I know there's been no kind of assault on Spiros Angelis. But speaking the truth isn't what I came here to do.

I'm not expecting George to go straight for my groin but that's what he does. What he finds there he grips and after a moment of trying to wrench it free he hooks into my guts with his other arm and I double over and then a knee strikes me twice across the skull and I go down again.

They pile in. Leather sandals and naked fists strike in succession, so fast and so intense that I can't even push up to all fours.

Then George tells them to stop. And they stop.

In the numb silence it's my balls that hurt most.

George leans over and he says slowly, 'What did you say, cunt? About my brother? I would like you to repeat it because I didn't hear you.'

I get up to my knees and I reach out and get George by the buckle of his leather belt, pull him a couple of weak inches closer.

'I said, what they really love about Spiros is how he cries out for his mother while they're fucking him. They say that makes it so much sweeter.'

There's nothing in his eyes when I look up at him and smile.

He whispers, 'You're fucked now, cunt.'

George shudders and waves his hands for Jimmy and Ross to move out of the way. They move.

George takes me by the collar, holds me bent over and runs me across the room, my feet scraping against the floor. Looking up, there's me hurtling towards me. I can hear George screaming and someone else is screaming and just before my head collides with its own reflection I see my eyes and I see that the other person screaming is me.

2

There are two of them, a tall one and a short one, both in their late twenties and both with a heavy layer of acne on their necks like an infection one contracted from the other. The short one is ginger-headed, freckle-faced, neckless and about as Scottish as a person can be without an accent. The other is obviously Italian but he also talks like he was born here, sports close to a full growth although it's only midday. Despite all this, the uniform makes them look like brothers.

The short one says, 'Had you had dealings with George Angelis prior to Sunday night?'

The tall one says, 'You knew the bloke, right? At least tell us you knew the bloke before you wrecked his car for him.'

They're talking to me as I stare at the ceiling. Ceilings in hospitals are covered with power points. I've been here three days, but until this line of questioning I never noticed the power points. I've got an icy sheet pulled up to my chin but it's no defence against these cops.

'I'd never met George before,' is what I say. And that's the truth.

Until right now, I've had this entire ward to myself for all of those three days. Propped in a corner bed, I've watched the sky through the window to my left, or I've watched the TV that's bolted to the roof, or I've watched the heads move past the windows in the doors at the far end of the room. Between here and there has been a sea of empty beds, which has meant solitude, which has meant paradise. Now, most of the beds are hidden from view because the curtain is drawn on the bed next to mine. I don't remember anyone moving in there, but twenty minutes ago I woke up to find myself in a private little grotto these uniforms are using for an interrogation room.

The short one says, 'Yeah, Mister Angelis claims that *you* inflicted the damage to his car. With acid, sort of thing. That right?'

Demetri, slouching on the dressing table beside me, says, 'John's in no condition to be interrogated regarding anything for which he might later be charged.' He glares past his bushy eyebrows at the tall one. 'You know that.'

What I'm in no condition for doing is anything other than sitting in this bed and watching that TV. Someone must have switched it off while I was asleep. This is the first time I've seen it switched off in all these last three days and I've been watching it all that time: I can tell you exactly when each network schedules a current affairs show or a news bulletin. All that terrible stuff, you can't help but think that whoever it happened to deserved it. I even caught a glimpse of George Angelis, a story on how the AFP had seized a pile of illegal steroids.

The short one says, 'Did you have any prior knowledge of…of the Federal Police?'

'Prior to last Sunday night? Yes, I had heard of the Federal Police.'

'I mean, of their intention to execute a warrant.'

'No.'

The tall one says, 'You didn't get a tip-off from someone? Like your mate, Detective Burke?'

'No. And he works for Victoria Police.'

'So it was just a coincidence that you were there at that time?'

'Yes.' That's the truth, too.

'Come on, matey. For real. How did you find out?'

You'd think they'd go easy on someone with this many stitches in his forehead. My scalp is shaved and my eye sockets are swollen from the surgery, so I look worse now than I did when I arrived at this place, unconscious and bloodied. Today the swelling is starting to recede, leaving a grey patch where my cheekbones should be. I look pitiful, but I hadn't expected these cops to *doubt* me. At least, not the parts that are true.

'He's already answered that question,' Demetri says, examining his fingernails.

Last night I saw Demetri on the TV. He was interviewed about a criminal trial that ended a month ago. They overlaid the interview with footage of Demetri exiting the County Court, following his client: a middle-aged woman with blonde hair and dark roots who high-heeled her way along William Street, ignoring the questions yelled by reporters, ignoring the cameramen who ran to get ahead of her. What the stations love to do is play the footage of her when she was first arrested, covering her face with her jacket as she was driven into the city holding cells. They played that repeatedly over the interview with Demetri. It makes her look so guilty. Who cares that she was acquitted.

Next to me, Demetri wriggles against the wonky white cabinet. If he peeked behind it he'd see the bottle of whisky I've got stashed back there. I was surprised when the nurse agreed to smuggle it in for me, but I guess they get weirder requests than that. I guess they'll give the patients anything to keep them manageable.

Demetri says, 'Did they find what they were looking for?'

The short one says, 'Hey?'

'Your mates in the raiding party.'

The short one looks at the tall one, makes his fucking-lawyers face.

Before Demetri got here, these two had already filled me in on what happened Sunday night. In between telling me over and over how lucky I was to be alive, enough times that I almost apologised for it, they said that three men were in the process of beating me to death when nine federal officers sauntered into George's enormous shed at the end of George's enormous driveway and suggested that, rather than beating me to death, these three men should instead provide access to areas of the property listed on the Magistrates Court warrant the officers had brought with them. This list included the attic above George's gym where George kept a commercial quantity of blaxitarine. According to them, George snuck in a good last kick to my groin and stomped to death my mobile phone before he was properly restrained and charged, but I didn't notice because I wasn't conscious. If I'd been conscious, I could have told George that a commercial quantity of blaxitarine means jail.

'Has it occurred to anyone to charge Angelis with assault?' Demetri asks.

'There's plenty of time for that, matey,' the tall one says. The way he says it, he'd sneak in a good last kick to Demetri's groin.

When I saw Demetri interviewed on TV last night, I wound the volume up loud. You can do that when there's no one else in your ward. At one point the good nurse came in, the one who bought me the whisky, and asked if I was having trouble hearing. She thought it might be an effect of the surgery. I told her that I knew the guy on the TV and wanted to hear all of what he said, because I knew nothing about the case except for what I'd read in the newspapers. When she realised what the case was, she shook her head and tut-tutted, 'Oh, she didn't do it. Those kids are having everyone on.' Then she waddled away, leaving me to sip my whisky and watch the TV all alone.

The short one says, 'On the night in question, had you been drinking, or any drugs…sort of thing?'

'I might have had a couple of drinks.'

'Celebrating something?' the tall one asks.

'Just life.'

He says, 'Can you at least tell us what you were doing there at George's gym?'

I'm thinking about the interview I saw on TV last night because

I don't want to think about the one that's happening right now.

The reporter who took the interview introduced the story like this: 'A year ago, Belinda Norman was a well-respected art teacher at St Ninian's, an exclusive private school in Melbourne's eastern suburbs. Since then, Belinda's world has fallen down around her.'

And again, there was Belinda in the backseat of the police car, jacket up to her face. Slow-motion. Dramatic music.

'Last month, a jury found Belinda Norman not guilty of unlawful sexual intercourse with two male students. Her victory was short-lived, however. The very next day, civil proceedings were launched in the Federal Court by lawyers acting for the boys seeking damages for psychological injury. The writs allege that Norman engaged in a sexual relationship with the then-year-ten boys late last year, and as a result, the students suffered post-traumatic stress disorder and depression.'

The TV showed two boys loitering outside the County Court, both in suits, their faces blurred.

'With that trial beginning only five days from now, I sat down with Demetri Sfakiakopoulos, Belinda Norman's solicitor, to find out more about the case that has transfixed a nation.'

What this journalist means is that the case has transfixed the nation's *news media*. If Belinda Norman were even remotely unattractive, this would be another sad story buried on page eight among the overseas riots and the celebrity marriages. But these two boys claim to have scaled the Mount Everest of the male libido: sex, repeatedly, with their *desirable* high school teacher. Old men in editorial positions are transfixed, so the rest of us have to be too.

There was Demetri in his crisp charcoal suit, wispy white hair and bulbous nose, smiling awkwardly. Offscreen, the reporter said, 'Mister Sfakiakopoulos, thanks for joining me.'

'You're welcome,' he croaked. Then he coughed. You could tell he was sitting on the bottom edge of his jacket so it didn't bunch around his shoulders. He's done this kind of interview before.

The reporter asked, 'Hasn't this question already been decided in the criminal courts? Why are these proceedings any different?'

Demetri smiled. He'd been tossed a sitter for starters.

'Because the standard of proof is lower in civil proceedings. Rather than prove the case beyond all reasonable doubt, which, as we all know, is the standard of proof in a criminal case, in these proceedings the allegations need only be shown to be likely on the balance of probabilities. It's an *easier* standard for Belinda's accusers to attain. Proving guilt is very difficult in a criminal trial.'

And I thought to myself, tell that to Spiros Angelis.

I say to the tall one, 'I know George's brother, Spiros. He's in prison. I was asking after him.'

'Why not just go visit him in prison?

'I kind of helped put him there. I don't think he'd be happy to see me.'

The short one asks, 'What'd you expect to find out?'

'Nothing.' My voice is a hoarse whimper. I've hardly spoken at all in the three days I've been here. I look the tall one right in the eye. 'I guess I was after some kind of closure.'

There's a creak and a rustle from the bed next to mine. The curtain wraps all the way around that bed, cocooning whoever it is, trapping them inside our soap opera.

I guess I can't play the television as loud as I want from now on.

During the interview with Demetri they played a clip of Paul Norman, Belinda's husband, addressing the media pack after Belinda's acquittal. He had a naturally dishevelled look and a flushed complexion and it was more than the strain of the trial that you could see in his eyes. I picked him for a committed drinker.

He said, 'If they pursue damages, a claim for damages, I'm

confident their story will be shown to be entirely fictitious. *Again*. But, you know, some comfort that'll be. This has all had a terrible effect on my family. On Belinda, her mental state, and financially we're ruined. These kids have ruined us.'

Then it cut back to the interview with Demetri and he said, 'I believe Paul has a point there. Lying to a court is difficult. That's where I think the Crown's case fell apart. The boys simply lacked credibility. People don't generally realise how difficult it is to falsify evidence convincingly under the glare of a jury. It's hard enough lying to the police.'

Now, when the short one asks why George and his friends attacked me, I say, 'I don't remember.' So I guess *I'm* not having much trouble lying to the police.

The Italian one rolls his big brown eyes and says, 'Mate, we're just trying to figure out what happened.'

'You think I don't want to?' My voice cracks.

The short one says, 'You could be a little more, like, cooperative.'

I push up on my elbows. 'You think I don't want to know how I ended up here? Look at what they did to me.' I point with one dainty hand to my face. 'I am scarred for *life*. I almost *died*. This has been the worst thing to ever *happen* to me. And I can assure *you*, officers, that I am just as keen as you are to get to the bottom of what took place that *terrible* night.'

I drop flat onto the bed. My head hits the pillow hard for emphasis.

Demetri, standing there next to me, pats me gently on the shoulder.

'Obviously John's still recovering from the surgery. How about we give him a chance to rest, you blokes come back later...'

The two of them look at one another. Conversing without words.

I say, 'I *really* don't remember what happened...'

Demetri says, 'I think that's enough for today, boys.'

But the way he pats my shoulder again, he's speaking to me. That's enough from *me*.

The short one rests his hand on his gun. 'I suppose we'll come back then.' He heads for the door.

The tall one uncrosses his arms and steps towards me. 'If your memory miraculously returns, do let us know. And if I find out you had anything to do with that shit George Angelis was selling, I'm going to put you in the same prison as him, right in the same fucking cell. Understand me?'

'Yes, officer.'

Their footsteps trail off and leave a silence. Now the room seems brighter. The sun has come out from the clouds and it pours in through the window, turning the grey walls a clinical blue. Demetri waddles over to that side of the room where the window is, his hands deep in his pockets, staring down at his shoes.

'That was cute, what you told them. *Closure.*' And he makes exaggerated bunny ears with his fingers. 'You make it sound like you went there to put the whole Spiros chapter behind you.'

'I did.'

'Come on, John.' He holds a gaze on me, but it's interrupted by two self-conscious glances at the next bed, where the curtain is. His voice drops.

'You and I both know what you went there for.'

I peer right back at him, for long enough until he turns away, takes another step closer to the window, looks out. The sunlight across his face burns white and he's hard to look at, so I almost don't catch his soft startle.

He's seen something, or someone, three storeys down where the carpark is. Or maybe I'm the one who's seeing things. There's still a load of drugs in my system.

I say, 'Did you know Kevin Tomlinson's out of prison?'

He takes several seconds to react. When he does he speaks gently into the glass and it fogs. 'Christ. Is there any good news?'

'He's working in real estate now. Or that's what he says. Wears a suit and everything.'

He sways a few steps away from the light towards me, still with those hands in his trousers, a remnant of his private school childhood. He's got wrinkles where he used to have dimples and his nose somehow lacks the nobility it once glowed with.

He says, 'Yeah, well, hey. Things change. Speaking of blasts from the past, you remember Leo Spaske? Your opposite number at the Neil Bighuty trial?'

'Sure,' I say. 'He got defrocked just like I did.'

'He was given leave to reapply for his licence. Which he did. He's working again.'

I show Demetri no reaction to that.

He pouts and raises his eyebrows in a familiar way that used to be fatherly and is now grandfatherly. 'It might be time for *you* to reapply, John. Get back on the horse.'

This morning, on one of those TV breakfast shows, they reported that the two boys had started a Belinda Norman fan club on Facebook. This is before their alleged sexual relationship with her, and they didn't use their real names. One of them called her a MILF and the other one wrote a dirty limerick about what it would be like to literally be her underpants.

It was a journalist who found that out. But it's just the sort of thing a private investigator would be asked to find out.

'I can't do that shit anymore,' I tell Demetri.

'I can get you work. You know I can.'

Demetri doesn't drop the paternal stare, so I turn away to face the curtain.

'Come on,' Demetri's voice raises slightly in pitch. 'You haven't been out of the game that long.'

'I felt this way before the Pioneer Hotel,' I say to the curtain. 'I can't do it anymore.'

'What about the money you owe me?'

This is where I'd turn away dismissively if I hadn't just done that. But even with my back to him, I can still see his shadow, thrown against the curtain from the brightness of the window. And even in his shadow I can see the disapproval in his face.

After I lost my licence Demetri kept up the rent on my office and sometimes I did work for him but mostly he just gave me cash so that I could maintain the supply of vodka that was, some weeks, the only reason I ever left the office. I kept the blinds drawn and the whole place was a flood of newspapers I meant to throw away but never did and when Demetri came by he'd always say how it was worse than the studio apartment I used to rent in Footscray. He'd drop a few fifties on the desk, the desk I didn't use for work anymore, and he always did that at the end of his visit, on his way out, so I could pretend not to notice, so I didn't need to get all proud and insist he keep his crappy money. After he'd gone I'd clutch at it and stagger downstairs, hunched and allergic to sunlight, every muscle in my face taut and reddened. I'd buy alcohol and noodles and another newspaper and scutter back to thaw out again in the dark.

Demetri says, 'I tally it to be approximately five thousand dollars.'

There was some kind of conversation, when he first began to pay my rent for me. I think I promised to work the money off.

'I'm not in a hurry for it, John. I'd just like you to think about it the next time you go looking for *closure*.'

His shadow makes those bunny ears again and I exhale sharply. It earns me a jag of pain in my forehead.

Demetri says, 'Let's drop it. You see me on TV?'

The room dims, the sun goes behind a cloud and Demetri's

shadow folds back into the hospital curtain. I turn my head back to him. He's smirking at me.

I say, 'Yes.'

Demetri was smirking on TV when he said, 'The boys had a crush on Belinda Norman and this lawsuit was prompted by their sense of rejection. The male ego is a delicate thing.'

Still smirking, he swings away and wanders proudly towards the beds on the far side of the room. I won't tell him that for part of the interview his jacket was bunched around his shoulders. The male ego is a delicate thing.

'They're claiming for post-traumatic stress disorder. Can you believe that? Not only are they asking us to believe that Belinda actually shagged these two drongos, they want us to believe they're traumatised by it.'

I push myself around to face him. 'You don't think she did it?'

Demetri doesn't hesitate. 'Nope. This woman is gorgeous. Have you seen her? If she wanted to cheat on her husband, she could have any man she liked. It's inconceivable that she'd do it with a couple of pimply kids.'

'So the boys are lying?'

'If ever I met teenagers who could lie about it, it's those two. And that's exactly what the jury thought. We're not talking about a couple of confused children here, John. They have a history of fabricating sexual encounters with the girls in their class. They are savvy and sharp and they smell money. Or at least their parents do.'

I sit up in the bed now, feel the throbbing in my forehead peak and combine with a soft sting. These are the first real sensations I've had since I woke from the surgery. I put my hand to my forehead, feel the scabbing around the stitches.

'Thanks for coming to see me,' I say. 'You must be busy. With all this going on.'

'Yeah,' he says. His voice sounds distant. He ambles back to the window and looks out, back down to the carpark.

'Actually, I came along for more than one reason. I wanted to see how you were, but...' He twitches a smile at me, then chases it away with his serious face. 'Something's come up.'

What I think he's going to say is that he can't afford me anymore—not the rent on my office or the handouts I live on. I prepare for it, readjust myself in the bed. But what he says next is nothing like that. What he says next, through the telescope of time, will have a much more powerful effect on me than mere homelessness and bankruptcy.

'Belinda and Paul Norman have a son. He's sixteen and he attends the same school, St Ninian's, where all this is supposed to have happened. So far he's remained mercifully uninteresting to the journos covering the story, but who knows how long that's going to last.'

Now that I'm sitting up in the bed there's room at the far end where my feet used to be. Demetri sags onto it, swivels to face me, carefully arranges his suit jacket.

'He didn't give evidence at the criminal trial because he's got nothing to give evidence about. And even if he had something, there are compellability laws that would keep him off the stand. But that's not the case in a civil trial. And the plaintiffs have subpoenaed him.'

'Even though he's got nothing to say?'

'That's right. They know how tough it will be for the poor bastard, giving evidence at a trial where his mother is accused of having sex with his classmates. And we're talking about a boy who's already a mess. He's on a bunch of antidepressants, he's been hospitalised for depression more than once, he's an ongoing suicide risk. And that's *before* any of this happened. The plaintiffs figure if they threaten to get him up on the stand, to examine him publicly about his mother's alleged sexual escapades, his parents'll cave. Settle rather than go to trial. To save the kid from that nightmare.'

I give another sharp exhale, get another jag of pain in my head. The numbness of the medication is wearing off, but not the other numbness. About what these litigants are doing to each other, I simply do not care.

Demetri says, 'His name's Troy. I only met him once. From what his parents tell me, he's got problems. But right now, so do they.'

'What did you come to see me for?'

There's a creak from the next bed. Maybe the person in there wants us to know they can overhear us. Or maybe they're wriggling in their sleep and all this talk is falling on deaf, sedated ears.

Demetri rotates his body as far as it will go and lowers his voice again. 'Belinda and Paul found out that Troy was going to be served, so they sent him off to stay with his Auntie Caroline in Colac, hoping the process server wouldn't find him there. Sending Troy away was against my advice, I should add.' Demetri gives another nervous look to the curtain. 'Not that it matters. The process server showed up in Colac. And guess who the process server turned out to be.'

It's Demetri's ironic tone of voice that gives it away.

'Leo Spaske.'

'Risen from the dead. Newly re-licensed. And the retainer he's on must be enormous.'

I can't help but rub my fingers along my scar again.

'So the kid got served. Sounds like there's nothing you can do that isn't going to be in contempt.'

'That's just it. He didn't get served. Leo rolled up in his big blue Valiant, screaming and threatening, telling the old woman if she didn't open the door he'd kick it down. He even slashed her tyres in case they tried to do another runner. Brought the old girl to tears. But when they got to Troy's room, Troy was gone. He'd packed a bag, swiped the old lady's purse, and no one's seen him since. That was three days ago.'

'Leo scared him off?'

'Nope. Troy was gone before Leo showed up. He's not running because he doesn't want to give evidence. He's running because he's just running. Like I said, the kid's a mess.'

'Why did Leo slash her tyres?'

Demetri shrugs. 'He's got to do something to justify what he charges.'

'You don't really think I'm going to take a job, do you? Look at me.'

'Come on. You must have tracked down a hundred runaways in your time.'

'Why don't you get someone real? With a licence.'

'There's no one better than you.'

'Even if I took the job, Leo's had three days' start on me. He'll find Troy before I do.'

'I don't think so.' Demetri tips forward off the bed. His worried eyebrows lead the way across to the window. 'I think Leo thinks we know where Troy is. That we've got him stashed away somewhere, keeping him hidden until after the trial. For the last two days, I've been seeing blue Valiants in my rearview mirror, outside my home. It's as if Leo thinks I'm going to lead him to the boy.'

Demetri points out the window. 'There's a blue Valiant down there, parked opposite my car…'

I prop up more rigidly against the pillows.

'If he followed you here, then he must think you've got Troy in the hospital. Which means he's in the hospital.'

And now, perfectly on cue, there's another creak from the bed next to mine.

Like carnival clowns, Demetri and I turn and stare at the nylon curtain that's been floating beside us all this while.

Demetri whispers, 'You're joking…'

He takes a step across the room and gazes at the doorway, then comes back to me.

'What do you think?'

'I don't know.'

We stare at the curtain like Leo is about to reveal himself: giggling and dressed in a hospital gown because he really does go that extra mile for his massive fee. But instead there's just silence. Nothing but the noise of the ventilation system carrying diseases from one ward to the next.

'Fuck him,' Demetri says finally. 'None of this is anything he doesn't know already. The more time he spends in that bed, the less time he's out there looking for Troy.' He turns back to me. 'So what do you say?'

'Leo's got too much to prove. And he's a nut.' I don't care if he can hear me. 'I'm not in any condition to go up against that.'

'He might be crazy, and he might be a *fucking arsehole*,' Demetri hisses this at the curtain. 'But he's not crazy enough to hurt you. He'll lose his licence for good.'

'How long until the subpoena terminates?'

'That's the good news. He's only got four days left. After that, they might request an adjournment, but by the grace of God we've pulled Justice Weir, who never gave an adjournment for anything in his life. So I think it's safe to say that the trial starts Monday whether Troy's been served or not. Time is on our side.'

'Then why go looking for Troy at all? Let the subpoena lapse and wait for him to come home when he runs out of money.'

'I put that same point to Belinda and Paul, but understandably, they're worried about their son. We're talking about a boy with serious personal problems. He's got about a thousand hang-ups and phobias. Anything could happen to him.'

'If I find Troy and try to keep him out of reach of a process server, that's perverting the course of justice.'

'You're being retained to track down a missing child. No one's asking you to keep Troy away from Leo Spaske.'

'But that's actually what you want me to do.'

'Absolutely not. No one's asking you to do that and you're not getting paid to do that.'

'Won't his parents get charged with the same thing, perhaps even for suborning a witness, by sending Troy to Colac?'

'That's not your problem. The way they see it, it was a worthwhile risk, to save Troy the experience of taking the stand, and they're prepared to face the music if it comes to that. It was their only option in the face of blackmail, which is what this is. The worst kind of blackmail, because it's directed at their son.'

I nod at the curtain.

'If Leo has been following you around, and if he knows you're here, then he knows you've asked me to do this. He might stick on my tail, wait for me to lead him to Troy.'

'That's what I'd do if I were him.'

'And you're telling me not to do anything about that?'

'I'm saying, I can't ask you to stop a witness being served with a subpoena. It's illegal and I could lose my certificate. That's what I'm saying.'

Demetri pulled that same trick last night on the TV. The journalist asked him, 'The school in question sacked Belinda Norman on the very day it heard about the allegations. If you're successful at trial, will she bring a compensation claim for unfair dismissal against St Ninian's?'

Demetri gently closed his eyes and opened them. 'Our focus right now is on the proceedings brought against Mrs Norman. There'll be plenty of time for other things after the trial.'

The journalist smirked, put on his fucking-lawyers face.

'Surely you're considering it. Belinda was marched off campus and a letter was sent to parents calling your client a woman of loose moral character and implying that she was a sexual predator.'

'And I'm saying to you, our focus right now is on the trial that begins next week.'

Then there was a long pause while Demetri stared back at the reporter, and the reporter loved it. He let it linger as long as he could. Then: 'Demetri Sfakiakopoulos, thanks for your time.'

Now, when Demetri stares back at me with that same face, I say, 'You only want me for this because I've got less to lose if I get done for hiding a witness.'

He scowls, incredulous. 'That's not true—'

'You *are* worried about your certificate, and since *my* licence is gone, you think I'll be more manageable than a real private investigator—'

'You're the best. That's why I want you to do it.'

'Bullshit. You want me because if it goes sour, you've got a patsy—'

'Oh, just spare me the scattergun hatred, will you, John? Who do you think you're talking to?'

The jag of pain, this time it isn't in my forehead. I feel it even before he points out the obvious, his voice a scratching whisper. 'We worked together for, what, eight years? Did I ever fuck you over? Ever once? I've been paying your rent and keeping you alive while you have your little breakdown. What have I been doing that for? So I could rip you off? Jesus…'

I put away my fucking-lawyers face. I think I even hear Leo sigh on the other side of that curtain.

Demetri shakes his head, staring across at the window, the dark clouds beyond it. He exhales silently. 'You're so fucked up, you can't even see when…' He pushes a thumb and forefinger into his eyes. When he looks at me they're slightly red—part angry, part imploring.

'Try to imagine what this kid has been through. Those two

boys are the legends of St Ninian's. The rest of the school treats them like movie stars. You should hear some of the jokes the kids are making—'

'I don't need the sob story,' I say, scratching into my bald head. 'One more confused teen runaway isn't enough to get me up from this gurney. If I do it, it will be to repay my debt to you. And that's the only reason.'

'Repay your debt to me? This is one missing kid. You owe me for a bloody sight more than that.'

'I'm the best, remember? My rates just went up.'

Bustling footsteps enter the room and both Demetri and I turn to see a nurse, muscular and businesslike, oblivious to us. She makes for the bed directly opposite mine and pulls back the sheets, presses a button on a small remote control. The bed rises hydraulically.

Floating in silently behind her is a man so pale and so gaunt that there's a tinge of blue in his face and his hospital gown hangs off his body like it would hang off a wire coathanger. You can tell that the hollows of his cheeks are echoed in his stomach and hips. He senses the two of us and snaps his head around, eyes so bloodshot they're really two perfect pools of red. There's a small nose ring in one nostril and around his neck are ligature marks. Where the rope burned into his throat is now a purple line, neat and undeniable.

He locks eyes with me, knows what I'm looking at. He stands there and waits for the nurse to finish making up the bed and he stares right back at the scar on my forehead.

I wonder if I look as shattered as he does.

The woman sing-songs, 'In you go.' He climbs into the bed and the nurse shuffles away, leaving him weakly arranging his pillows.

Demetri interprets this activity as his cue to leave. There's a finality in his voice as he lowers it so the new patient can't hear.

'This place is like the Addams Family. You should have been out of here days ago. Come by the office this afternoon and meet

Belinda and Paul. You'll like them. They're drinkers.'

He rises off the bed, steps back to the window for one more look outside. His face tells me the Valiant is still there.

'I had a client once who thought Leo Spaske was after him for some unpaid invoices, so he booby-trapped his front door and all his windows. He actually had a nail bomb hidden inside his porch light. Leo Spaske can do that to you.'

The new patient lies in his bed, unmoving. A rock under a sheet.

Demetri turns to face me again, his hands thrust back in his pockets. 'One more thing. The nature of a Victorian subpoena is that it's considered to have been served if the person in question has actual knowledge of its contents. Troy doesn't know they're trying to get him to take the stand and if he finds out, then arguably, technically, he's been served.'

My throat burns from all this talking. 'What does he think he was doing in Colac?'

'Just that his parents thought he needed a break. Because school was tough for him.'

'So if I find him I shouldn't tell him?'

'That's not your job. You're just the delivery man.'

I nod. I'd happily do this job as Marcel Marceau. If I'm lucky, Troy will be the silent type too and the whole thing will be over in a few quiet hours.

'After this, we're square, right?'

'Yeah,' he says, disapproval written across his face like toilet graffiti. 'After this you can go looking for all the closure you want.'

He doesn't do the bunny ears this time. Instead he bows his head, makes a theatrical shrug and turns to leave, then stops.

'So long, Leo,' he calls into the curtain.

From inside there comes silence. Demetri pivots to grin at me. 'Always was a rude bastard.'

Then he disappears. I hear his footsteps pad out the door, the door swing shut. The moment he's gone I hear a creak and a thud from behind the curtain. Someone shifting, perhaps sitting up. The rustling continues and I realise they're standing now, whoever they are. I watch, waiting to see if Leo shows himself or if he sneaks off the other side, out of sight.

But no. The curtain yanks open right in front of me.

She's in her early twenties, shockingly thin, with long brittle hair and bags under her eyes. The beady sternness of her gaze has nothing to do with me; it seems to be just her natural disposition. She hovers there in front of a metal bed and a tall table with nothing on it, then gingerly reaches to a cabinet this side of the curtain and opens a door, takes out a book I can't see the title of. Just before she draws the curtain shut she falls back onto the bed and looks at me with only a shade of curiosity.

I glimpse her wrists, thickly bandaged from the base of each hand to halfway up her forearms. Then she's gone from view.

The man in the bed across from me hasn't moved.

Maybe the idea is to put us all in here together.

3

Some guy gets on at the first floor and stares at me. I don't look back. It's just the two of us in here and, compared to the buttons and the marble-pattern floor, I'm probably the most interesting thing. My head is shaved. I've got a scar on my brow the shape of a question mark and it's big and recent enough to look like I came straight from the asylum, freshly lobotomised. I won't grow hair in that spot for at least twelve months, is what the surgeon said. I'd stare at me too.

He's a tourist, wealthy, maybe Korean. Like I'd know. There must be a pool on level one because that's where he's come from, cloaked in a hotel robe and squeaky with chlorine. When the doors opened and he saw me, he didn't hide his revulsion. He wore it right there on his face and hobbled into the elevator and pushed the button for the eighth floor and then turned back to me to stock up on more revulsion and maybe that's how it goes in Korea. Maybe, in Korea, people are honest about how you make them feel.

Though I doubt it.

At the third floor the doors open again and I step out and walk straight down the corridor. The man in the elevator probably came to Sydney for the koalas and the sunbeams. Probably he doesn't speak English and would feel no obligation to contact the front desk and tell them that a strange man with a messed-up face and a dusty black coat is wandering the halls, looking furtive. Still, and maybe only from habit, I walk with a purpose, not glancing at the room numbers, not appearing to be on this floor for the first time in my life.

When the elevator rattles closed I glance casually over my shoulder to be sure the Korean man didn't alight here too, but I'm alone in a narrow, sky-blue hallway lit by halogens and a window at the far end with a view of Sydney tower. Quiet. There are no sounds of voices or television and no shoes or trays laid out on the carpet. A couple of DO NOT DISTURB flyers are about the only indication there's anyone occupying the rooms. Following the trail of numbers, I reach 302 and open my jacket pocket.

The last time I picked a lock was so long ago it appears in my mind as the action of someone else. Someone reliable, non-threatening. Someone who doesn't even drink. A car alarm was wailing outside my home one night. This was back when I lived in what you'd call a home, which is how long ago this was.

I got the car door open, killed the alarm and was walking back to my flat when someone, a neighbour, appeared on the other side of the panelled fence that lined our driveway. In the dark I heard the man's voice say approvingly: 'About fucking time.'

Then he said, 'Cunt.' And I realised he thought it was my car.

At least, that's how I remember it. For the first couple of days after I got this scar on my head, I was remembering things wrong.

'Your memory,' the surgeon said, 'will improve.'

'That,' I told him, 'is a shame.'

Finally the plug rotates and the lock snaps open. Inside the room is black: the blinds are drawn tight and the day is getting dark. I flick the light switch but no light comes. I flick it twice more, then push the door all the way open to at least illuminate the nearby parts—a short corridor with a door to the toilet and, immediately to the right, a wardrobe. I open it, hoping for a torch or even a matchbook, but all that's there is a lonely wire coathanger, swaying at me. I pull it out and fold it in half, flatten off the shape where the two points meet and mould it into something vaguely similar to an oblong tile. The slot above the light switch, where you'd usually insert your oblong tile to give power to your room, that's where I jam in the coathanger.

The lights come on and I close the door behind me, lock it.

Past the bathroom and the wardrobe is a room not much bigger than the massive bed set against the wall. The sheets are twisted up and a blue backpack sits open like a massive hatched egg. Socks and underwear and a t-shirt are piled near the window, and on the bench next to the television are the remains of last night's dinner, maybe today's lunch. It's a plate smeared with tomato sauce, decorated with charred fat, a fork and a steak knife. Also there are two beer cans, both of them crushed by hand and balanced side by side, bowing to greet me.

I lurch forward to the bar fridge. Inside there are juices and soft drinks, no beers. There are no mixed drinks and no miniatures of liquor to be seen and even if there once were, it looks like the kid would have drunk them. I kick the fridge door shut. A shade of daylight borders the heavy curtains so I yank them open, but that only seems to make the room darker. The view from here is of grey cloud and the grey roof of the warehouse next door. Nothing to drink and nothing even to look at. Between now and whenever it's just me and what's in my head.

So I pack Troy's things.

There isn't much. A crumpled shirt, a pair of new sneakers dug in under the bed. I stuff all of it into the backpack, realise this is his school bag. There's a pencil case in here and an exercise book with Troy's name on it. There's a toilet bag with a toothbrush, toothpaste, an old-fashioned razor, shaving cream and moisturiser. There's a handheld game device, but I'm not so desperate that I'm going to play it. I slump down onto the bed, look up at the roof for a while then over at the opposite wall and there I am in the mirror. Me with my hair shorn off, strange stitches in my forehead, numbness in my eyes. I have crows feet. I look old. This is you now, John. Soak it up.

What's merciful is I don't have to soak it up for long. There's a scratching noise outside the door, a key fitting into the lock, and I get up and position myself this side of the bathroom. It's possible that the kid will see the coathanger, wonder why the lights are on in here, maybe run for it and then this whole game will start over. But he doesn't. He shuts the door and strolls right in, doesn't see me, doesn't notice his bag is packed and zipped up. The room key drops onto the bench and he pulls his jacket off. His headphones must be playing something irritating, judging by his face. Or maybe that's just his face.

Pimples are stippled across his brow, down his temples to his neck, seemingly enormous against the pale of his skin, a lot of which is hidden by the long hair you grow when you want to hide your acne and your face. He's got a pronounced lower jaw like a prehistoric fish and eyes set deep in his skull like his father. He didn't get his mother's looks.

I sidle into position between him and the door.

He senses the movement, sees me and whinnies like a startled horse. It's an instinctive response, summarising the shock of finding someone in your room who looks like me. His palms come up, the international symbol for 'Stop', but I can't stop because I'm not doing anything. He takes two steps back and trips, whinnies again as he goes down and his body hammers shoulder-first onto the carpet.

I say, 'Relax. Your parents sent me.'

He's back on his feet, wrenching away the earphones, his face transformed from an irritated child's to a terrified one's.

'*Fucking what do you want?*' he screeches, his hands up to stop me again.

'I'm going to take you back to Melbourne.'

'*What?*'

'My name's John. I've got your things ready. Let's go.'

He pulls the hair from his eyes, shows his teeth, seething.

'*I don't fucking want to. Get the fuck out or I'll call the fucking police.*'

He's well dressed for a hate machine. Shiny blue denim and a hooded sweatshirt where the hood is a different colour from the shirt. Beneath it his limbs and torso are so thin they may not even be there. But some kind of muscle makes his arms hack and gesture at me.

'*You can't make me go…*'

'Yes, I can.'

'*You fucking can't. I'll call the fucking police…*'

'Go ahead.'

'*I'll…*'

Helplessness crashes over him and his clenched face scans the room for options. What he sees is the steak knife on the dinner plate. He snatches at it, but rather than threaten me he whisks the blade to his own chest, over his heart, clutched in both hands. He bugs out his eyes.

'*Get the fuck out or I'll fucking stick it in. I'll fucking kill myself.*'

'That's your breast plate,' I say, tapping the same point on my chest. 'You don't have the strength to break through that. Not with a blunt knife.' He seems to choke on the words as I say them.

Someone claiming they were going to kill themselves was, back when I did this sort of thing more often, an invitation for me to sit and read the newspaper, let them blow themselves out like Cyclone Bertha. They were already missing persons, so they probably had a dramatic streak long before I came along. I thought of it as a cry for attention: what you did instead of an Oscars speech. And despite their wailing and their threats and their warnings for me to keep away, none of them was ever not bluffing.

But now, Troy starts to drag on that knife, drawing the point millimetres into his shirt. His face becomes an angry ball and he presses the blade harder, perhaps enough to pierce the skin; his teeth grind against each other, all of him vibrating. If he doesn't have the strength, he wants me to believe he does.

So I step across the room and clutch at the knife, pull it from Troy's body and with the back of my other hand I strike his face, not hard, mostly across his forehead. It's more gravity that sends him to the bed but he falls theatrically, screeches an unintelligible word and ends with his face pushing into his hands and his hands pushing into the bunched bedsheets. I put the knife back on the plate and wipe beef grease off my fingers onto the pillow.

'*I wanna do it*,' he cries into his palms. '*I wanna do it…Let me do it…*'

'All right,' I say. 'Change of plan. We're going downstairs. Leave your bag.'

We take the elevator to the ground floor. He rubs at his chest and there's a smear of blood on his shirt the size of a gooseberry. I guess the blade did break his skin. His face is the kind I make right before I vomit: pale, pained. He's rubbing that too, where I slapped him.

We come out to the reception desk which is opposite the bar. It's exactly the kind of bland hotel that makes a mint out of people who don't mind blandness, who demand it and pay outrageous prices for it. I scan the bland tables and the bland lobby and the quiet city street beyond the sliding bland doors, my hand held up to indicate Troy should stop and wait while I do this.

I'm looking for Leo Spaske.

Not that I need to. Since Demetri's moment at the hospital back in Melbourne I've not had so much as a whiff of Leo's Scandinavian musk. I'd think the story of Leo and Troy's subpoena was entirely made up if it weren't for how it feels true. Threatening to put a teenager through a teenager's worst nightmare—public, predatory humiliation—is about as evil as I've known plaintiff law to get. And it's a surefire winner. I'm surprised they don't do it all the time.

After ten seconds of analysing everything I lead Troy into the bar. It's not big, not crowded. There are prints by Matisse decorating the place, with Matisse's name in big letters underneath them, like it's really important you *know* that it's *Matisse* they've got on the walls. I'd say it's very Sydney except that there's a million of these pictures hanging on walls in hotels in Melbourne. A single barman stacks the fridge and outside dusk is slowly drawing down. The plate-glass wall is lined with tables and ordinarily I wouldn't sit anywhere so open, but there are only five tables in the place and I don't want to sit where we can be overheard. I direct Troy to a chair and he slumps towards it. I go to the bar.

'Do you have lime juice?' I ask.

The barman stands slowly, looks at me with no expression. Then he says, 'Hey?'

'Lime juice. From limes. Do you have limes?'

'Yeah.'

'I need a double vodka tonic with lime juice in a tall glass. Is that all right?'

'Sure.'

I turn to Troy. He's pulled his hood up over his head and seems to be staring at the table top.

'Troy,' I say.

He doesn't respond.

'Troy,' I say again. I need him to look up so that the barman will be able recognise him. If it comes to that.

Troy does look up. His eyes are barely open and he still looks like he's going to puke.

'What do you want to drink?' I ask.

He shakes his head, lowers his eyes again.

'Troy,' I say, louder.

His eyes come back to me, wider this time. It's my own fault, but I hate it when people are scared of me.

'I'm going to get you a juice. Is an orange juice okay?'

He nods softly.

I turn back to the barman. 'And one orange juice.'

He keys this into the register.

'Doesn't seem to be feeling too good, poor kid,' I mutter. The barman just nods, takes my money, sets about making the drinks. I'd hate to rely on him as a witness. He has blond tips and a goatee and he's so disengaged it's possible he's under hypnosis. Working in a hotel like this might do that to you.

There's a middle-aged loner at the table by the door. Maybe she's seen Troy, maybe she's not the observant type. But that will have to be good enough.

I set the drinks down on the table and sit opposite him, drink in gulps. His orange juice gets no attention. I survey the emptiness beyond the plate glass. The hotel's name, The Royale, is written vertically above me, a little gaudy for such a narrow city street. When I look at Troy, he looks away, his hands in his pockets, skinny frame almost rigid.

'I'm sorry I hit you,' I wipe a drip from my chin. 'But I can't have you hurting yourself. Not right there in front of me.'

'Why do you fucking care?' It's dry and full of hate, but it's the first calm thing he's said. His eyes flit between the scar on my head and the table.

I take another long drink. 'Because I'm the one who'd have to stop the bleeding, put you onto the floor and pump your heart for you. For one thing, I'd get blood all over my clothes. I'd have to get your tongue out of your airway, keep it out of there while I called an ambulance. Then I'd have to give you rescue breaths. Mouth to mouth.'

I expect him to recoil, but he doesn't. He says, 'No one's making you.'

'Not true. If you stuck a knife in your heart with me watching, and if I didn't do anything about it, the cops would want to know why. And your parents would sue me. Or they'd sue the guy who got me this job. He'd be angry with me and I don't want to make him angry. He's been good to me.'

Troy stares with his studiously sleepy eyes back at the table, tips back in his seat, unmoved. He's probably heard a few speeches in his short life.

I finish the tall glass and weigh it in my hands. The ice cubes inside crash against each other, the familiar rattle of finality. *You have finished your drink, sir. What are you going to do now?*

I say, 'It's different, though, if I'm not there.'

From my jacket pocket I take out the room key, drop it onto the table in front of him. He tips forward on his seat. 'What?' His voice croaks because of all the screaming he's been doing.

'The man at the bar, he's seen you. He'll say you left, went to the elevator, I stayed. I can say I thought you just went upstairs to get your bag. Then I go back up, wondering why you're taking so long, find you but it's too late. I call the ambulance and do some pilates until the police show up. The whole thing's over good and quick and I don't have to try and…whatever.'

'Don't fucking dare me to,' he says, his eyes steady. 'I'll fucking do it.'

'I'm not daring you. You want to, so I'm giving you the chance.'

His face seems to lose its contempt. He picks up the key and looks carefully at it, like maybe I swapped in a fake one. Then his eyes come back up to me, big and hazel and intense, like maybe I've been swapped in for the guy who just smacked him across the face.

I lean forward, lower my voice.

'What I said about puncturing your breast plate, I meant that. If you want to do it right, get the blade in behind your adam's apple, from your right hand side, then wrench it out longways. You've got to do it in one quick movement though. That'll cut your carotid artery and your oesophagus, and there's no coming back from that. Understand?'

There's a moment while he absorbs, then he nods quickly.

I stand up. 'You're not going to have long, so be quick. And for Christ's sake leave the door unlocked.'

I carry my ice cubes to the bar, set down the glass. The barman is stacking the fridge again, hasn't noticed me. When I peek over my shoulder, Troy is staring at the key in his hand.

I say loud enough for the barman to hear: 'All right, Troy. You go get your bag and I'll wait here for you.'

This gets the barman's attention and he approaches. When I look back to Troy, he's moving through the tables, back towards the elevator.

'My friend's just getting his bag,' I say to the barman. I do my best to smile. 'But I think I've got time for one more, don't you?'

He mixes it for me with his characteristic mindlessness and I take it back to my seat, opposite Troy's lonely yellow juice. I keep a watch on the entrance to the hotel, just in case he tries to run for it. But I don't think he'll do that.

I finish my drink in one long draught and as I lower the glass a minuscule speck of liquid splashes back against my face. It hits the scar on my head. Makes it sting.

I'm about to go back up to the room when I see a big blue car come around the corner at the far end of the street. Instinctively I'm up and away from the table, out of the car's view, sheltering behind a thick pillar. I make myself as thin as possible.

The car chugs past, slow enough for Leo to get a good look at the hotel. But for all I know it's a rockabilly hipster letting a blind man cross in front of him.

When I chance a look, the vehicle is gone. Magically. I might think I was hallucinating except that I'm two drinks down now, enough to keep me sharp. I didn't see the driver, maybe it wasn't even a Valiant. But here I am, hunkered under a Matisse.

If it was him, he must have followed me up from Melbourne. He did well for me not to spot him, but I guess I'm a little rusty. And now he's parading his big dumb car down a Sydney street where it barely fits. I guess he's a little rusty too.

But if Troy's dead upstairs I guess none of this matters anymore.

I take the elevator to the third floor and I try to make it seem like a casual saunter along the hallway back to room 302. I knock gently.

No sound from inside.

Maybe he's done it.

The plan is that I should go inside, but I can't seem to take my hands out of my pockets to turn the handle. I wait several seconds for that to happen. Eventually I hear the tone from down the hall and I seize the handle and push inside before the elevator doors can open.

Troy sits on the bed. Hands clasped in front of him, almost praying. He jerks his head up, pained and squinting, trying to read my reaction to how he's still alive. I shut the door and approach slowly, glance around for where the knife might be.

It's on the carpet in the corner, unbloodied, still greasy and brown. There's a brown smear on the wall above it. He must have thrown the knife and there's where it hit.

'I suppose it sounds stupid,' Troy says, fidgeting with the webbing in his hand. 'It's just…I can't handle the sight of blood.'

As he speaks he lowers his head again, lets the hair fall protectively across his face and thrusts his thumb into his palm like he's trying to stigmata himself. But when he sweeps his hair away and suddenly he's looking at me, his eyes don't hold any agitation. He's already forced it back, beyond anything I can see. The bland expectancy in his face is like he just asked me to renew his gym membership.

None of them was ever not bluffing.

I peer through the peephole. Whether that was Leo coming out of the lift really does matter now. But the corridor is empty.

4

It's night. Beyond our headlights there's just the reflectors on the road and the shifting shades of black that are actually the trees and the sky. Sometimes there's a spark of something more—the lit window of a farmhouse through the sticks or a fire that doesn't burn bright enough to reveal the people who must be tending it. For an hour now the only other vehicle on the road has been the distant pair of fat orange headlights in my mirror. I'm not driving fast, just under the speed limit, but that car's keeping its distance. It's too dark to see what kind of car it is.

Apart from those headlights, the whole world is me and Troy

and a conveyor belt of animals pulverised on the bitumen. Possums and wombats and kangaroos, crushed and forgotten by an endless stream of humans.

About half an hour ago Troy asked me to pull over so he could throw up. He said he always got fucking motion sickness in a fucking car at fucking nighttime. I glanced at those orange lights in my rearview and suggested he vomit into the clean-up bag that hung from the glove box. It was wrapped in red cellophane that matched the deep red in the rental company's logo, and through the cellophane you could make out the words: FOR YOUR CONVENIENCE.

So Troy vomited into the bag. After that he just flopped there beside me, listless, while the whole car stank of sick. I suggested he take the antidepressants that his mother gave to me to give to him. They're called Lexaprine and I was surprised that he took them without protest. He didn't ask why I refused to pull over. I'd tell him there could be someone following us, but that might make him throw up again.

Now the listlessness has worn off and he's playing with the cellophane, pinching it between his fingers and rubbing it to make it squeak, huddled forward like he would be if his arms were only as long as his wrists. He's been doing it for a while and mostly it hasn't bothered me but the only other sound is the metallic whisper of the engine and now he's getting the knack and that squeaking is making me grind my teeth. When I realise how tightly clenched my jaw is I raise a hand and say, 'Cut that out?'

Immediately he thrusts himself back in his seat, jerks his head to face the window, making it obvious he was squeaking the cellophane so that I'd be annoyed, so that I'd tell him off, so that he could be annoyed too. He turns to look at me, challenging. His quiet resentment has evolved into plain old resentment. After a long stare, he says, 'You're fucking weird.'

He waits for me to ask why, and when I don't, he says, 'Telling me to go kill myself.'

We drive over the remains of something big with wings.

'I didn't tell you to do anything.'

'You told me how. You helped me. Man, that is fucked up. Do my parents know how fucked up you are?'

'Right now I think they're more concerned with how fucked up *you* are.'

He goes back to playing with the cellophane, quietly now, focusing hard on it. 'My mum's a fucking slut,' he says, half-mumbling.

Then he says, with forced humour, 'Want to hear a joke? What's the difference between my mum and a bowling ball?'

I don't answer.

'You can only fit three fingers in a bowling ball.' He laughs through his teeth.

I'm hoping that's the end of the talking. He seems to ponder his own words for a while. There's just the sound of the car slipping along the road and the soft buzz in my head that seems to be the sound of the headlights trailing behind us. We go past a lumpy kangaroo, dragged to the side of the road by the thoughtful motorist who ran it down.

'So you do this, like, for a job?' he asks, louder than necessary. Instinctively I decelerate, in case he's about to flip out.

'No. I'm unemployed.'

'Well, what did you do before you were unemployed?'

'I was a private inquiry agent.'

That makes me smile. Whenever I used to tell people that, no one knew what it meant. That's not why I said it, it was genuinely what I thought my job was, but having to explain it gave me some control, depending on who I was talking to and why. Troy doesn't know what it means but he doesn't want to show that because he thinks it'll make him look dumb. He nods.

'How come you don't do that anymore?'

'I lost my licence.'

His face slackens as he thinks.

'Want to hear a joke?'

'I'd rather we didn't talk. I need to concentrate.'

'Why does my mum wear underpants?' He doesn't wait for me this time. 'To keep her ankles warm.' And he snorts.

We drive over two foxes, parallel, like one of them couldn't bear to live without the other. Though what's more likely is one fox was eating a dead fox and got hit by a car because he didn't see it coming because he was distracted because the other fox was so delicious.

Troy says, 'How did you lose your licence?'

'Something bad happened.'

'Is that when you got that scar on your head?'

'No. That was something different. I don't want to talk about my job. I don't do it anymore.'

'If you don't do it anymore then why the fuck are you here?'

'Your parents needed you to come home quietly and I know how to do that.'

'Fuck *that*,' he says feebly.

We're approaching a service station, one of those miniature cities with fast food restaurants and trucks lining the carpark. It isn't exactly bustling at this late hour. If that is Leo behind us, his Valiant is going to need petrol soon enough.

Troy senses my thoughts. 'Is there someone after us?'

'I don't know.'

We pass the rest stop and I slow down to get a good look in the mirror. As the orange headlights reach the carpark the full body of the machine is illuminated. A long, cornflower blue Valiant rolls into the driveway, headed for the pumps. I can't see the driver. Even so, I press hard on the brakes and pull onto the mud shoulder.

'Stay here,' I say.

'What are you doing?'

'Shouldn't be long.'

It takes only a few seconds. I run back along the highway, spot the Valiant at the pumps. No sign of Leo. I scurry past the gas tanks and the ice machine, get a view inside through the glass. A skinny blond figure all in black is waiting in line. If that is Leo, he's even taller than I remember him. Casually, I walk to his car, squat and use the corkscrew on my keyring to drill into his front tyre. After a heady moment of pushing and wrenching, the black rubber hisses at me with relief. When I get back to the car, Troy says, 'What the fuck, man?'

I bear down on the accelerator, refocus on the road ahead. I hope we can find a motel before Leo catches up.

'Is it something to do with my mum?'

'Yes.'

Then Troy says, 'What do you call my mum with a runny nose?'

I exhale.

He says, 'Full.' But he doesn't laugh this time. He hunches forward again, fiddles with the cellophane that hangs from the glovebox. I let the awkward silence seep into the cracks that are starting to show in his bullshit façade. Then I say, 'You know, you could give your mum the benefit of the doubt. The jury found her not guilty.'

'She is guilty.'

'You don't know that. Just because they make jokes about her at school—'

'I do know. I saw her.'

We're going so fast I don't want to take my eyes off the road. But I have to, for a moment.

'What did you see?'

'I saw her. With Tyler. In the darkroom at school.'

'Did they see you?'

'Yeah.'

'What did they do when they saw you?'

'Mum was really angry. You're not supposed to go into the darkroom when the red light's on, but I didn't know. I don't do art. I just like to go to the darkroom sometimes. She said they were developing pictures, but...'

'What did you see?'

'I don't know. He was pulling his pants up when I came in. Her shirt was unbuttoned.'

He hasn't taken his eyes off the red cellophane. After three more seconds I realise there's no point driving like this now. I ease my foot off the accelerator.

'Did you tell anybody?'

'Nuh.' Troy shrugs.

'They want you to give evidence. In court. Do you know that?'

He shrugs again.

I say, 'Do you think you can talk about it in court?'

'Yeah.' Another shrug. He still doesn't look at me. 'I don't care.'

I wait for him, don't speak, give him the space to volunteer more. He doesn't, and silence becomes our default.

We drive over a koala. Maybe a koala. Car tyres, one after the other, have rendered it a mess of grey fur and dried blood and a ribcage. The people keep coming, me and everyone else, each of us gives it another trampling, transforming it into something more than just dead.

I don't know what time it is when we cross the Murray. The water is black and quiet, so much so that the only way I know we're crossing it is there are 'no diving' pictograms lining the road, and then I realise the road is actually a bridge. On the south side is Victoria and a roadsign that says WELCOME TO YARINDARRA, held up by two long metal stilts angled comically back from the road like the sign is meant more for aeroplanes than for cars. Almost definitely this was caused by a car colliding with the stilts, but if you needed proof, there's a bunch of dying daffodils in pink paper taped to one of them and the other has a football jersey dangling from it, orange and blue and clean, seemingly new. I slow to look at these items as our headlights pass across. I bet the local TV news covered it and said it was a senseless waste and I bet it failed to mention the hypocrisy of small town culture that combines a motor-vehicle fetish with a collective alcohol abuse problem and then wonders why its teenagers finish up mutilated and facedown in puddles of their own shit and blood. The local news probably didn't mention the shit and blood either.

Troy doesn't seem to see it. His head rests against the window and I'd say he was asleep if it weren't for how no one could sleep like that. He might be pretending to be asleep.

The main street is well lit but empty. It isn't quite a ghost town, though, because of the hospital at the far end that seems to be open. Or at least there are people coming and going and all the lights are on. It hulks over the shopfronts like a pitbull over kittens, seemingly airlifted out of the 1960s and dumped here because they needed somewhere along the river that could treat more than footrot. On the opposite side of the road is a town hall and a massive clock tower lit up by the hospital and it's saying that it's just gone ten.

We pass all this and suddenly we've left the town. The road tilts up a not-steep hill through more black, which I suppose is dried-up farmland, and there's no sign of the orange headlights behind us. Suddenly in the blackness there's a motel, graceful and long and flaunting a neon lamp that says VACANCY. The office lights are on. An oasis in outer space.

I pull into the driveway. Through a glass door that's almost entirely papered over with warning signs, advertisements and credit card stickers, there's the office lit deep yellow by two tired bulbs poking out of the ceiling. Behind the desk, itself another drift of notices and disclaimers, a heavy woman is perched on a high stool wearing a man's striped shirt and glasses. They're attached to a thick black rope that loops back around her neck and disappears into bushy hair, tinted with a loud brown to hide the grey.

Troy straightens and looks around at where we are. Ahead of us is a flat stretch of motel edifice, punctuated with fluorescent lights along the narrow path that runs past fourteen or fifteen closed doors. It's too cold in the year for the flurry of bugs and lizards that would usually be attending those lights like they were trendy new bars in the city, but it's not so cold that the windows are fogged over with the warmth of the people asleep inside. If there are people inside. Between the path and the road is a gravel carpark where no cars are parked. Opposite the motel, on the opposite side of the highway, is a solitary phone booth, lit blue by the fluoro inside. Beyond that is just nighttime.

Troy looks at me like I just flicked him with a lacker band. 'Can't we just drive through?'

'I need a rest.'

He licks his lips, dry from the journey.

'Fine then.'

I get out of the car. As I open the office door I hear the chime of an electronic bell in a distant room. The big woman is transfixed by a small television on the desk and she doesn't look up, but her brow creases and I guess she's not happy that I've intruded. The office smells intensely of roast beef, but there's no sign of meals or used dinner plates or sandwiches, so the smell must come from her. She finally looks up to me and says, 'G'day,' but the last syllable trails off a little as she clocks the long scar across my head and comes to terms with it. We've been driving in the dark just long enough for me to forget it was there, and I take a second to come to terms with it myself. I'd wear a hat if it didn't hurt so much.

I say, 'Hello. We need one room, two beds.'

She shoots a glance through the glass at Troy, looks back at me over the thick-rimmed glasses, then removes a small blue card from a stack on a bulldog clip. She hands it to me along with half a biro. The other half has been chewed off.

'It's two hunge and twenny-five for the night,' she rasps.

I'm about to fill in the form when I pause. Our eyes meet and she shakes her head, not scared of a confrontation, wobbling the loose skin beneath her jowls. 'It's the only way I can be open real late like this.'

My guess is that she thinks I'm here with my underage boyfriend and if I'm going to break the law in her motel then why shouldn't she make some money out of it?

Past her, on a cluttered bench, I spot a bottle of cheap gin almost hidden behind another television and stacks of ringbinders and brochures. There's only three or four fingers inside, but it must be the only thing to drink between here and the nurses' station in the hospital.

'You can make it two-fifty if you throw in that bottle.'

'Not much in it.'

'No, there isn't.'

'You want it or not?'

'Yes, please.'

And she can see how badly. It's in my sudden politeness. Her thumb and forefinger needlessly adjust her glasses. 'Got to be three hundred, then.'

I point weakly, say, 'You could buy a full bottle for thirty dollars.'

'Yeah, but it's me husband's. For when he sits the night shift. I shouldn't be selling his grog to just any bloke that come in here.'

I get it. Maybe the occasional car pulls into this place late at night, having reached the psychological milestone of the Murray River, but the real reason it's open so late is the married couple who run it can't bear to be around one another. Twelve-hour shifts keep them apart and maybe it wouldn't matter if no one ever pulled in after dark. He drinks and she smells permanently of roast beef, and if that king-size shirt she's wearing is her husband's then it's likely they can't both fit in the bed at the same time anyway. Win–win.

I say, 'Can you put it all on one receipt? Without itemising it?'

'Sure. You got to pay now, but. Not check-out.'

She rings it up on the till and I pay in cash, clutch the bottle and the room key and leave. It's suddenly cooler outside, or at least there's a breeze I hadn't noticed before.

'We have separate rooms, right?' Troy asks as I get into the car.

'One room, two beds.'

He hangs his head, doesn't say anything. I motor the car forward, park on the worn gravel outside room five. When we left Sydney I planned to find a motel like this and park behind it, so the car wasn't visible from the highway. There's no point in that now.

The room is bigger than I expected. The two beds are both doubles and there's a writing desk with plastic flowers arranged across it and two ceiling fans. Troy slumps onto the first bed and lies still with his eyes closed. The crusty cream walls look like you could chip into them with your fists and the floor is an arrangement of bright orange tiles that maybe were supposed to fade over time but never did. So, like any motel, it's decorated in a way that even a mad person couldn't stand for more than a week. I go to the bathroom at the far end and that's big too. There's a deep porcelain bathtub and a picture of flying ducks hanging next to the toilet. The only light is a weak bulb on the wall, diffused by an opaque plastic dome spotted with the silhouettes of bugs that long ago crawled in there to die.

I piss and flush and when I come out of the bathroom Troy's still lying on the bed. His eyes are open now, peeking out past the hair that conceals the rest of his face in what has become more or less his signature pose.

I say, 'I'm going to the phone booth outside to make a call. I'll be watching the door so don't try to leave, and the window in the bathroom doesn't open so I wouldn't bother there either.'

He says nothing, keeps staring. He might be dead but for the long, healthy breaths he's drawing. I leave him like that, close the door and lock it, cross the white gravel and the black tar of the highway and glance back: in the motel office she's still gazing at the television, dispassionate, like it's a propaganda film she's already been forced to sit through over and over for days. I screw the cap off and sip gently from the seventy-five-dollar bottle of her husband's backwash. I have to save some for after this phone call, when I may be required to think more precisely about what I'm taking Troy back to.

The phone booth is the old-fashioned kind, with a door and full protection from the elements. They got rid of these in Melbourne years ago because they couldn't have homeless people finding actual shelter at night. Corrosion eats at the bottom half of this one but the interior is well maintained or else it's just never used. The handset is green under the blue fluoro and it's cool like it's been refrigerated. As I press it to my ear I feel the cold seep into my brain and down into my shoulders. I shiver.

A phone rings in Melbourne. She answers after eight of them. 'Hello.'

'It's John Dorn. I've got Troy. We're in a motel on the Murray.'

A hand goes over the receiver. Voices. When she comes back on the phone there's sleep and whisky in her voice.

'Bloody hell, that was fast. Any sign of...you-know-who?'

'He's around, though we're yet to be formally introduced. And on that subject, Troy told me a secret tonight.'

There's a long silence. I listen to the wind whistle through the booth.

She says, 'Don't...Don't say it over the phone. We don't know who might be listening.' Her voice is full of that earnest victimhood she's mastered after a thousand press conferences.

'But you understand what I'm talking about?'

'I think so.'

'Demetri doesn't know?'

'Ummmm...No.'

'Lying to him seemed like the best course of action to you?'

'Wait, no...we thought it was better—'

'If he knew, he could have told you that they'll probably get an adjournment if Troy's not there. He's central to their case now, so if no one can find him, the judge will put the hearing off until they do.'

'I know, it's just...Look, Mr Dorn...John...I'd rather not talk about it like this. Just bring Troy back and we'll chat about it then, okay?'

'Sure,' I say. 'But you better hope Leo Spaske doesn't find us before then. Because I'm not going to lift a finger to stop him serving Troy with that subpoena.'

Wide orange headlights appear over the hill, as if, by the speaking of his name, he has been summoned. They cut mercilessly through the white haze that emanates from the hospital on the other side of the hill, approaching.

Speaking very slowly, Belinda says, 'I never said you *should* stop him. That would be illegal.'

'It would be illegal,' I echo her words and her tone. 'And yet it's what I've been doing since I found Troy. This phone call is to let you know that I won't be doing that anymore. See you tomorrow.'

'Wait...' Her voice breaks as she speaks. 'I'll...' She's searching for a solution, almost as if she can feel the car's headlights as they pierce the dark.

She says, 'Where are you?'

'We're at the Yarindarra Motor Inn on the Hume Highway.'

'Okay. We'll come. We'll come there right now. You just wait there.'

'If that's what you want. We're in room five.'

'I want my son home safe.'

'I'm sure you do.'

'Just stay there and don't...do anything. We'll be as fast as we can.'

'All right. But you better hurry. Something tells me Leo is just around the corner.'

I hang up.

Through the immediate quiet comes the sound of the Valiant closing in, engine grinding, all four tyres properly inflated. The headlights loom in the dark like an alien invasion and I step out of the phone booth, linger on the dirt verge this side of the road, watch the car reach the soft brown light thrown by the motel onto the highway.

The blue Valiant flicks by at a startling speed, too fast for me to glimpse the driver. But he glimpses me.

I know this because of the sudden screech of brakes.

Its momentum carries it on, smoke rising from its rubber, long tracks scorching black on the black tar. The pig squeal seems to last hours, getting louder the further the car goes. When it finally comes to rest the machine's body has drifted gently in its desperation, skewed against the straight lines of the road, panting.

I step onto the bitumen and stand there in the stink of the clearing smoke. I know Leo must be watching me in his mirror and I wait for him, screw the cap off the bottle and brace myself with a short swig.

Finally, the driver's door opens. A figure with ragged blond hair steps out, stands to his full, remarkable height. He wears a black suit that doesn't quite fit because no one makes clothes for people like Leo—long and skinny with limbs like he spent years stretched out on a rack. He doesn't shut off the motor and he doesn't close the car door. Just towers over his vehicle, faces me with an odd stillness, too far away for me to hear him if he speaks.

The calm gives this all a sense of showdown.

I can't help but smile at him, at the slight absurdity of this black wasteland where we've come face to face for the first time since we both got kicked out of the same profession, two stick figures on a barren highway, either end of a sad motel. There's no sound of anything but the soft meter of the Valiant's engine.

Then I see there's something in his hand and I stop smiling. It's a blade, several inches long, bouncing soft light from where it hangs by his lower thigh.

He's too far away to hear, but I say, 'Leo?'

Now he goes, beelines across the carpark, crane legs striding metres at a time. I recognise vengeance in the sharp crack his shoes make on the white gravel, in his face as he moves into the light.

'Wait!' I break into a run, knowing I won't get there in time.

With one powerful overarm action Leo buries the knife into the Mitsubishi's rear tyre. There's a hiccup and a hiss and the car sinks.

All I can do is shout, 'No, Leo!' and throw up my helpless arms.

He silently yanks the blade out and turns serenely to face me as I approach. 'I owed you that much, didn't I, John?'

'Put the knife away. You don't need it.'

'Goodness me, John, I don't intend to use it on *you*. I am perhaps more likely to get what I came for while I've got it in my hand, though, wouldn't you say?'

I keep a distance, raise the bottle and my other hand in the air. 'You win, Leo. I'll take you to Troy. Just put away the knife.'

The planes of his white face, that black coat; his yellow hair and long limbs. He has the look of a scarecrow that's climbed down from its hoist on some nearby farm to terrorise Yarindarra in the nighttime.

Now he strikes a casual pose, enjoying the power of his knife.

'So you're working again, Johnny old boy?'

'Nope.' I take another hit of the gin. The tipping back of my head causes me to lose balance and I gently reposition myself. 'This is a one-off.'

Leo looks me over, from my feet to the scar on my brow.

'Probably just as well. You don't look as though you could take much more.'

I scratch my nose, force a glum smile.

Leo says, 'I didn't expect you to stop for the night. It's not like you to be so sloppy.'

'Can you put the knife away?' I wave the bottle at him. 'It's making me nervous.'

Leo shakes his head and is about to say something when the sound of footsteps and a familiar shucking noise turn him towards the motel office.

She must have heard the Valiant's brakes and me shouting. Now she's standing outside room two with her glasses dangling from the rope around her neck and an old pump shotgun held up with one hand.

'I don't want this shit going on here, boys. You understand? Bloke with the knife, that your car sitting out on the road?'

The gun is a Remington eight-seventy, but it's hard to be sure in this darkness. It's levelled at the scarecrow who's frozen in place, grimacing at her, knowing by her appearance and her rural inflection that she could pull the trigger and sleep fine tonight.

'Yes it is, as a matter of fact.'

'Well, off you go then. Enough mucking about.'

He turns to me, his face demanding an explanation. I'm just as surprised as he is.

'Madam, I am awfully sorry for the intrusion. I'm here on court business. I've got documents to—'

'I don't give a rat's what you're here doing. I'm not having you shouting and waving that thing around in the middle of the bloody night. Acting like a bloody idiot. Now I'm telling you to *piss off*.'

'Very well...' He folds the switchblade and drops it into his jacket pocket, edges past me, his hands raised in surrender.

As he passes I say, 'Give me the subpoena.'

He stops and eyeballs me, inches away.

I say, 'I'll serve it.'

His face is all wrinkles and he smirks. 'No fear.' But he lingers there like he's considering it.

'I'm not going to tell you again,' she yells, takes another step forward. There's a biro behind her ear; it's pointed at Leo, too. 'You've got a vehicle sitting plum in the middle of the bloody highway. You'll get someone killed.'

Leo shouts over his shoulder, 'Don't shoot.' But he doesn't go anywhere. He squints at me, at my scar, at the bottle in my hand, at how I'm offering to do his job for him. Then a smile comes across his face.

'Poor old John Dorn. Something happened to you, didn't it?'

And he slowly backs away towards the road.

'Keep going,' she says, following him with the weapon.

As he steps backwards he sneers, thrusts his chin out, raises his voice so she'll hear him. 'I'll return with the police.'

Then he turns and starts the trek to his car.

We watch him in silence, a loping black-clad nightmare trying to hide his defeat. He folds expertly into the driver's seat like a spider through its trapdoor and the engine responds with a dip in its whirring beat. He puts it in gear, slams the door shut, straightens the machine on the road and stamps down. The tyres screech goodbye. His lights sweep south, crushing dead animals in their path.

Some showdown.

When I turn back to her she's tucked the Remington under her arm, taken the biro from behind her ear and she's writing on a scrap of paper, noting Leo's plate number.

Then she peers at me over the glasses that are back on her face. 'Lucky I don't run you out of here, too. All that carrying on. You got a spare?'

'A what?'

'Spare tyre.'

'I don't know.'

'Else you'll need a tow to Nigel's.'

'Okay.'

'He's over in Severington but, so you'll need a tow. In the morning.'

'Okay. Someone's going to meet us here. Tonight. We'll figure out what to do after that.'

'Better tell 'em to behave.' It takes several shuffling steps for her to rotate and face the motel office again. She lumbers off, the shotgun swinging by her side. 'Had enough idiots for one night.'

There's no light on in room five so I assume Troy's asleep. I don't know how, given all the noise from outside, but my experience of teenagers is that they can sleep anywhere. When my eyes adjust to what is more or less pitch darkness I see there's no one lying on the bed.

'Troy?'

'Yeah?' A bored drawl from the bathroom. There's the dimmest red glow leaking out from under the door.

I knock. 'Troy?'

'Fucking *what*?' He's just as annoyed as ever.

'What are you doing?'

'I'm taking a bath.'

'Can I come in?'

'Whatever.'

I reach to the wall and switch on the living-room halogens, but he says, 'Leave the lights off.'

'Why?'

There's a silence in which I can almost hear him shrug. 'I'm setting a mood.'

I switch off the light and push the bathroom door open. My eyes go immediately to the source of the red glow—Troy has laid the red cellophane from the car, the envelope that contained the rental company's tidy bag, over the bathroom light and he's used chewing gum to hold it in place. The entire space is a spectrum of deep reds and blacks. Troy lies in a full bath, his head and naked shoulders surrounded by a pale raft of bubbles. He barely looks at me. It's too dark to see steam rising from the water but I can feel the heat.

'You know...' he says, trying to sound conversational. 'They wanted to get rid of the school darkroom. Because photography is all, like, digital now. But my mum fought for it. She's the one who said the school should keep it.'

I linger at the door with nothing to say. Troy's hair is still dry and his face is drawn like he's been crying. Though maybe it's just the poor light in here.

He says, 'I used to go in there sometimes. I liked the smell of the chemicals. I spent a lot of lunchtimes in there.'

I glance around at the darkroom he's sitting in now.

'How is my mother?' he asks, because he's clever.

'She's on her way.'

Troy blinks at me. 'She's coming here?'

'Yep. Both of them.'

'When'll they get here?'

'Before it gets light, probably.'

'Fucking excellent.' Troy shakes his head and smiles sarcastically, then tilts his head back against the red tiles. The white ceiling is red and the white walls are red. This room is like a submarine movie. I slouch to the toilet and sit down on the lid, catch my face in the mirror above the sink. My scar is more pronounced in the red light.

'Why don't you like to talk about your job?' Troy's grin is gone. He's suddenly serious.

'I don't know. I don't care if I talk about it, really.'

I unscrew the bottle cap and shrug. 'Anyone's job gets to them after a while. What I did for a living...You kind of become an expert on the shitty things people do to each other.'

'Right. Things like abducting people from their hotels. And taking them places they don't want to go?'

I smile. 'Yeah, that's right.'

He nods slowly, still watching me.

'I know you're, like, doing your job. I'm not cut with you.'

His eyes seem to have thawed. The darkroom setting has relaxed him. Perhaps we can be friends for the very short term. Or at least not enemies.

'Good,' is all I say.

'If your work was so bad, tell me something horrible. Tell me a really horrible story.'

I wag my head. 'I'm going to bed. And so are you. You're tired.'

'I'm not tired. I can't sleep when I take Lexaprine. I'll be awake for ages.'

If that isn't tiredness in his eyes, maybe it's resignation. Probably because his parents are on their way and there's nothing for either of us to do about it.

Leo is coming. The police are coming. Paul and Belinda are coming. All I have to do is sit here and see who arrives first. Just a few more hours at most. After that, this will all be over and nothing else will matter. I don't even have to go back to Melbourne. I could just lie down in this motel room and I'd never have to get up again.

'You want a story?' I say.

'Tell me the worst thing…'

'There are lots of worsts.'

'Choose one.'

I try to identify some criteria. At any given moment I have a dozen bad memories bumping around my head, looking for an exit.

'There's a thousand of them…' I say. 'I wouldn't know where to start.'

'Just pick one and tell it to me.'

He rests his head back against the tiles, gives me an encouraging smile. He wants a bedtime story for while he falls asleep, and he wants it to be proof that the world is as miserable as he is. The opposite of a bedtime story. I go to turn the cap on the bottle but there's no cap there. It's in my hand, waiting for me to drink. When I do I feel the unconscious stab of knowing there are only two or three mouthfuls left. Then I peer up at the ceiling and I wonder what I'm going to say.

5

I'm staring at the tiles between my feet. The bottle has been empty for a while now, hanging from my hand low enough that it travels only an inch or two when I place it on the floor. The sound of my voice as I've been speaking has bounced around the room like a PA system, echoing back my words. Now it's finally quiet.

I look at Troy and he's asleep, so I guess his drugs didn't keep him awake like he thought they would. He might have been like that for a while, I don't know. He mustn't have heard all of my story. I want to wake him just to tell him he didn't miss much.

The police haven't come. Leo hasn't come. Belinda, I suppose, is on her way. Might as well go and lie down, wait for them like that. I'm wondering if I should wake Troy up or leave him sleeping in the bath when I realise something's wrong.

Something in his expression, or his position. Something in the stillness of the water he's soaking in.

I stand up to look closer.

My bones crack and then I know what it is. It's the water. I can't see through it. Everything in this room is bouncing back the red from the red light, but the water isn't just red.

It's opaque.

I clutch at the cellophane over the light dome and though it's only stuck with chewing gum I have to claw at it to pull it free. The room brightens. I squint. The sudden whiteness of the tiles stuns me but the bath doesn't turn white. It stays red. Troy is lying in a bath of red.

I step closer, reach and feel the chill of his skin, searching for a pulse. The water that was once so hot has gone stone cold. Troy's corpse has chilled it like an ice block. I press two fingers against his damp adam's apple and wait.

Is that the ragged thread of a heartbeat? It's the thinnest pulse you can have if you have one.

I inhale. Stare. Curse under my breath.

On the steel soap shelf there's a razor blade: he must have done it before I even came in, while I was outside with Leo. After he stuck the cellophane over the light because he can't stand the sight of blood. Then he lay back and listened to me as I blabbed away. Sank into my bedtime story, dying all the while.

And it's exactly what I asked him not to do. This kind of suicide falls squarely in the category of ones that require *action*. This isn't Troy going upstairs and leaving me drinking in an overpriced hotel bar. Everyone's going to ask about what I do next, and there will be people who want to prove that I didn't do enough.

I pick the bottle up off the floor, like the bright new light in here will reveal one last mouthful of gin. And though I knew it was empty before I picked it up I hurl the bottle through the doorway and it lands softly somewhere in the dimness, denying me even the satisfaction of a smash against a pine wall.

Listening now. If Leo or the police or Belinda arrive, then helping Troy can be their problem. But there's no sound. No approaching car, no footsteps. No wind or birds or insects. Outside might as well be outer space.

I blow a sigh at Troy. His skin is even paler than it used to be, bloodless, almost translucent. His eyes are gently closed and there's a glisten of drool at his lips like he's sleeping. I roll up my sleeves and plunge my hands into the blood-water, get a grip on his thin legs and under his neck, yank at him and almost topple into the bath myself. My second attempt raises him from the water. I feel how weightless he is, put him down on the bathroom tiles.

He's wearing underwear, standard dress for a cry for help. There are two cuts on his right wrist and three on his left, weakly oozing blood. There are old cuts on his arms too, on his biceps and thighs, some a week or two old, some years.

For a few seconds I consider using the fresh towel on the rack to stop the bleeding but I know I won't be able to tie it properly. I'm already soaked with pink water and I trudge out to the closest bed, pull off the oversheet. I bite into one edge, trying to tear at the overlocking there, chew and chew and fidget with the spit-soaked hem and finally get a footing. Tear a long strip. For the second strip it occurs to me to use the razor blade, which makes the process easier.

With the two lengths of white cotton sheet I wrap Troy's wrists, pulling the knots as tight as I can.

I check for a pulse again. Can't tell. Clasp my hands over where I think Troy's heart is and give five good pumps. They do nothing, but more than five feels like too many so I slap his face, lean over and shout his name into his ear.

Nothing.

I pump his heart again, put my ear to his mouth and try to sense breathing. Maybe I feel something but I can't be sure. I pump again, shout '*Wake up,*' listen for breathing. Still can't tell. I clamp his nose shut, place my lips on his blue ones and breathe. The air goes somewhere, but Troy doesn't seem to react. I pump his heart again, breathe again. Pump again. Nothing.

I stand up, look around the bathroom and walk into the main room and turn on the light and look around some more, as if there's a solution to the problem around the place and it's just waiting for me to notice it.

I go to the door, outside, trudge along the buzzing path of fluoros, watch the road in case a car happens by.

As I approach the motel office I see that the lights are off inside. She must have packed it in, gone to sleep somewhere beyond the office. I hammer my knuckles against the glass.

'*Hey,*' I yell, using my cracks on the door to emphasise the rhythm of my voice. '*Hey! Help! I need help!*'

There's no response.

'*Hello! Help me, please! Please wake up!*'

Silence. No light. The excitement of waving a shotgun around must have taken it out of her. If she's in there at all.

'*Someone's dying! Can you wake up, please!*'

I linger, hopeful she's slowly rousing, hopeful she can take over this problem like she did the last one. But nothing happens. I trundle back to room five and Troy is still dead on the floor.

I take the oversheet from the other bed and lay it out on the carpet, drag Troy's body onto it, bundle him up and lift him, carry him outside. Then I'm halfway through the balancing act of unlocking the car door and gripping Troy's body when I remember Leo Spaske stuck a knife in the rear tyre.

Looking at it now, the tyre is slumped flat and the car lists. I kick the passenger door and shout at it, turn away before I kick it again.

An ambulance would take an hour or more, if it came at all. Over the hill I can still see the white haze from the lights of the hospital. It won't have anything approaching an emergency room but it might have someone in a uniform who'll take this child out of my hands.

I shift the weight in my arms and set off across the carpark to the highway.

Troy's eyes are still shut and he's still unresponsive, even to the cold air that must be even colder given that he's naked and wet. The white sheets are as pink as his underwear. Trudging out of the motel light into the dark of the highway, I know I'm wasting my time. I'm kidding myself that Troy has a pulse. You only have to lose a litre of blood to die from it and that much must have already pooled in my jacket pockets.

Starlight is all there is to see by on the highway and there's just enough of it to bounce off the reflectors on the road, black-grey squares showing me the path.

Probably Troy didn't intend to die. He let me into the bathroom, had me sit there and talk, all the while expecting me to notice that he was slipping away. Which I didn't. Troy was counting on me to save him. Instead I just drank and talked.

I walk faster.

Something is trickling down my legs and into my socks, squelching out a small fart sound with every step. I'm starting to feel the weight of Troy now despite all the blood he's lost. One of his arms has broken free of the sheet and it dangles, tapping on my hip with each squelch. A macabre one man band.

Really, the worst thing I've ever seen is a man with his head so far up his own arse that a boy died right in front of him and he didn't even notice. The story I should have told Troy is the story of right now. It's the kind of story that usually gets me melancholy and drunk. Only it was being melancholy and drunk that made it happen.

I wish Demetri were here. I'd tell him *this* is why I won't reapply for my licence. Because *this* happens.

Only Demetri isn't here. I'm alone on a black road and there's nothing to drink. Nothing to do but get this package to the hospital. And it's taking too long. I force my legs to give more with each step, to move faster, to solve this problem sooner. Despite the strain in my knees I'm jogging now and looking over my shoulder in the hope that there are lights approaching.

There are not.

The first time I checked for a pulse there was one and I'm not kidding myself about that and maybe I was too impatient when I checked again because I was flustered because Troy was dead. I'm not kidding myself that he might survive this and then I wouldn't have killed a fifteen-year-old using only my self-importance and then the worst thing I've ever seen one person do to another person won't be what I've just done out here in this place but fuck it. If I were Troy I'd want to die too so who am I to stop him and maybe it wasn't a demand for attention and maybe he just wanted to slip away under the red light so he couldn't see his own blood and I'd be a fool to rush him to the hospital so fuck it. I'd be just a sucker to run this skinny corpse to a farmers' hospital where they'll tell me he's been dead too long and didn't want to live and look at yourself all covered in blood and out of breath because you thought you stood a chance do you really think you stand a chance, John?

A shiver crashes over me and the muscles in my thighs yawn with pain and my calves cramp up but I can keep going because that's all I can do I have to go to the hospital so then I can nod along with everyone in there when they tell me I did everything I could to save Troy when really I was only saving myself and I want them to think I did my best and my right calf is on fire and there's pink liquid soaking through my sleeves and chafing my stomach and the undersides of my elbows and they'll all think I was trying to save the boy when really I'm only saving myself I'm not trying to save Troy I'm not trying to save Troy but look at me *look at me* my knees are burning through Troy's blood is acid and it's burning into all of my body and there's more acid on my face but it isn't blood and I have to blink it away but it doesn't stop but it's too dark that radiation shiver hasn't stopped I'll do anything I don't know how long it takes to die from but this has to keep going these knees are burning through but they have to keep I wish Demetri were I'll do anything the worst story won't be me it won't be talking about me and there he was bleeding and there was me talking about me and not even seeing that black shapes move past me the dead roadkill on the road just blotches because there's nothing to see but the white glow over the hill is brighter now because it's closer I can tell it's closer I'll do anything not every story is about John Dorn not every story is John Dorn but it was because that's I'll do anything I promise I'll get my licence back if we just say that Troy will and the light from the hospital breaks over the hill and out of nowhere there's the town hall clock and it's ringing out and it's sounding the alarm and I can see it and I can see the road and Troy and his eyes are shut there's something squeezing my arms but it's just my arms I'm blinking and squeezing out the liquid from my eyes because I need to see my knee has burned through but I'm running and the bell is pounding and the shiver's still I'll get my job back I promise I promise there'll be a thousand more stories I promise if we can just say that Troy will if we can just say then I promise there'll be a thousand more stories and if we can just say that Troy will then I promise there'll be a thousand more stories but this time none of them will be about *John Dorn.*

ACKNOWLEDGMENTS

The author wishes to express his appreciation to the following people for their generosity and support:

Margaret Lovitt
Colin and Marcus Lovitt
Mieko Higano
the Freeman family, especially Larry
Simon Saunders
Craig Robertson
Michael De Robbio
and Nic Frame

A special thank you to Mandy Brett, and a very special thank you to a girl who used to be called Katie Freeman.